little black dress
· IT'S A GIRL THING ·

ar Little Black Dress Reader,

anks for picking up this Little Black Dress book, one
he great new titles from our series of fun, page-turning
mance novels. Lucky you — you're about to have a fantastic
omantic read that we know you won't be able to put down!

hy don't you make your Little Black Dress experience
en better by logging on to

www.littleblackdressbooks.com

where you can:

- ❥ Enter our **monthly competitions** to win
  gorgeous prizes
- ❥ Get **hot-off-the-press** news about our latest titles
- ❥ Read **exclusive** preview chapters both from
  your **favourite** authors and from brilliant new
  writing talent
- ❥ Buy **up-and-coming** books online
- ❥ Sign up for an essential slice of romance via
  our **fortnightly email** newsletter

We love nothing more than to curl up and indulge in an
addictive romance, and so we're delighted to welcome you
into the Little Black Dress club!

With love from,

The *li*

Five interesting things about Nell Dixon:

1. I once crashed a Sinclair C5 into a tree. (Sinclair C5s were weird little concept cars that looked like go carts.)

2. I'm scared of heights and got stuck on a rope bridge on an assault course and had to be rescued by a very nice army man.

3. I used to be a midwife and have delivered over a hundred babies.

4. I sing to the music in supermarkets, loudly and tunelessly. Strangely, my family prefer me to shop alone.

5. I have dyscalculia which means I can't remember numbers and often read them back to front.

By Nell Dixon

Marrying Max
Blue Remembered Heels
Animal Instincts
Crystal Clear
Just Look at Me Now

Just Look at Me Now

Nell Dixon

little
black
dress

Cataloguing in Publication Data is available from the British Library

ISBN 978 0 7553 5437 5

Typeset in Transit511BT by Avon DataSet Ltd,
Bidford-on-Avon, Warwickshire

Printed and bound in Great Britain by
Clays Ltd, St Ives plc

HEADLINE PUBLISHING GROUP
An Hachette UK Company
338 Euston Road
London NW1 3BH

www.littleblackdressbooks.com
www.headline.co.uk
www.hachette.co.uk

Just Look at Me Now is dedicated to The Romantic Novelist's Association without whose collective help, advice and support this book would not have been written.

Acknowledgements

Many thanks to the many beauty experts who took the time to answer all kinds of questions. Special thanks to Charlotte McClain who answered lots of questions about how magazines work and provided invaluable information and insight. Any errors are entirely my own. Thanks to my wonderful and talented cp Kimberly Menozzi and thanks also to the Coffee Crew, Phillipa Ashley and Elizabeth Hanbury, for keeping me relatively sane and caffeinated.

Saffy continued to talk, waving a stick-thin fake-bake tanned arm in front of the whiteboard to jab home her points. Tia sighed and doodled another flower on her notepad, shading the petals with tiny, fine blue strokes from her pen. The editorial meeting had only been going for ten minutes and, much as she loved her friend, she'd already begun to lose the will to live. Overhead, the air conditioning whirred quietly, its chilly efficiency making the bare skin of her arms pimple into gooseflesh.

The hot summer sun beat against the tinted windows of the meeting room and the remains of Tia's pink marshmallow melted gloopily on to the surface of her hot chocolate. The large smoked-glass table in front of her was festooned with tinsel, baubles and shiny silver Christmas crackers in a tawdry display of unseasonal festivity.

The door of the meeting room crashed open, causing every head to turn. Sir Crispin Stanford-Hope, proprietor and Chief Executive of *Platinum* magazine and Hellandback Press Telecommunications, made his entrance. He was accompanied by Helen, *Platinum* magazine's editor and organiser of the pretend Christmas in June. Tia slid a blank sheet of paper over her flower doodle and sat up a little straighter in her seat.

Sir Crispin strode around the table to take Saffy's place in front of the whiteboard. Helen trailed after him, her usually forceful personality dwarfed by Sir Crispin's ego. A third person accompanied them: a tall, slender, blond-haired woman dressed in a deceptively simple plain black sheath dress that Tia knew had cost more than her monthly salary. It was a woman she hadn't seen in person for many years and had always hoped she'd never have to see again.

She swallowed hard and dropped her gaze down to the pile of papers in front of her. A horrible sense of nauseous unreality began to sweep through her, making it hard to focus on Sir Crispin's announcement. She raised her head again as he began to speak.

'Okay, people, I see you're all busy finalising the plans for the Christmas and New Year anniversary edition of *Platinum* magazine. Good stuff, we want a big push over the winter season to grab those new subscribers. This is our twenty-fifth year – a landmark. As you know, the post of fashion editor recently became vacant.' Sir Crispin glared around the room as if challenging one of the editorial staff to point out that it was only vacant because he'd fired the previous fashion editor for being photographed at lunch with his brother-in-law and rival press magnate, Rupert Finch. 'So, I'm delighted to intro-duce your new fashion editor, fresh from our New York office: Miss Juliet Gold, who has graciously consented to return to London to steer the fashion section through this important time.'

The elegant blonde bowed her head to acknowledge the polite ripple of applause from the assembled staff around the table.

'I know you'll all make her feel very welcome.' Sir Crispin scanned the room once more.

Saffy's cheeks had turned a dull red under her tan and her eyes were suspiciously bright at Sir Crispin's announcement. She'd stepped into the vacant fashion editor's post after her senior's inauspicious departure and Tia knew her friend had hoped the move might become permanent. They'd even speculated together that Helen's request that Saffy chair this month's staff meeting might be an indication of an imminent appointment.

'Right, Helen, I'll leave you to get on with the meeting. Nice to see everyone getting into the seasonal spirit. Just the ticket, splendid, carry on. Juliet, good to have you on board, my dear.' Sir Crispin swept out of the room leaving behind the new fashion editor and an awkward silence.

Tia concentrated on her breathing and tried to control the rising nervous tide of panic in her stomach. It had been twelve years, there was no way Juliet should recognise her. Even so, her mind flitted miserably through all the conceivable consequences if Juliet were to suddenly see through her new image and denounce her in front of all her colleagues.

'Well, erm, take a seat, Miss Gold. I think we should

go round the table and introduce ourselves before we crack on with the business in hand.'

Helen frowned at Saffy to indicate that she should vacate her seat for Juliet. Saffy duly stood and took the empty chair to Tia's right as the new fashion editor installed herself next to Helen at the head of the table. Juliet's lips curved upwards in an ill-concealed smirk as she surveyed the rest of the editorial team with her dark grey eyes.

An icy trickle of sweat ran down Tia's spine as, one by one, her colleagues announced their names and roles while Juliet nodded and made brief notes in a navy-blue Moleskine notebook. Little black spots danced in front of her eyes and her grip tightened round the pen she'd pinched from Saffy's desk on the way to the meeting.

'Tia Carpenter, beauty editor.' To her relief her voice at least sounded calm and steady. Her breath hitched in her throat as she waited for Juliet to recognise her, and tell the room that her name wasn't Tia at all. Instead, Juliet made a note in her book while Ravi from Features made his introduction.

The rest of the meeting passed in a blur. Her pen automatically jotted things down but most of her concentration was devoted to staying conscious and waiting for the new fashion editor to denounce her as a fraud.

Finally the torture was over and Helen swept Juliet off to her inner sanctum to give her a full brief on *Platinum* magazine's anniversary and seasonal edition. The other staff drifted back to their desks, hoping to catch the sandwich delivery service before it left the building, leaving Saffy, Tia and Ravi huddled around the water cooler.

'Well, that was drama, darlings.' Ravi helped himself to a beaker of iced water and leaned nonchalantly against the wall. His tailored cream linen jacket still miraculously uncreased despite the long meeting.

Saffy vented her feelings on the water dispenser, jabbing the 'on' button with her thumb. 'Cowbag; I never even got to interview for the job. Who is she, anyway?'

'She was the fashion editor for *Ritzy*, and before that she worked on *Vogue*. She's been in New York at *Platinum* mag's sister office for the last six months.' Tia took a long pull of her drink, the icy chill of the water soothing her frazzled nerves.

The other two stared at her round-eyed.

'How come you know about her? Did you have some goss that you didn't share?' Ravi demanded.

Heat flamed into Tia's face. 'No, don't be silly. How would I know anything? Her name rang a bell, that's all. A friend of mine used to know her.'

Ravi shot her a glance and Tia held her breath, hoping she hadn't given anything away. She'd been following Juliet's career for years, breathing a huge sigh of relief when she had headed overseas.

'It's not fair, and I'll have to fetch and carry like a lapdog all over again. I really thought it would be my big break when Trudie got the chop.' Saffy scowled at her cup of iced water, her expression an unhappy contrast to her brightly coloured hair.

'I'm sorry, Saf. I thought you'd get it too, you've done

some great spreads.' Tia patted her arm. She'd been convinced her friend would secure the post. Saffy was really good at her job. 'We'll go out after work to the Pink Pagoda, commiseration drinks are on us.'

'Thanks Tia, I'd better get back to my desk; no doubt Helen will be after me to show this new woman the ropes.' Saffy grimaced and finished her drink, tossing the empty plastic cup into the waste bin.

'You honestly didn't know about this Juliet woman getting the job?' Ravi murmured as soon as Saffy was safely out of earshot.

'No, I told you, how could I? I'm only one of the minions, remember?' Tia discarded her own empty cup. She wished she had known, and then she might have been better prepared for her old tormentors' reappearance in her life.

'Mmm,' Ravi replied and followed her back into the main office where the new appointment was the topic of conversation on everybody's lips.

Tia couldn't help feeling relieved when Ravi was summoned by one of the temps to sort out the photocopier which appeared to have run amok, copying and stapling two hundred copies of the latest marketing report instead of the two it was supposed to produce.

She slipped away to the toilets to try to pull herself together. She'd always feared fate would throw her and Juliet together again one day. With Juliet working in fashion, and her own career in beauty it was always a possibility. She just hadn't thought that today would be the day. She ran some cold water over the pulse points in her wrists to calm her nerves and popped open her handbag to retrieve her make-up.

Being the beauty editor for *Platinum* magazine, the trendiest glamour publication for the twenty-something's, had its perks. One of them was the volume of free samples of luxury products that regularly arrived on her desk. She selected a lipgloss which was allegedly guaranteed to plump and moisturise your lips for twenty-four hours with one application. So far, it hadn't survived the banana and low-fat yoghurt she'd had for breakfast and the iced water from the machine.

Tia reapplied the lipgloss, taking care to define the edges of her mouth. It would be difficult not to let her secret slip if she were working with Juliet on a daily basis. She stared at her reflection, trying to picture herself as Juliet would see her now. It still took effort on her part to see herself as everyone else saw her. Slim, attractive, with her brunette hair in the latest cut, and wearing flawlessly applied make-up to highlight her best features. Why should Juliet recognise her? She was a totally new person.

The remainder of the working day slipped away even more slowly than the unappetising mince pies that Helen had thought would help the staff to 'think Christ-massy' on a hot June day. As Juliet was shown around the offices by Saffy to meet the other, more junior members of the team, Tia covertly followed her progress through the cubicles. She needed to be ready for the inevitable moment when her nemesis would appear in front of her computer monitor.

Saffy halted in front of Tia's desk, with Juliet next to her. 'This is the beauty department. You met Tia this morning; she's head of beauty. Her assistant, Anna, is on maternity leave at the moment so she's managing with temps. This is Poppy, her intern, and Ravi, over in Features, is helping out here and there.'

Tia sucked in a deep breath and pinned a smile to her face. Her heartbeat kicked up a notch. 'Lovely to have you join us, Juliet.' She hoped she sounded sincere but not arse-licking.

'It's nice to be back in the UK. New York was fabulous but I'd begun to get a touch homesick.' Juliet's smile didn't reach her eyes and Tia decided she'd definitely had some Botox injected into her forehead.

Saffy pulled a face behind Juliet's back and Tia fought the urge to giggle.

'I'm sure you'll find it a little less hectic here than in New York.' Tia hadn't had Juliet marked down as the kind of woman who would get homesick. Okay, she'd had a much nicer home than Tia when they'd been growing up but, even so, the small provincial town where they had both lived couldn't possibly hold that great an attraction for Juliet.

'Oh, I can see that already, but darling Crispin was so persuasive about getting me to come here. I'm sure I can do great things to put some sizzle back in the Fashion department.'

'Well, I'll look forward to working on some ideas with you.' Tia hoped Juliet wouldn't turn around. Behind her, Saffy looked positively murderous at the implication that the fashion department had lacked sizzle under her direction.

Juliet gave another humourless smile. 'That's very sweet of you. Well, come on, Susie, we've work to do.' She gave Tia a nod of dismissal and swept off back to her own department with Saffy following mutinously in her wake.

Ravi scooted his chair across the office to lean on her desk. 'Darling Crispin! Get her, the cow, hate her already, and where does she get off calling Saffy "Susie"? Bitch.'

'I think we'll all need that drink tonight.' Tia rolled her shoulders, trying to ease the tension knot from the back of her neck.

'Poor Saf will need a permanent hip flask full of tequila at this rate,' Ravi muttered. 'Do you think Jools is very pally-pally with our esteemed owner? Helen didn't look too impressed this morning, did she? Maybe old Cris has parachuted Juliet in over Helen's head. It would be so typical of the old boy; he's always thought of *Platinum* as his own personal plaything.'

Tia smiled weakly as Ravi hugged himself with speculative delight at his new theory. 'I don't know. We're stuck with her, though, and if she *is* a close personal friend of Sir Crispin's, then we'd better tread carefully.'

Ravi grinned at her. 'Wouldn't you love to know, though? Old Sir Crispin must be thirty or forty years older than dear Juliet, and there were all those rumours about him and Helen.'

'There were only rumours about Sir Crispin and

Helen because you started them after last year's Christmas party.' Tia picked up a bundle of paper from her desk and smacked him playfully on the arm.

Ravi loved to gossip and if there was none to be found, then he wasn't above inventing something. The uncanny thing was that there was more often than not a grain of truth in his stories and Tia often wondered how much he really knew about everyone at *Platinum*.

'Darling, you flatter me. Uh oh, wicked queen alert at ten o'clock, look busy'. He scooted away back to his desk as Helen emerged from her glass-fronted office to stride off in the direction of the fashion department.

There were other rumours about Helen that hadn't started with Ravi. Mainly they were about the bottles of Jack Daniel's hidden in the plant pot of the large fronded palm behind her desk. If Ravi was right and Sir Crispin had appointed Juliet without consulting Helen, it looked as if *Platinum* might be getting a new senior editor too.

2

The Pink Pagoda was filled with the usual crowd of escapees from the nearby office buildings. If anything, the hot weather seemed to have driven even more people to seek refuge in the stylish air-conditioned teak-and-chrome interior to sip cold imported beer and glasses of chilled white wine.

Tia joined Ravi and Saffy at their usual perch at the far end of the bar next to a stainless-steel dish of complimentary peanuts which appeared promptly at their arrival. Her friends had managed to escape from the office before Tia and from their seats they had a clear view of anyone entering or leaving the bar. A strategic position which had proved very useful in the past when Helen had decided to stop by.

'If that bloody woman calls me Susie one more time I swear I will not be answerable for my actions.' Saffy picked up her glass and knocked back her third double shot of vodka in what had to be less than thirty minutes. The little stack of empties next to her told their own story. 'It's not fair, that job was mine. Helen had virtually promised it to me.'

Ravi raised his eyebrow at Tia, an unspoken 'told you so' over his earlier speculations.

Saffy signalled to the bartender for a refill.

'Go easy on the shots, Saf,' Tia cautioned. 'You don't want to face Juliet tomorrow with a pounding head.'

'My head already aches from her constant bossiness. She's reorganised the desk, moved all my stuff so I'm working out of a damned wire basket, and she even took down my Johnny Depp picture. I had to save him from the wastepaper basket. I barely had time to rescue him before she dumped her yoghurt pot on his face.' Saffy drummed her immaculate French-polished nails on the wooden bar top.

'She's a new broom, darling, you should know what that means.' Ravi gave Tia another meaningful glance before returning his focus to Saffy. 'Anyway, have you spoken to Helen about it?'

Tia took a sip of her white wine. Ravi must know full well that Saffy hadn't spoken to Helen. What could she say? 'Oh, by the way, I thought *I* was going to be appointed as the new fashion editor'?

'Not yet. I will, though. At least, I think I will as soon as I've figured out what to say. Maybe I should just start looking for another job.' Saffy stared woefully at her replenished drink. Even the top of her artfully styled magenta hair looked droopy.

'I wonder what's brought Juliet home from New York?' Tia mused. It had been playing on her mind ever since the staff meeting. New York was a much bigger pond than London in fashion circles. She would have thought New York's glittering social life would have been perfect for a wealthy single girl like Juliet.

'Oh, so you didn't buy that homesickness crap either, darling? I agree, I mean who would give up a job in NY to come back here to be at Sir Crispin's beck and call?' Ravi adjusted his cuffs and flicked an imaginary piece of lint on the floor.

'I think it's a man,' Saffy announced. 'She was on the phone to him all this afternoon, reorganising the next photo shoot so that it takes place at one of his hotels. She was all giggly and flirty and "Oh Josh".' Saffy effected a grating titter, then grimaced.

All the blood in Tia's veins turned cold and for a moment she thought she might fall from her perch on the art deco chrome bar stool. Saffy had to be mistaken, fate couldn't be *that* cruel, surely. 'Josh Banks? The Oakleaf chain of hotels?'

Saffy nodded and knocked back her vodka shot, shuddering as it went down. 'That's the one. Apparently he's an old friend.'

Tia pressed her fingers against the stem of her glass in a bid to stop them from trembling. An image of Josh straight from their schooldays entered her head. She could still see his dark hair, the dimple in his cheek when he smiled and those amazing blue eyes that had turned her sixteen-year-old insides to mush. Not that he'd ever noticed her, at least not until the awful ghastly last night of the leaver's party. Juliet had ensured then that he'd noticed the shy, fat girl with the bad skin and braces.

'We're scheduled to do a piece on him for the

Christmas special – well, him and eleven others. "*Twelve Christmas crackers you might want to find in your stocking*"; Ravi said.

'And would you? Want to find him in your stocking?' Saffy slurred.

'Oh, I've seen him, darling; very nice, but straight, alas.' Ravi heaved a mock sigh of regret and finished the last of his drink.

'Probably into weird sex stuff or lives with mummy, then. Must be something wrong with him if he likes Juliet.' Saffy looked hopefully at her once more empty glass.

Juliet and Josh together for ever. Juliet had scratched it on the green metal railing at the back of the science block and written it on the covers of all her school books. Twelve years ago when Tia hadn't been Tia at all. If she were to close her eyes now she could see the playing fields stretching out before her, the grass parched to a pale yellow by the summer sun. She could almost smell the asphalt melting in the sunshine and see Juliet, golden-haired and beautiful, sneaking an illicit cigarette before gym.

So Juliet was still in touch with Josh after all this time. Tia had kept track of Josh over the years too. It would have been hard not to, since he'd turned his family's small chain of hotels into a massive success story. The media had been quick to pick up on the irresistible combination of youth, good looks and money. Ever since then he'd been pictured in the tabloids and a variety of celebrity magazines dating different stars and models.

'Tia, my sweet, are you going to nurse that empty glass for ever?' Ravi's cultured tones cut across her thoughts.

She shook her head as the barman collected her glass. 'No more for me. I should get off home.' She slid down from her stool and smoothed her pale green cotton skirt.

Ravi raised his eyebrows as Saffy ordered another vodka shot. 'Oh, don't mind me, Tia, I'll see that the lush here gets home safely.'

Saffy stuck her tongue out at him and Tia laughed.

'I need to go; Ginny will be wondering where I am.' She'd sent her godmother at least five texts since the morning's fateful editorial meeting but Gin hadn't replied to any of them. It wasn't unusual for her not to reply, it probably meant she'd embarked on another one of her home improvement projects and hadn't checked her phone.

'See you tomorrow, then. At least, I will; if Saffy has any more vodka, she'll probably end up in A and E.' Ravi rolled his eyes and grinned.

Tia smiled back in response and made her way out of the Pink Pagoda and on to the high street, leaving Saffy and Ravi to bicker between themselves. Even though it was almost seven o'clock, it was still hot. The tube felt clammy and fetid with the smell of overheated bodies and stale sweat and she was glad when she reached her stop and was able to escape upwards into the sunshine.

'Gin, I'm home,' Tia called out as soon as she unlocked the front door of the large Edwardian terraced house she shared with her mother's old friend. Gin had been happy to give her a home when she'd left her old life behind. Without her constant loving support, Tia hated to think what her life might have been like. The only downside to living with Gin was her constant need to change her surroundings, and as if to prove her point the smell of fresh gloss paint and the dull thud of a rock beat hit her as soon as she entered the hall.

'Gin, where are you?'

She headed along the hallway to the kitchen, As she pushed the door open, the pulsating sound of the Flying Monkeys' latest album kicked up a notch. Her god-mother was halfway up a stepladder clasping a paint roller.

'What are you doing?' Tia turned off the CD player and stared at the kitchen, every spare inch of which was shrouded in dust sheets.

'Do you like it? I got so sick of looking at that manky pale blue colour. I thought we'd go white, minimalist.' Gin beamed at her, while a blob of white paint adorned the end of her nose and specks of blue dust shook down from her grey hair.

'You only decorated in here twelve months ago,' Tia pointed out.

Gin descended the ladder and replaced the roller in its tray. 'I know, but really, it was pretty awful, totally wrong for this room. Anyway, I haven't done much, just refreshed some gloss work and emulsioned the walls and ceiling. I was about to finish now.'

Tia picked her way carefully across the room and surveyed her friend's handiwork. She knew it would be useless to try to persuade Gin to stop her home improvements, at least today it was only paint. Before Christmas she'd returned from work to find a large hole in the bathroom wall. 'It does look better,' she conceded.

Gin beamed and started to roll up the dust sheets from the kitchen countertops. 'Super. By the way, you're late; have you been to the Pink Pagoda?'

'If you ever looked at your phone you'd know why I was late.'

Gin looked sheepish. 'I think I've lost it again. It's probably under one of these covers'

Tia moved a sheet from the wicker chair in the kitchen corner and took a seat. 'Juliet Gold arrived today as the new fashion editor at *Platinum*.'

Gin stopped clearing and straightened up to stare at Tia. 'I thought she was in New York?'

'Well, now she's back. Sir Crispin arrived with her today for the planning meeting. Saffy's gutted.'

'You saw her? Juliet? Did she recognise you?' A worried frown creased Gin's forehead.

'No, she didn't recognise me.'

Gin sank down on the chair opposite Tia and absent-mindedly scratched her nose, smearing the blob of white paint on to her cheek. 'What are you going to do?'

Tia shrugged. 'There's not much I can do. She's there to stay and so am I. I won't let her force me out of my job.' Despite the bravery of her words she felt a little sick. Seeing Juliet everyday and working alongside her was going to be hard. Even harder if she was still involved with Josh.

'What was she like? Has she changed much?' Gin asked.

Tia picked at the white-painted wicker arm of her seat. 'She's still tall, slim, blonde, gorgeous and an absolute *cow*. She's been calling poor Saffy Susie all afternoon.' Maybe it had been too much to hope that Juliet might have changed in the years since they'd left school. What was it they said about leopards never changing their spots?

'Same old, same old, then. Do you think she will recognise you?'

'I don't know. I mean I have a different name, different everything. It won't make for a comfortable working life, though, that's for certain.' Tia trailed to a halt.

Gin continued to watch her through shrewd blue eyes. 'There's something else, isn't there?'

'Saffy thinks that Juliet is still involved with Josh Banks. Saffy heard her talking to him on the phone. She's switched the next photo shoot, the big anniversary one, from the Milano Spa to Josh's flagship hotel, the Broadoak.'

'But you won't have to go to that, will you?' Gin asked.

Tia sighed. 'I don't know. Ordinarily no, but this is a big product placement shoot for beauty products too. It's for the anniversary edition so Sir Crispin wants maximum advertising money and interest and of course I haven't got an assistant at the moment apart from Poppy.'

'Even so, it doesn't mean you'd be likely to run into

Josh. According to the gossip columns he's travelling all over the place these days, isn't he?'

Tia had often wondered what would happen if she did meet Josh again. She swallowed the lump in her throat as she remembered the last time she saw him. It had been the only time he'd ever noticed her, and she could still see the pity in his eyes.

'Tia?'

'Sorry, I was miles away then. Yes, I think so; according to the press he's here, there and everywhere but you know I never was very lucky.'

Gin's face was sympathetic. 'You still have a thing for him, don't you?'

'A bit, I suppose. Though doesn't everyone have that for their first crush? Maybe this will turn out to be a good thing. I'll finally put Longmorton High School and Josh and Juliet behind me for good.' She tilted her chin defiantly, wishing she felt braver than she did.

'Maybe.' Gin stood and pottered towards the open back door, dust sheet in hand, and left Tia with her thoughts.

It probably was time she put her past firmly behind her. She wasn't that scared, unhappy teenager any more and there had been plenty of other men since Josh to prove to her she wasn't unattractive.

She leaned back in her seat, lost in her memories. Josh playing basketball in the school gym, Josh handing her the pencil she'd dropped in art. The stub was still in her box of treasures upstairs under her bed, precious because Josh had touched it.

Tia smiled and shook her head. How melodramatic could you be? Perhaps Juliet had done her a big favour by turning up at *Platinum*. It was high time she shook off the last traces of the girl she used to be. She wasn't sixteen-year-old 'Big Barb, tub of lard' any more, she was Tia, beauty editor at one of the most prestigious magazines in the UK publishing world. Now was her opportunity to finally exorcise the ghosts of her previous life.

As usual, Tia was one of the first people to arrive in the office. The *Platinum* offices were on the sixth floor of a large block, owned by Hellandback. Other titles in the company's portfolio, such as *Stock Market Today* and *Musclemen*, occupied some of the other floors. There was something about the peace and quiet of that first hour – when she and the cleaner were the only ones there – that she really loved. She enjoyed taking the opportunity to sort out her emails and plan her diary before Poppy could burden her with tons of post and countless questions.

She placed her takeout skinny latte on the corner of the desk and pulled out her PDA to run through her appointments. The distinctive click of Helen's office door resonated over the dull background hum of the vacuum cleaner out in the corridor. Tia peeked over the top of her cubicle, curious to see who else had come in early.

To her surprise, Juliet emerged from Helen's office carrying a large brown envelope.

'Oh! I didn't know you were here.' Juliet's cheeks flushed dark pink under her *Gatineau* foundation.

'I always come in to the office at this time.' Tia stepped out from her cubicle wondering what her new colleague had been doing. 'I like to get a bit of a jump on the day.'

'I was, um, just leaving a message for Helen.' Juliet sidled away from the office door. 'There's so much to do; that girl, what's-her-name, has been quite helpful, but still.'

Tia recalled a time back at school when Juliet had liberally applied superglue to the deputy headmistress's chair, resulting in poor Mrs Johnson having to call for help and a change of clothes. Juliet had worn the same expression on her face then, part glee and part suppressed excitement.

'Your assistant editor's name is Saffy. She's very good at her job.' Tia was pleased her voice sounded so calm, even though her heart was banging against her ribs. She placed her hand against the cubicle partition to steady herself and looked Juliet in the eyes.

'Saffy, yes, of course it is. I must try to remember. You know what it's like in a new post, so many new names.' Juliet gave a little tinkling laugh that was clearly intended to disarm.

Tia forced a smile. 'Helen usually comes in around midday unless it's print week. Her assistant – her name is Milly – will be in soon.'

'I'll bear that in mind.' Juliet's smile didn't reach her eyes.

Tia fought the urge to dry her clammy palms on the legs of her cream linen trousers. 'Do you think you'll enjoy it here?' She couldn't quite believe she was having a conversation with Juliet after all this time and that the other woman still appeared completely unaware of her real identity.

'Oh, I'm sure I'll be able to get everything arranged to my satisfaction soon enough.' Juliet's lips thinned in another sketch of a smile as the tinny sound of a mobile rang out from the fashion department. 'Excuse me; no rest for the wicked.'

Tia sank back down on to her seat as Juliet hurried off to take her call. Her hand shook as she reached out to take a sip from her latte and she placed the cup carefully back down on the desk without taking a drink. The contents of her stomach rolled and she took a few deep breaths to try and calm her nerves.

What had Juliet been up to in Helen's office? There definitely had been something in the way she'd reacted when she'd realised that she'd been seen. Tia drew another breath, her stomach settling again now. Facing Juliet had unnerved her, almost as much as the day she'd seen her sneaking out of Mrs Johnson's office clutching the tiny tube of glue.

Back then she'd been too scared to challenge Juliet or to tell any of the staff what she'd seen. Not that it had made any difference; Juliet had known that Tia knew her secret and had exacted her revenge. Today at least Tia had corrected Juliet about Saffy's name and had managed to get in a barb over Milly's name too. Tia picked her cup up once more, steadying it with both hands while she drank. She could only hope Juliet wouldn't turn on her this time.

'Is *she* here yet?' Saffy appeared at her side.

'If you mean Juliet, then yes. If you mean Helen, then no. God, you look awful; how many more shots did you sink after I left?'

Saffy sank down on the vacant chair next to Tia. 'Dunno. Have you got some concealer?' She eyed the vast array of cosmetic samples on the table next to the desk.

Tia rolled her eyes. 'About seventy different kinds, but I don't know if any of them are industrial strength.' She rummaged amongst the products and selected a slim silver tube. 'Here, try this one. You can tell me if it's any good for a piece I was thinking of writing on cover-ups.'

Saffy eyed the coffee cup on the desk. 'Is there caffeine in there?'

'Latte.' Tia handed over the remains of her drink.

'Anything. How many paracetamol is it safe to take before they pump your stomach?'

'Go and stick your concealer on before Juliet realises you've arrived. Oh,' she said, rummaging again, 'borrow some of this blusher too; you look like a corpse.'

Saffy loaded up with products from the table and dragged herself off in the direction of the toilets while Tia fired up her computer. So much for getting a nice quiet jump on the day's work.

'Morning, darling, you look ravishing today.' Ravi rested his arms on top of the cubicle partition. 'I see Jools is here bright and early – obviously out to make a good impression – although quite what our esteemed fashion director will make of her ladyship messing about with all her photo-shoot bookings, I've no idea. I suggest you lay in a stock of popcorn ready for the fireworks show.'

Tia forced herself to remain straight-faced. It would be quite nice to see Juliet getting chewed up. 'You are so naughty. I'm sure Juliet would have cleared everything first.'

'Oh, really, darling? Well, pull up a pew, because here comes Penelope now and she doesn't look happy.' He slid away from the top of the partition to resume his seat in the next cubicle where he could lean out and discreetly watch Juliet's encounter with Penny. The fashion director was responsible for co-ordinating and booking all the settings and photo shoots for the magazine, and her demeanour was, indeed, anything but happy as she stormed through the office.

Tia chose not to look, forcing herself to concentrate on the screen in front of her while the sound of raised voices came from the fashion department. She hoped Saffy had remained in the toilets so she wouldn't get dragged into the row.

Her email pinged, signifying a message had arrived in her inbox.

You're missing the fun. R

Tia shook her head. She was surprised that Penny appeared to be unaware of Juliet's plans, especially as the two women shared a department. Then again, Penny had been out yesterday afternoon at a meeting and maybe Sir Crispin had given Juliet carte blanche to do as she liked. It wouldn't be the first time he'd completely turned office protocol and job descriptions on their head.

Ooh, gone quiet, do you think Penny killed her? R

Ravi was right, the sound of raised female voices had ceased. The cubicles around Tia were filling as the rest of the staff arrived for work.

You were watching. Where's Saffy? T

Haven't seen her since I poured her out of the bar and into a cab last night. R

Tia sighed and wondered if she should launch a search party in case Saffy had passed out in the toilets.

Her email pinged again: *News just in – Penny has intercepted Saffy. R*

This time Tia ventured a cautious peep out of her cubicle and spotted Penelope. Saffy's face wasn't visible but Penny was waving her hands about as she talked and her smooth chestnut chignon appeared to be aquiver with indignation.

Tia scooted her chair back under her desk and sent Ravi another email.

I wonder who'll be first in line to bend Helen's ear when she gets in? T

Fiver on Penny. R

Saffy disappeared into her department and Poppy arrived at Tia's desk with a pile of samples and advertising copy. Tia turned her attention to her work and tried not to listen out for any more excitement over in the fashion department.

By the time she'd sorted out the post and given her intern a list of instructions she realised she'd missed

Helen's arrival at the office. She checked her email to see a string of messages sitting in her in-box.

World war three over here. S

You owe me a fiver. R

'I've arranged a preliminary meeting at the Broadoak Oakleaf Imperial at 12 re the anniversary shoot. Would be helpful if you were there. Juliet.

Tia looked at her PDA, hoping she already had an appointment for twelve. No such luck.

The last email was from Helen: *Juliet has managed to secure us the promise of an exclusive at the Broadoak Oakleaf Imperial – use of their new spa for the anniversary shoot ahead of anyone else. Please prioritise your diary accordingly.*

It looked as if Penny had lost the fight. Tia took a deep breath and sent a reply back to Juliet.

Can only spare a couple of hours. Will meet you there. Tia

There was no way she could contemplate sharing a cab with Juliet all the way to the Broadoak Imperial. Despite Helen's instructions, she had no intention of allowing Juliet to think she could arrange her work plans for her.

She hit send and sat staring for a moment at the screen. Crap, what had she agreed to? Suppose Josh was there? Somewhere deep in the back of her mind she'd always had a fantasy of meeting Josh again one day. A day when she'd be wearing a gorgeous designer evening gown and fabulous shoes. He'd look at her and say, 'Do I know you?' and then he'd realise who she was, just as she was leaving and climbing into her limo like a modern-day Cinderella. He'd run after her, begging for a date.

Sighing, she glanced down at her pale-cream coloured trousers and pastel-green top – definitely not a glamorous look. At least, with all the products she had available, her make-up would look good. It was stupid to fantasise anyway, since it wasn't likely that Juliet would want her tagging along if Josh was going to be there. Instead of hoping that he would recognise her, she had to pray that he would be as oblivious to her real identity as Juliet seemed to be, if he did happen to be present at the meeting.

Across the city, Josh Banks had finished dictating his last letter of the morning to his PA. With his assistant gone about her duties he was alone in his office once more. He swivelled his seat to contemplate the panoramic view from his penthouse suite.

Juliet Gold: there was a name from his past. He hadn't heard from her for years until a few weeks ago, when she'd contacted him to say she was returning to London and to suggest that they meet up for old times' sake. Since then there had been a few emails and a couple of calls – then, yesterday, the proposal that *Platinum* magazine have an exclusive photo shoot in the new spa.

He'd looked her up, of course, on the Internet, wondering if she'd changed much since he'd broken up with her after the school disco incident. The one with that weird, fat girl . . . what was her name? Barbara.

Juliet had been sex on legs; he'd been the envy of the

school rugby team. He shook his head trying to clear his thoughts. Funny the things you remembered. Now Juliet was back in town and hinting she'd like to carry things on where they'd left off. Could you go back? And did he want to? The Barbara incident had shown him a side to Juliet he hadn't much liked and, even now, he realised he still felt a haunting sense of shame over the whole thing.

The publicity for the hotel chain and the spa was too good to turn down, even if it did come attached to Juliet. He was surprised Sir Crispin hadn't thought of it, especially as he had to have learned by now that Josh had acquired quite a few of Hellandback's shares. Still, he and Sir Crispin had never really seen eye-to-eye; the older man perceived him as some kind of threat to his precious publishing empire.

The new spa was important to him. He'd designed the project from scratch, intent on building the most glamorous and exclusive spa in the city with a limited membership of VIPs. While guests and the public could use some areas, there would be other parts which only those on the hot list would be able to access, ensuring its exclusivity. Publicity in a leading publication like *Platinum*, with a huge spread of photographs in the anniversary edition, would be a major advertising coup.

He'd have to see what happened when Juliet arrived for the lunch meeting. Would it be purely business, or would it be mixed with pleasure? At least he had Kim, his PA, and this other woman from the magazine, Tia somebody or other, to provide something of a buffer if Juliet should have more pleasure than business in mind.

*

'Did you want to do lunch, darling? We could Sushi or noodle?' Ravi popped his head over the cubicle partition once more.

'Sorry, Ravi. I'm going to the Broadoak Oakleaf Imperial with Juliet, Helen's instructions.'

'Get you, hobnobbing with teacher's pet.'

Tia rolled her eyes at him. 'Trust me: I'm really not looking forward to it.'

'Of course not, you poor thing, having to go and eat some lovely exotic lunch at the Broadoak's expense. Are you getting a sneak peek at the new spa? There are so many rumours going around about that place. The membership list is sooo exclusive even Her Maj couldn't get in there.'

'Who, the Queen?' Tia stared at him, wondering wildly why the Queen would be at the Broadoak and only half concentrating as her mind was still preoccupied with calculating the odds of running into Josh.

'No, darling, the other queen – Madonna.' Ravi tutted. 'What is up with you today? If it's anything catching, make sure you sneeze all over dear Jools.'

'I'm fine, just busy. I'd better go, I said I'd meet her there at twelve and it's almost twenty to, now.' Tia picked up her bag and checked she had her notebook, pen and camera – all the requisite tools of the trade.

'Well, have a nice time, remember to say please and thank you, and come back and tell Uncle Ravi all the juicy details.'

Tia shook her head in mock despair and headed for

the elevator. She wished Ravi could have accompanied her. He would have no problems keeping Juliet in her box.

She was ten minutes late when the cab drew to a halt in front of the Broadoak Oakleaf Imperial's stone-porticoed entrance. A uniformed doorman in dove-grey livery, white gloves and black top hat helped her from the cab, leaving her feeling flustered and untidy as she followed him through the chrome-glass front doors into the marble-floored lobby.

The reception area of the Imperial smelt of fresh flowers, beeswax and money. Tia made her way to the desk and gave her name. Her heart raced as the receptionist picked up the phone to make the call to inform the organiser of the meeting of her arrival.

'Please take a seat, Mr Bank's PA will be down to collect you in a moment.' The receptionist indicated one of the stylish leather-covered armchairs grouped together on the far side of the lobby.

'Thank you.' Tia took a deep breath and sat on the edge of one of the chairs, trying not to hyperventilate.

A million different thoughts raced around her head. Damn Juliet and Helen. Penny had obviously opted to boycott the meeting in protest. Maybe she should simply say she wasn't well and leave now before it was too late. Perhaps Josh wasn't here after all. Maybe it was only his PA that was handling the meeting.

The elevator doors opened and a well-groomed auburn-haired woman in her early fifties, wearing a smart pastel-blue suit, emerged and spoke to the receptionist.

Tia's grip on her bag tightened as the woman strode towards her.

'Hello, Miss Carpenter, glad you could join us. Miss Gold and Mr Banks are already upstairs in the meeting room. Please follow me and I'll take you through.'

Tia's heart banged against her ribs as she tried to summon up a smile.

'Thank you.' She trailed miserably through the sumptuously decorated lobby after the PA and wondered briefly if this was how prisoners had felt as they had gone to the guillotine. She'd never felt such a kinship before now, but as dread pooled in her stomach, each step she took seemed to be leading her closer to her doom.

The heels of Tia's 'so last season' shoes sank silently into the thick carpet of the corridor leading her to Josh's penthouse suite and office. In her head she composed her letter of resignation for Helen. This surely had to be the moment when she'd be exposed, face to face with Josh again after all these years.

Josh's PA opened a polished mahogany door and stood to the side to allow Tia to enter. Light streamed into the room from vast floor-to-ceiling sash windows temporarily dazzling her vision as she stepped into the room. Juliet and Josh stood together at the window looking at the view. Backlit by the midday sun they glowed like golden statues and Tia was immediately sent back to her teens.

'Juliet's going to marry Josh. Don't they look so good together?'

She'd been trailing behind a group of Juliet's cronies as they'd filed off the sports field. Juliet had been walking further ahead with Josh. He'd been carrying her javelin. The sun had glinted off Juliet's blond hair and her crimson sports skirt was short enough to reveal a pair of perfectly tanned long golden legs.

Tia had been alone, puffing along at the back of the group, sweat trickling down her spine while her hair clung damp and frizzy around her face. Later, in the changing room, she'd discovered her classmates had been amusing themselves by seeing how many sticky grass burrs they could attach to the back of her white sports shirt without her noticing.

'Miss Tia Carpenter, *Platinum* magazine,' the PA announced, jolting her back into the present.

Josh and Juliet turned to face her. Tia remained rooted to the spot, her tongue obstinately frozen to the roof of her mouth.

'Tia, I'm so sorry. I would have waited downstairs for you but you *are* rather late.' Juliet made a great show of looking at the tiny gold Rolex watch on her wrist. 'Josh and I are old friends, and we haven't seen each other for absolutely ages. We were so busy catching up on past times; I quite forgot you were joining us.' She laughed her little tinkly laugh, immediately setting Tia's teeth on edge.

'It's nice to meet you, Tia. I'm Josh Banks.' He walked over to her as he spoke, holding out his hand for her to shake. His shoulders appeared broader beneath the grey pinstriped Italian designer suit jacket than she remembered and she thought he might have added another inch in height. His eyes were still a deep piercing blue and his dark brown hair still fell on to his forehead in a wayward lock that made her pulse race and the blood sing in her ears.

'Nice to meet you,' Tia murmured.

He enclosed her hand in his and her heart skipped a beat. Her skin tingled at his touch and she had to fight the urge to snatch her hand back before she could betray herself.

'Let me get you a drink. Wine? Mineral water?' He released her hand and indicated a small bar she hadn't noticed before at the side of the room.

'White wine would be lovely, thank you.' She forced the words out, relived she sounded normal whilst inside her emotions tumbled about like clothes in a washing machine set on spin.

He hadn't recognised her. There had been no trace of surprise or revulsion on his face. Tia blew out a silent breath as Josh's PA moved to pour her a glass of wine.

Juliet strolled over to join Josh next to the bar, slipping her arm through his. 'Josh and I were at high school together. I called him as soon as I knew I would be moving back to London. Amazing, isn't it? Such a small world. We used to have quite a thing together back then.' She gave another little girlish laugh.

As Josh's PA handed her a glass of wine, Tia was pretty sure Juliet didn't have a fan there either. It wasn't in anything the older woman said or did particularly, it was merely a faintly scornful flicker of her eyes and a feeling Tia had.

'All quite a long time ago now.' Josh smiled and extricated himself from Juliet, making a point of moving his arm from her grasp. 'Shall we take a seat and get to business?'

Tia clutched her glass like a lifebelt as she followed

Juliet to a large oval glass-and-steel table that was clearly used for meetings. A small model of the new spa complex nestled amongst the scattering of papers spread over the tabletop. Juliet took the seat next to Josh, while Kim, his PA, sat on the other side equipped with a notebook and a glass of water.

'This is so exciting! I take it this is the model of the new spa? When is it expected to open?' Juliet leaned forward to peer at the 3-D model.

'We intend to fully open in November, in time for the Christmas and New Year rush. Although some areas will be in use before then,' Josh said.

'We would need to have pictures before then if we were going to use it for a shoot,' Tia commented.

Juliet frowned at her as she settled back in her seat. 'I'm sure some areas would be suitable for us to use. I mean it doesn't have to be fully functioning, it simply has to look good in the background – and Josh, you said some departments would be open.' Her tone was dismissive of Tia's concern.

'I can see it would be excellent publicity for us to have pictures in *Platinum*, especially as your anniversary edition would coincide with the opening. The Christmas and New Year period is a busy trading time for us with people visiting the city, shows, shopping, and office functions.' Josh picked up his glass and took a sip of his wine.

Juliet shot Tia a small, triumphant glance.

'Do you think you can have enough areas ready, though? I'm sure the designers would not be too happy if their wares were being shot on a building site. You do want to give the best impression both of the spa and of the products.' Tia was aware that she sounded negative but surely Juliet hadn't thought this concept through properly.

Josh stood and lifted off the top half of the model so that they could see inside.

'The ground floor is an exact miniature of what the finished building should look like,' he explained.

There appeared to be a reception area in a sleek modernistic style, changing areas, a suite of beauty rooms, a pool and a suite of various other rooms which seemed to have been given different themes.

'As you can see, we've gone for a lost world of Atlantis overall theme. The reception area will be finished in the next few weeks so we can use that for the shoot. The shell therapeutic suite of rooms would also be at a stage where I'd think you could use it for background.'

Tia peered at the model, trying to imagine herself moving through it, picturing the set-ups of the shoot. 'Will any of the beauty rooms be available? One of those would be good to use for the beauty product placement shots.'

It sounded as if it would make a change from the usual Christmas spreads which always seemed to opt for a 'Narnian winter' or 'Country House Christmas' look.

'I'm sure it'll be stunning. I adore the concept.' Juliet leaned forward once more in a calculated gesture, or so it seemed to Tia, to give Josh an ample flash of her cleavage in her fitted strappy black sundress.

'We can look at the schedule and push for one of the rooms to be ready if that would help you.' Josh placed the top half of the model back down, seemingly unaffected by Juliet's charms. He looked straight into Tia's eyes and smiled as he replied.

Tia's stomach did a mini-flip of excitement and her cheeks heated up as she forced her gaze away from his. There was no mistaking the faint sizzle of electricity that had just passed between them.

'Tell us more about the theme. It sounds fantastic.' Juliet moved her hand to rest the tip of a delicate pearl-pink polished fingernail on Josh's sleeve.

Tia wondered if she'd imagined the flicker of annoyance that crossed his face. The thought heartened her a little and she smiled to herself.

'If you ladies can cope with the dust and the noise we can go downstairs and take a look at the work in progress before we have lunch.'

'Lovely.' Tia was suddenly glad that she was only wearing her comfortable trousers and top.

'Super.' Juliet echoed in a superbright tone.

She wasn't convinced of Juliet's enthusiasm. The tailored designer dress and high heels that Juliet was wearing weren't exactly the most appropriate attire for a building site.

Tia walked beside Josh's PA to the lift, Josh followed behind her with Juliet. The tinkly, grating sound of Juliet's laugh irritating her every step of the way. Once in the lobby Josh took the lead and they walked through the main reception and out into a corridor through a door marked private.

At the end of the corridor a plastic sheet hung from the ceiling blocking the way and holding the dust created by the renovation and building work at bay. Placed on a small shelf on the other side of the wall was a stack of yellow hard hats. Josh reached through and passed each of them a hat, placing one firmly on top of his own head.

'Regulations,' he explained.

Tia slipped her helmet on and tried to hide her smile at Juliet's mortified expression. Josh held the plastic sheet to one side and they stepped through. Bits of plaster gritted beneath the soles of their shoes as they continued on along the corridor. Ahead of them Tia heard music blaring, tuneless whistling and the banging of hammers.

'Are you ladies okay?' Josh asked as they emerged into a round room filled with light, noise and workmen.

Tia smiled. 'Trust me, it's like being at home.'

Gin would have enjoyed this excursion. She would have donned a hard hat with alacrity and bounded about the room asking technical questions of all the workmen.

Juliet looked far from impressed. Her hard hat sat perched precariously so as not to disturb her hair and she looked as if there was a distasteful odour lurking somewhere under her nose. As soon as Josh repeated his question to her, however, she switched to a simpering smile.

'This will be the reception area. The walls are going to be floor-to-ceiling aquariums.' Josh indicated the area all around them, pointing out the various features with his hand.

'But you won't have fish in here when we come to do the shoot, will you?' Tia eyed the hive of activity wondering how on earth Juliet could be thinking of staging a glamorous shoot there in just a few weeks' time. Fish would make a great backdrop but if the tanks were empty it would look like it did now – a builders' yard – not very glamorous at all. Penny would freak out.

'Yep, will do. This area, although it looks as if there's a lot to do, is almost complete. I want the lobby open for preliminary sign-ups to whet the appetite of members. It's going to be very exclusive,' Josh continued to explain as he led the group through the lobby and on into what was to be one of the shell rooms.

'The shell rooms are intended to be a crowd pleaser, designed to make the clients feel as if they're encased inside a delicate pink pearl while they're being pampered and preened with aromatherapy.'

At the moment, however, even as he tried to sell the concept to Juliet and Tia, Josh had to admit it was hard to envisage the finished result.

Juliet's expression said it all; she really was not impressed by her surroundings. He'd wondered how he would feel seeing her again after all these years, whether he would still be attracted to her. Strange, but, despite her still-stunning face and figure, plus the 'I'm available' vibes emanating from her, he wasn't interested. The other woman, Tia, was a different story.

The petite brunette appeared to be completely unfazed by the state of the spa, nodding her head thoughtfully at his estimates of when the work would be completed as if computing in her head whether it would tie in with the magazine schedule. When he'd shaken her hand earlier upstairs, he'd felt a strange kind of connection, almost as if he knew her from somewhere. Although that was clearly crazy, he didn't know any beauty editors. Models and actresses, yes, but someone who wrote about lipsticks, no.

'Are you certain you can have rooms ready in six weeks' time?' Juliet voiced her doubts out loud as she picked her way over an electrical cable, the toes of her black patent shoes grey with dust.

'Quite sure.' Josh gave her what he hoped was a reassuring smile.

Juliet still didn't look convinced.

'You'll keep us informed of the progress, in case we need to change plans?' Tia queried. Her tone was businesslike and she didn't appear perturbed by the building work. He wondered what she'd meant earlier when she'd said it reminded her of being at home. Maybe she had a partner or husband who was into DIY. The thought was strangely depressing.

'Of course. Shall we go and get some lunch now? I'm sure you've had enough of the dust and noise.' To his annoyance Juliet insisted on clinging to his arm like a human leech as they made their way back along the corridor and out into the foyer, shedding their hard hats on the way.

'I'll show you where you can freshen up.' His PA led Juliet and Tia away to the cloakrooms while Josh went off to wash the dust from his own hands.

As he waited in the restaurant for the women to return he wondered if the publicity for the hotels and the spa would come at too high a price if Juliet intended hanging around. After all, he had already agreed to be interviewed and photographed for the magazine for some ridiculous article on eligible single men.

Josh took a sip of the mineral water the waiter had placed before him. He wasn't vain but he wasn't stupid either. He knew lots of women were anxious to become a permanent fixture in his life. Even without the lure of the money and the hotel chain he knew he wasn't exactly ugly. All the same, if Juliet's biological clock was ticking he had no intention of falling for her. They weren't sixteen any more.

'Juliet loves Josh for ever.'

It had been written inside a heartshape on the red cover of Juliet's history book. He'd taken some stick from the rest of the guys on the rugby team over that.

He stood as Tia and Juliet approached the table and a chill ran down his spine as if someone had walked across his grave.

5

Tia followed one step behind Juliet across the restaurant to where Josh stood waiting for them. Her cheeks were still warm with embarrassment from the fuss Juliet had made in the ladies' about the dust marks on her dress. Kim had borne the brunt of the complaints when she'd kindly offered to sponge away the offending marks. Now, as they neared their table, and Josh, Juliet was all smiles once more.

As soon as they were all seated, Josh turned his attention to Tia. 'I know Juliet has just started at the *Platinum* offices, but what about you, Tia? Have you been working there long?'

'A little over two years. I worked at a number of magazines before then, you know, first as an intern, then as an assistant, before finally working my way up to beauty editor.' Tia reached for the water jug, anxious to pour herself a drink to hide her nervousness. She felt like a candidate at a job interview, trying to make a good impression.

His bright blue gaze made her uncomfortable. 'I was

trying to think whether we've met before somewhere. You seem familiar.'

Her hand shook as he spoke and the heavy crystal water jug wavered in her grasp. Iced water spilled in a cascade on to the table and splashed over the edge.

'You clumsy idiot!' Juliet jumped up from her seat, a large water stain on the front of her dress.

Tia's cheeks burned under her colleague's furious glare, mortified by the disaster. 'I'm so sorry. Truly, I didn't mean to spill it. Here, let me help you. The jug was heavier than I thought.' She grabbed a pile of napkins from the table.

'It was an accident,' Josh soothed, proffering Juliet another of the linen napkins to mop up the water, even as two waiters scurried across to replace the dripping tablecloth and all the place settings.

'I'm soaked.' Juliet dabbed ineffectually at the front of her dress with angry stabbing movements.

Kim rose from her seat. 'If you'd like to come with me, I'll get housekeeping to sort it out for you.'

Juliet contented herself with a last furious look at Tia before marching off with Josh's PA.

Tia bit her lip, trying to control her emotions as the waiters departed with the sodden tablecloth. Once more it seemed she was destined to be on the receiving end of Juliet's temper.

'I'm so sorry; I've made such a mess. My godmother always jokes about my clumsiness. Poor Juliet is soaked; maybe I should head back to the office. We can always sort out the details for the shoot over the phone.'

Tia's heart thumped painfully in her chest. Juliet's anger and Josh's earlier statement had sent her mind reeling.

Had he recognised her because of this accident? She had always been clumsy at school, dropping her books and her pens, tripping up on the stairs. Perhaps it would be better if she left before Juliet returned. She picked up her handbag, anxious to make her escape.

'Don't worry about a thing; it was an accident, it could have happened to anyone. Juliet always was a bit hasty, and besides, Kim will soon have her all dried out and perked up again. Stay and enjoy your lunch. I insist.' His eyes smiled into hers and reluctantly Tia replaced the strap of her bag on the back of her chair.

He passed her a menu and refilled her water glass.

'Thank you.' She took a deep, calming breath to steady her nerves and tried to pick something to eat that she wasn't likely to drop down her front or choke on and require the Heimlich manoeuvre.

'It's funny, I'm sure I would have remembered you if we'd met before. Tia is an unusual name.'

She shuffled in her seat and pretended to focus on the menu, even though the print was swirling in front of her. She should have left while the going was good.

'My godmother chose my name; she always says it seemed to suit me.' She gave a small shrug. Josh wasn't to know that Ginny had spent hours with a pile of baby name books trying to find something as far from Tia's original given name of Barbara as possible. It had all been part of the plan.

'It sounds as if you're close to your godmother?' Josh asked.

'I live with her. My mother died when I was sixteen.' Tia closed her menu with a snap.

Memories of that horrible last summer rushed into her mind. The awful humiliation of the end of term disco, Josh and Juliet, and then, only a few weeks later, her beloved mother finally succumbing to the illness that had dogged her for all of Tia's short life.

Ginny had stepped in to rescue her by taking care of the funeral arrangements, packing up the house and selling it before whisking her away to London and a new life. A fresh, new start, just as she'd promised Tia's mother.

'I'm sorry. That must have been a very difficult time for you,' Josh's voice was warm with sympathy. His gaze locked with hers sending a tingle of awareness through her body.

'Thank you, it was.' Just for a split second she wished her past had been different. That she had never won the scholarship to Longmorton High School and had never met Josh or Juliet before this week.

Much to her relief she spotted a now-dry Juliet returning to the table, putting an end to any further discussion about Tia's past.

'We haven't ordered yet, you're in the nick of time,' Tia gabbled, offering Juliet her menu.

Juliet waved her away with an impatient flick of her wrist. 'Oh, do keep still, Tia, before you knock something else over.' She took her seat next to Josh while Kim took the place next to Tia.

Tia noticed Kim sharing a meaningful look with Josh, but Juliet, busy with the menu, appeared oblivious to the exchange.

Juliet dominated the conversation for the remainder of lunch. It didn't seem to matter what subject was raised, she had a knack for managing to turn every topic to the wonderfulness of Juliet. Tia was content to sit and listen, with no desire to draw any more attention to herself, despite Josh and Kim's attempts to include her in the conversation.

'I'll have to leave you ladies with Kim, now, as I'm afraid I have another meeting to get to. Please stay and enjoy your coffee.' Josh dropped his napkin on to the table and pushed his chair back.

'Call me later, and we can go over the details,' Juliet suggested, her voice rich with meaning.

Tia tried to hide a smile as Josh's cheeks turned slightly red. 'Erm, sure, catch you later. Tia, it was very nice to meet you. Hope to see you again soon.' He shook her hand briefly, taking her by surprise. The warm pressure of his fingers sending tiny sparks of desire into her bloodstream, still lingering long after he left.

'Actually, I do need to leave too.' Tia seized her bag and stood. She really didn't want to spend any more time in a tête-à-tête with Juliet, and Josh's touch had unnerved her.

'If you're going back to the office, we can share a cab.' Juliet placed her tiny china coffee cup back on its saucer. Her tone made it clear that she wasn't prepared to allow Tia to escape quite so easily.

'Thank you for looking after us today, Kim.' Tia smiled warmly at the older woman. She still felt guilty over the water juggling incident. Poor Kim had probably had to endure another dose of Juliet's bitching, thanks to Tia's clumsiness.

'Not at all, it was my pleasure.' Kim assured her.

Juliet didn't comment at all. They left Kim in the restaurant and waited at the entrance of the hotel while the doorman hailed a taxi. Tia followed in Juliet's wake as she swept out of the lobby and into the black cab without speaking. Tia wondered if it was too much to hope for that she might get the silent treatment all the way back to the office.

'Don't think I don't know what you were up to,' Juliet hissed.

'Sorry?' Tia stared at her.

'Little Miss Innocent. You tipped that water over me on purpose. I suppose you think you have a chance with Josh Banks? I saw the way you two were looking at each other when I came back from the restroom. Well, you're barking up the wrong tree there. He was mine once and he will be again, so stay away.'

Tia was aware she was probably gaping like a goldfish. 'I spilled the water by accident, the jug was much heavier than I expected. I'm sure Josh Banks has plenty of women he's interested in, and I don't think for a moment that I would be one of them.' Judging by the glances she'd seen exchanged between Josh and Kim, she wasn't sure that Juliet was one of them either. Still, Tia had seen Juliet in action before.

Juliet's eyes narrowed and her voice took on a more conciliatory tone. 'I'm sorry, maybe I was a little bit snappy.'

She sighed and produced a tiny white lace-edged handkerchief from her bag, dabbing at the corner of her eyes. 'After all, you and I are colleagues; I'd like us to get on well together. It's simply that Josh and I have such a history together; he's my Mr Right, and, after meeting up with him again today I can tell that spark is still there between us.'

Tia barely managed to restrain herself from rolling her eyes at this outrageous piece of theatre from her companion.

'Well, if that's the case, I hope it works out for you. Is he the reason you came back to London?'

Juliet stopped patting at her face and darted a sharp glance at Tia. 'Partly, but I have to admit I was a little homesick after being away for so long, and, of course, Sir Crispin was so insistent that he wanted me here.' She slipped her handkerchief back inside her bag and drew out a blinged-up gold coloured Dior mirror which she used to check her eye make-up.

The cab drew up outside the office and Tia pulled out her purse to pay the taxi.

'It would be nice if you and I could be friends, Tia,' Juliet said, packing away her mirror.

Tia almost dropped her change and the receipt from the driver. 'Um, sure.'

She scrambled free from the taxi, wondering if she'd heard Juliet correctly. Friends? With Juliet! Her head buzzed as they entered the building and walked towards the elevators. How could she be friends with Juliet?

'Perhaps we could go out for drinks one evening, I'll check my diary. See you later.' Juliet wiggled her fingers at her in farewell when they reached their floor and headed off to her own department.

Tia made her way back to her desk and clicked on her email, hoping a dose of normality might sweep away the surreal conversation she'd just shared with Juliet. It was no use, nothing made any sense. She closed her in-box again.

Juliet had warned her off Josh, as if they were sixteen again. Then she'd said she wanted to be her friend and suggested a drinks date. Talk about keeping your friends close and your enemies closer. She remembered Juliet's friends at school. Sasha, doe-eyed and a bitch of the first water, now married for the second time to a stockbroker who was at least twenty years older than she was; Melanie, blond-haired and blue-eyed with a reputation for sleeping with the entire rugby team, including the subs bench, was working in TV; then there had been Yasmin, Juliet's yes-woman. Tia had no idea what had happened to Yasmin.

'Well, come on, darling, tell Uncle Ravi all about it.' Ravi's voice preceded him before he appeared in her cubicle and dropped down into the spare seat her assistant had always used.

'The spa will be gorgeous – when it's finished. At the moment it's a building site, and I'm not sure enough of it'll be done in time for the shoot. I'm going to ask Penny to go and take a look. I think she's the best person to make a judgement even though she's livid with Juliet for mucking up her arrangements with the Milano. Lunch was delicious, but Juliet is still a cow and I accidentally threw a jug of iced water into her lap.'

Ravi's cheeks pinked with excitement at the last part of her statement. 'Accidentally? Oh fabulous, I would have paid money to see that. I'm only surprised she didn't melt when the water hit. Wait till Saffy knows – you haven't told her yet, have you?'

'There's more. Juliet said she's still in love with Josh Banks and that's partly why she's back in the UK.' Tia waited for Ravi's response.

'Really? Wow, from the column inches on that guy I don't see any signs of him having been pining his life away over her. Do you think they have it going on?' He arched an eyebrow as he posed the question.

Tia shrugged. 'I didn't get that impression either, but she warned me off him. Can you believe it? Like we were little kids at school or something. As if he'd be interested in me anyway.'

Ravi hugged himself with delight. 'Oh, darling, you must have *really* got on her tits.'

'Anyway, after all that now she claims she wants to be my friend and wants to set up a date for drinks.'

Ravi laughed aloud, only stopping when Tia gave him a withering look. 'Sorry, sweetie, but that is positively too priceless for words. You and Jools – bosom buddies, fabulous.'

'Not funny.'

'No.' Ravi attempted to suppress a smile and failed.

'I'll be glad when this whole bloody anniversary edition is put to bed,' Tia muttered.

'I'm interviewing your main man next week for that Christmas Crackers piece. Is he as gorgeous as his pics?'

'Yes he is, and he's straight.' Tia's body warmed at the memory of Josh's hand touching hers. She wondered briefly how she would feel if his hands touched more of her.

Ravi grinned at her. 'Good job, or Juliet would be warning me off next and offering to be my friend.'

Tia smiled back, her spirits lifting at her friend's good humour. 'You should be so lucky.'

6

'Spill.' Saffy slipped on to the barstool next to her. Her eyes were bright with anticipation at a juicy piece of gossip.

Tia waited until the bartender had placed two tall glasses of gin and tonic in front of them and moved away before replying.

'I'm sure Ravi's already told you what happened.'

Saffy poked the lemon slice inside her drink with her twizzle stick, making the ice cubes clink against the glass.

'Yeah, but I want details. Tell me everything, but especially about chucking water over the bitch queen from hell.'

Tia smiled and shook her head. 'It was an accident.'

'Wish I'd seen it. She was in a foul mood this afternoon. She and Penny had another stand-up row. They were so loud, Helen came out of her office to calm them down.' Saffy slurped noisily on her drink.

'How did I miss that?'

'You were in the loo.' Saffy licked her lips.

'Have you drunk that already?' Her friend's glass was already miraculously devoid of liquid. The ice cubes hadn't even had a chance to melt.

Saffy shrugged and rattled her glass on the counter to attract the bartender's attention. 'I've had a bad day.'

Tia watched as the bartender replaced Saffy's empty glass with a full one.

'What could be worse than having Juliet tell you she wants you to be her friend?'

'Having her walk through the bloody door!' Saffy gestured towards the entrance with her glass, spilling droplets of gin on to the polished top of the bar.

Tia's heart plummeted floorwards as she watched Juliet pick her way through the crowd at the entrance of the Pink Pagoda.

'I swear if I find out who let on that we drink in here, I'll kill them,' Saffy muttered as she pasted a false smile to her face.

'And I'll help you bury the body,' Tia added under her breath, watching as Juliet drew closer.

'I wondered where all you busy little worker bees buzzed off to when you left the office.' Juliet gave a little tinkling laugh. 'Oh, and look, the gang's all here,' she added as Ravi made his way across the bar.

Tia suppressed an irrational urge to giggle at the expression of dismay on Ravi's face when he noticed their companion. No one responded to Juliet's comment. She rapped on the bar to attract the bartender's attention and ordered a Champagne cocktail without bothering to ask what everyone else was drinking.

'Well, this is fun, isn't it?' she remarked as she turned back to face them.

'Lovely,' Saffy said brightly and not very convincingly as she took a long slurp from her gin.

Tia frowned at her, while Ravi managed to catch the bartender's attention to order his drink and extra tonic to top up their glasses.

'Tia was telling me this afternoon that you and Josh Banks knew each other at school. I'm interviewing him next week for the Christmas Crackers feature on eligible bachelors, is there anything I should know?' Ravi smiled disarmingly at Juliet.

Juliet sipped her cocktail. 'Well, Josh *was* head boy.'

Ravi's smile widened. 'And I bet you were head girl. I can just picture you now in your little white ankle socks.'

Saffy pulled a sour face behind Ravi's back.

Juliet blushed. 'Actually, I *was* head girl. Josh and I were boyfriend and girlfriend.'

Tia fidgeted on her bar stool. The conversation had taken a dangerous turn.

'And which school was this?' Ravi asked.

'Longmorton High School. Well, it's Longmorton Independently Endowed Preparatory School, to give it the full title. It's a private day school.'

Saffy muttered something unintelligible into her glass.

Ravi gave Juliet another smile. 'I bet you two made the sweetest couple.'

Tia took another large gulp of gin. Ravi's blatant

buttering-up of Juliet, and all the talk of Longmorton was making her acutely uncomfortable.

Juliet sighed and gazed dreamily into her cocktail glass. 'We were together all through sixth form, we even talked about getting married at one point.'

Saffy choked on the lemon slice in her drink and Tia patted her on the back.

'Ah, first love,' Ravi said. He sighed gustily.

'There's still a connection between us. When we met today, it was as if we'd never been apart.' Juliet sighed, too, and drained her drink.

Ravi looked suitably impressed as Saffy recovered her composure. Tia could only wonder if she'd been at the same meeting. Josh hadn't seemed very smitten with Juliet from what she'd seen – unless, of course, she'd read the situation wrongly.

Juliet glanced at her tiny gold wristwatch. 'Dear me, look at the time. I must dash. Lovely chatting with you all, see you tomorrow.'

She placed her empty glass on the bar and made her way to the street through the crowd.

'What the hell was that all about?' Saffy stared at Juliet's empty glass as if it might give her a clue.

'Darlings, I think that might have been dearest Jool's attempt at being our friend.' Ravi raised his hands and made quote mark signs in the air around the friend word.

'Jeez, we need to find a new place to drink,' Saffy muttered, shaking her head. 'What was she wittering on about? I can see her as head girl at some poofy private school. You might know she wouldn't have gone to the local comp like the rest of us.'

Tia wished she could have gone to a normal school like Saffy, instead of Longmorton with its snobbery and elitism.

'Well, it sounds as if she's definitely still got designs on the luscious and filthy rich body of Mr Banks.' Ravi sipped his drink.

'I think she's delusional. It'll probably turn out to be like that film, *Fatal Attraction*, where the woman boiled the rabbit.' Saffy drained her gin and looked hopefully down the bar, trying to catch the bartender's eye.

'What do you think, darling?' Ravi turned to Tia. 'You saw them together today. Is it an affaire du coeur?'

Tia forced a smile. 'You are such a fool, Rav. I don't know. She certainly seems keen on him. She warned me off, remember?'

'You didn't tell me that.' Saffy stopped trying to get another drink and stared at Tia.

Tia shrugged. 'It seemed weird. I mean, I only met the guy today but she thought I'd chucked water over her so I could get him to myself and have my wicked way with him.'

'Hussy.' Ravi clicked his tongue and grinned at her.

'By the way, I went and saw Helen today.'

Now Tia and Ravi stared at Saffy.

'About the job? What did she say?' For once, Tia managed to beat Ravi to the punch.

'Hmm, there's something very fishy going on. I mean, I was tactful and everything. I didn't just go barging in there saying she'd promised the job to me, what happened?' Saffy paused.

'Go on.' Ravi leaned in closer to hear Saffy more clearly over the noise in the bar.

'Well, we chatted, as you do. You know what Helen's like, you go all around the mountains before she gets to what you want to know. Anyway, the magazine in NY where Juliet was working is part of Hellandback Publications. Apparently, her move is all a bit hush-hush and complicated, something to do with shares and recent acquisitions.'

'And?' Tia asked.

'Helen was totally vague as usual, but this job is kind of a secondment. I got the impression that Sir Crispin forced Helen to take Juliet, but there was something of a cloud in the NY office.' Saffy sat back, a triumphant smirk playing on the corners of her purple-lipsticked mouth.

'Ooh, scandal! How delicious, darling.' Ravi, too, sat back, relaxing his elbow against the bar. Tia could almost see the wheels in his head turning as he filed away this latest tit-bit of information.

'How do we find out more?' he mused.

'I'm going to call the NY office and see what I can dig up,' Saffy announced, finally catching the bartender's attention for another drink.

'Do you think that's a good idea?' Tia asked.

'What? The drink, or Saffy snooping around digging up the dirt of dear Jules?'

Tia frowned at Ravi. 'I'm serious. Juliet is already

being a cow to you, Saf, you don't want to make her worse.' Memories of how much of a cow Juliet could be crowded into her mind. She knew Saffy could probably take care of herself but she would hate to see her friend on the receiving end of Juliet's malice.

Saffy shrugged and accepted another gin from the bartender. 'Look, she already hates me but since I do all the actual work I'm too valuable for her to ditch me. Besides, I can take Miss Poncey-pants, job-stealing ex-head girl any day.'

'And her little dog, too,' Ravi added with a witchy cackle.

Across town, Josh smiled for yet another photograph and shook the hand of yet another well-wisher. As patron of the cancer charity for the illness that had killed his father he attended many evenings like this one. Tonight was a black tie fundraising dinner. Tickets had been sold to the wealthy, the glamorous and the good to raise much-needed funds for a new piece of equipment for the X-Ray department at one of the teaching hospitals specialising in searching for a cure.

Standing in line next to the charity's chief executive and treasurer, he kept a smile fixed to his face as he greeted the guests while his mind wandered. He kept recalling the morning meeting with Juliet and her colleague. He knew his PA hadn't been overly impressed with Juliet and, truthfully, neither was he. She might still be beautiful and still just as willing to let him into her knickers but personality-wise nothing had changed.

Back then his hormones and the prospect of hot sex on tap had blinded him to Juliet's true nature for a long time. It had taken the incident with that fat girl to show him what his girlfriend was truly like. Now the other woman who'd looked around the spa, Tia, he wouldn't mind getting into her knickers. There had been a real connection when he'd shaken her hand and looked into her stunning brown eyes.

Dimly, he became aware that someone had asked him a question and he forced his mind back to the present. Despite the open windows and several strategically placed fans, the room was hot and stuffy. Beneath his dinner jacket his crisp white shirt had stuck to his back. His bow tie was strangling him and he wriggled his neck to try and ease the discomfort. He glanced around the room, pleased to find most of the white-linen-clad tables now had guests seated at them.

'Josh, darling, I didn't expect to see you here tonight. What a delicious surprise.' A soft familiar feminine voice dragged his attention back to the receiving line.

'Juliet, how nice.'

She smiled up at him, ensuring he got a good view of her cleavage, displayed to perfection in her dark-red evening gown. He smelled the rich heady scent of her perfume and knew from the glint in her eye that she had been perfectly aware that he would be there that evening. To his surprise she was accompanied by Sir Crispin Stanford-Hope. He knew Sir Crispin from other events and he usually arrived accompanied by women young enough to be his granddaughters.

Josh wondered why Kim hadn't alerted him to Juliet's name on the guest list. Never mind, it had probably said 'Sir Crispin Stanford-Hope and guest'. He shook hands with Sir Crispin and Juliet murmured, 'See you later,' as she passed down the line.

The ordeal of the receiving line over, Josh followed the chief executive to take his seat only to realise that as one of the major donors, Sir Crispin and Juliet were seated at the same table.

Juliet sent him a smouldering glance and shook her napkin out on to her lap as he sat down opposite her.

'All alone, this evening?' she asked as Sir Crispin buttonholed the charity's chief executive with a long and involved golfing story.

'I don't usually bring my dates to these kinds of functions.' He gave her a brief smile back and wondered how quickly he could eat a five-course meal and escape without indigestion setting in.

'Crispin very generously asked me if I'd care to accompany him this evening and, as I've always been keen on supporting *this particular* charity, I took him up on his offer.' Juliet leaned forward as she spoke and he caught a glimpse of a tiny brown mole on her left breast. He recalled the other one, equally as familiar, on the inside of her right thigh and swallowed hard.

The first course arrived – a cold summer soup – and, thankfully, Sir Crispin returned his attention to Juliet. Josh took a gulp from his glass of mineral water. The drink reminded him of the drenching Juliet had received at lunch and he smiled to himself at the memory.

Suddenly he found himself wishing it were Tia opposite him now, with her large dark eyes and the dimple that flashed in her cheek when she smiled. He wondered if she might have any moles that would be worth exploring. Under the linen trousers and silky shirt she'd worn at lunch she appeared to have a very nice little body. There had been something there when he'd shaken her hand, an uncanny sense of familiarity that he couldn't explain. Somehow he would have to work things out so that he could see her again.

As the waiter cleared away the empty dishes, the unmistakeable touch of Juliet's foot caressing his leg bought him sharply back to the present.

7

It was widely rumoured amongst the *Platinum* staff that Helen's usual near midday arrivals gave her time to have a snifter of 'the hair of the dog' before she showed up for work. However, the following morning Tia discovered that Helen had also decided to start her working day early.

Within minutes of settling in her chair and switching on her computer, an email summons to Helen's office appeared ominously in her in-box. Frantically trying to think of some misdemeanour she might have committed, Tia collected her notebook and diary and walked reluctantly across the office floor to rap on Helen's door.

'Ah, Miss Carpenter, take a seat.' Helen's eyes remained trained on the work on her desk as Tia entered the room.

Perched nervously on the edge of the large leather office chair opposite Helen, she wondered what was coming. She wished she'd had time to grab her usual cup of coffee before coming in. Uncaffeinated, she felt woefully ill-prepared.

Seconds expanded into minutes without Helen

looking up or speaking. Tia fidgeted on the edge of her seat, her pulse racing and her palms growing sweatier with every tick of the office clock.

Unable to bear the silent suspense she tried a discreet cough. Helen raised her head to blink at her thoughtfully through her glasses. Tia immediately sat up a little straighter in her seat and hoped Helen wasn't about to interrogate her on the amount of stationery her department had gone through or want her to justify all her expense claims.

Helen leaned back in her seat and tapped her dark blue Parker pen against her teeth, keeping her gaze fixed on Tia.

'How long have you been with us now, Miss Carpenter?'

Tia swallowed, and hoped this wasn't the prelude to being fired.

'Um, about two years.'

Helen lapsed back into silence and continued surveying Tia with an inscrutable gaze.

She couldn't stand the tension any longer. 'Is there some kind of problem?'

Helen placed her pen on the desk and sighed. Tia waited for her to speak, but instead, Helen stood and crossed to the plate-glass walls of her office and pulled the cord to lower the blinds, screening the room from the rest of the floor.

Tia was now convinced she might as well go and look for a cardboard box to carry her belongings home in, even though she couldn't think of anything she might have done that would warrant her dismissal. After all, misappropriation of a few stamps and envelopes was hardly grand larceny.

Helen retook her seat. 'Unlike your friends Mr Patel and Miss Patterson, I've always found you to be quite discreet.'

Tia struggled to stop her jaw from dropping open with surprise. Not at Helen implying Ravi and Saffy had big mouths, but at the secretive turn of the conversation.

'Thank you.' Tia wondered if her senior editor really did drink as much as everyone thought.

'I am relying on your discretion with what I'm about to tell you. You *must* keep this information to yourself. I cannot emphasise the need for confidentiality enough.'

Tia wriggled a little more upright in her chair.

Helen leaned forward and rested her elbows on the polished ash top of her desk. 'You may have felt that Miss Gold's appointment was somewhat unconventional? I understand Miss Patterson certainly feels a little aggrieved.'

'I think we were all a little surprised. I mean Saffy is very good at her job,' Tia ventured. This was not the conversation she had expected. At least, it didn't sound as if Helen were ready to sack her.

Helen's gaze flickered around the office as if she expected spies to pop out from behind the filing cabinets. 'Industrial espionage,' she hissed, the words streaming out in a paranoid rush.

Tia blinked, lost for words.

Helen nodded sagely. 'Exactly. So you see the need for discretion.'

'I don't know what to say.' Tia had never spoken truer words in her life. She tried to resist the temptation to look around the office for hidden cameras.

'I'm not in possession of all the details as Sir Crispin is operating on a "need to know" basis, but there is skulduggery afoot. The share prices for the Hellandback corporation have been behaving in a very odd manner. Sir Crispin thinks Miss Gold may be able to assist with his investigations, so arranged for her to join us here.'

Tia decided she would definitely make time for coffee before coming into work in future. If ever there was a need for a girl to be caffeinated it was now.

'How can Juliet help? What has she got to do with the shares? And what's it got to do with me?' Tia wondered if Juliet might still be in touch with Sasha. Perhaps Sasha's stockbroker husband had some insider knowledge that Juliet might be privy to. It all sounded very James Bondish and far-fetched.

Helen gave her a humourless smile. 'The stock market is a very volatile place, powered by rumour. One whiff that Hellandback might be vulnerable and mayhem would ensue. Sir Crispin is endeavouring to find out who is behind the attempts to lower the share prices but the culprit has been pretty clever.' Her dark eyes narrowed and became shrewd behind her glasses. 'I need someone on the inside, someone Miss Gold may take into her confidence, someone who can monitor her dealings and contacts without arousing suspicion.'

Tia's stomach gave another nervous lurch. It sounded as if Helen didn't trust Juliet. 'I don't see—'

Helen didn't let her finish. 'Sir Crispin thinks Mr Banks of Oakleaf Holdings may be implicated. It's no secret that they have diversified their portfolio recently outside the leisure business and now it would seem that Miss Gold and Mr Banks have some history together. I'll be frank with you, Miss Carpenter, my hands are tied over Miss Gold's appointment, but I'm not certain of her motives for joining us. I need someone who is on the spot, so to speak, to observe.'

Tia swallowed the hot bile that surged into the back of her throat. Surely Helen hadn't uncovered her connection with Juliet and Josh?

'But Hellandback is more than just *Platinum* magazine, there are the other publications and the radio and TV productions. I mean, it's not as if Juliet and I are close, we've only just met.' Her cheeks flushed at the last little lie. Besides, it was common knowledge that Sir Crispin's brother-in-law and arch rival Rupert Finch was keen to take over Hellandback.

'Very true, but *Platinum* magazine is the high-profile face of Hellandback, especially with the twenty-fifth anniversary coming up. You have the perfect opportunity to work closely with Miss Gold and Mr Banks over the spa photo shoot and the other promotional events that Sir Crispin has planned.'

Tia stared at her employer. 'I couldn't spy on a colleague!' Not even one as horrid as Juliet, she thought. It was all wrong.

Helen winced. '"Spy" is rather too strong a word, don't you think? What I'm asking you to do is to be alert to anything that may appear unusual or untoward between Miss Gold and Mr Banks, and to keep me informed of any developments.'

'But I don't think Juliet even likes me. Surely Penny would be better placed?' So Sir Crispin wanted Juliet to spy on Josh, and Helen wanted her to spy on both Josh and Juliet? It was enough to make her dizzy.

Helen raised an eyebrow. 'I don't think that would work out very well, do you?'

Tia closed her mouth. Helen had a point.

'Good. Remember, this is highly confidential, so you must refrain from discussing any aspect of this conversation with your colleagues. This of course includes Miss Patterson and Mr Patel.' Helen picked up a sheaf of paper from her desk and lowered her gaze.

Tia sat for a moment still dazed then realised she had been dismissed. Her head still whirling she left Helen's office and headed for the coffee machine. She needed caffeine and she needed it now.

Tia studied the menu on the front of the machine and decided her usual lattes and cappuccinos would not cut the mustard after her interview with Helen. She selected double espresso and hit the button.

'So, have you been a naughty girl, having to go and see our beloved leader at this ungodly hour of the morning?'

Tia startled at the sound of Ravi's voice behind her, making him snort with laughter at her surprise.

'Ooh, someone must have been naughty, jumping like that. Come on Tia, 'fess all to Uncle Ravi.'

'God, Ravi, you made me jump.' Tia retrieved her coffee from the machine, her hand trembling.

He peered at her drink. 'Espresso? Oh dear, it must have been a real chewing up.' He clicked his tongue sympathetically as Tia took a tentative sip of the scalding liquid.

'No, it wasn't. Sorry to disappoint you.' She forced a smile. 'Busy day today, I need a boost to get me going, that's all.'

He pressed the button for his usual morning hot chocolate and looked at her with a level expression. Tia knew her cheeks were pinking under his surveillance.

'Really, everything was fine. Helen wanted to talk about the photo shoot, that's all.' At least that wasn't a complete lie.

'Mmm.' His brow crinkled and he didn't look convinced.

'Hi, what's up?' Saffy appeared as though out of nowhere, materialising over Ravi's shoulder.

'Tia's been called to the office to see Helen and won't say why.' Ravi blew the steam from the top of his cup.

'I did say why. It just wasn't anything exciting,' Tia protested.

'But you're drinking espresso,' Saffy observed as she collected her own cup of hot water from the machine.

'Helen said I have to work closely with Juliet over this photo shoot thing.' Tia took another cautious sip of coffee and turned to head back to her desk, anxious to escape any further questions.

'Fair enough. Maybe I should have got a caffeine hit too.' She heard Saffy remark as she left.

Tia sat back down at her desk with a grateful sigh. Somehow she didn't think her explanation had fooled Ravi. His keen journalist's sixth sense would probably bring him sniffing back around her cubicle before the morning was out to try to prise the truth out of her.

She took another sip of her espresso, shuddering at the unaccustomed strength of the drink. Poppy deposited a pile of post into the tray on her desk and Tia opened up her in-box once more to check her emails. She scrolled down the screen, deleting junk mail as she went.

Dear Tia,
I hope you won't mind me dropping you this note to say what a pleasure it was to meet you yesterday. I look forward to seeing you again at the hotel soon. Perhaps we could meet for lunch. Let me know when you might be free. Hope to hear from you soon.

Josh

Tia's heart skipped a beat as she read it through once more.

'Tia, can I speak to you about the photo shoot?' Juliet's imperious query gave Tia her second start for the day, causing her hand to jerk from the mouse and knock the remains of her espresso all over her desk.

Juliet stood back, an expression of distaste on her immaculately made-up face as Tia frantically attempted to mop up the spill.

'Really, you are extraordinarily clumsy!' Juliet commented as Tia lifted her tray of post down on to the floor and stemmed the tide of coffee with some tissue.

'Sorry, what can I do for you?' Tia finally asked once she'd restored some order to her desk. She hoped Josh's email wasn't visible, otherwise, fairly innocent as the contents were, they might trigger Juliet's jealousy once more.

'Helen and Penny are insisting that we liaise over the photo shoot at the spa. I've appointments with designers to choose the clothes next week. You need to decide on products that will presumably complement the choices. I planned luxurious nightwear and obviously evening glamour with a retro twist to reflect the anniversary.' Juliet's tone as she consulted her Moleskine notebook implied that she couldn't understand why a bit player like Tia should even be considered.

'I thought we'd have skincare products, anti-ageing creams, lipsticks will be a strong feature, and maybe Fifties glamour for the hair. I need to consult Penny over booking the stylist. Who are you using for the pictures?' Tia asked and fished a piece of paper from her desk drawer ready to make notes, closing her in-box.

'I'm hoping to get Dino. I usually find his work

adequate but I've left that with my assistant. Penny is insistent on viewing the spa so I've arranged for you to go with her on Monday,' Juliet replied, making another note in her book.

'I've appointments on Monday, surely it would be better if you went with her?' Tia clicked on her calendar, exasperated by Juliet's high-handed ordering of her day.

'I couldn't possibly, I'm far too busy and Monday is the only time Penny has free,' Juliet said and closed her notebook. 'Eleven-thirty a.m. Josh will meet you there.'

It would clearly be a waste of time arguing with Juliet and, bearing in mind her recent talk with Helen, Tia decided it would be simpler if she moved her own appointments around.

'Fine.'

Juliet favoured her with a gracious smile. 'Thank you, Tia. I knew you'd be accommodating. It's very generous of Josh to give up some of his time to see you and Penny. I told him so last night while we were at dinner.'

Tia digested this nugget of information. 'Fortunately, I can move things around this time, but please check with me in future,' she said.

Juliet smoothed her black linen dress with her free hand. 'I'll let Penny know you can make it and I'll email you details of the fashion appointments and an invitation to diary share.'

'Thank you.' Tia wondered where Josh had taken Juliet for dinner. She certainly seemed to be in a good mood. Oddly, her own spirits had drooped ever since Juliet had mentioned going to dinner with Josh.

'I'd better go and see if my assistant has made a start on her work yet this morning.' Juliet half turned ready to leave.

Tia felt a pang of sympathy for poor Saffy.

'By the way, you still have coffee dripping down the side of your desk,' Juliet remarked and exited for her own department.

'It all sounds very odd to me,' Ginny said from the top of the ladder.

Tia sighed and held the steps steady while her godmother made her way carefully back down from where she'd been painting the coving on the hallway ceiling. She'd figured Helen's insistence on confidentiality didn't apply to Ginny. Besides, she needed to tell someone what was going on as it had all sounded very odd to her, too.

'I wish Juliet had never joined *Platinum.*' Tia stretched out a hand to help Ginny down the last step.

Her godmother shot her a sharp glance. 'Darling, you knew when you found out she was working on *Platinum*'s US sister magazine that there was more than a slight possibility your paths would cross.'

Tia heaved a sigh. 'Yes, I know. I suppose I'd kind of shoved it to the back of my mind, a bit like knowing where Josh was and what he was doing but never expecting to bump into him.'

Ginny rested her paintbrush on the tray and wiped

her hands on a piece of rag. 'Ah, now we get to the crux of the matter.'

Tia smiled and shook her head. 'No! Josh Banks is and always has been on a different planet to me. I'm long over my teenage crush.'

Ginny peered at her over the top of her paint-speckled glasses and Tia couldn't help but giggle at her doubting expression.

'Gin, stop it. It's true. Honestly.' Well, it wasn't absolutely true, but there was no way anything could ever happen between them.

'Hmm, if you say so.' Ginny dropped the rag down on to the dust sheet next to the paint tray. She strolled down the hall and into the kitchen with Tia following behind her.

Tia automatically switched on the kettle to make a cup of tea. 'It is true. Josh is still cute and sexy but totally not into someone like me. You've seen the kind of press coverage he gets and the women he dates. Besides, Juliet is back on the scene and what she wants she usually gets.'

Ginny turned on the taps and began to wash the remains of the paint from her hands. 'Methinks the lady doth protest too much.'

Tia shook her head and pulled two mugs from the cupboard. 'What do you think about what Helen said regarding the shares? Could Juliet be involved in anything odd like that? I mean, after seeing her with Josh, if there is a relationship, it seems to me that it would be more likely to be business, at least on his part.

Unless, of course, they're both very good actors. I would have thought Rupert Finch would have been the most likely suspect in any dodgy dealings. He and Sir Crispin hate each other. You'd never think they were related.'

Ginny reached for the towel and dried her hands. 'You told me that Juliet said she'd had dinner with Josh.'

'Yes.' Tia dropped tea bags into each of the mugs and tried to suppress the image that flashed into her mind: Josh and Juliet seated in an intimate restaurant somewhere. It made her feel irritable and, if she were honest, jealous.

'I don't know what to think. I mean, Juliet has always been unscrupulous, hasn't she? And you said you wondered what she'd been up to in Helen's office that morning you went in early. She could be double-dealing.' Ginny collected the milk from the fridge and passed it to Tia.

'I suppose it's possible. I forgot to mention that to Helen. Do you think I should have done?'

Ginny watched as Tia poured boiling water on to the tea bags and added the milk. 'I don't know. I mean, you've no proof that she was doing anything wrong. She may have had a perfectly good reason to be in Helen's office.'

'I guess.' Tia knew from Ginny's expression that she didn't believe Juliet had been there for an innocent reason any more than she did.

'Well, if she *is* up to no good, it'll come to light eventually. I'm bitterly sorry you have to go through all this again. I'd hoped that when you moved here with me and, well, made a completely new start, you'd have put all the bad things behind you. You've done so well, your mum would have been very proud.' Ginny's voice held a tell-tale tremor.

Tia wondered if that were entirely true. Yes, her mother would have been proud of her degree and her job and the way she looked now. The identity change which had been part of that new life had perhaps been a step further than her mother had intended. She slipped her arm around Ginny's waist and gave her a hug while Ginny wiped her eyes with a corner of the tea towel.

'I'm sorry, hun.' Gin gave her a watery smile.

'It's okay. I miss her too.' The ache around Tia's heart when she remembered her mother never quite went away. Sometimes, when she had dark moments she wondered what her life would have been like if things had been different, if her mum had been well. Or even if her father had bothered to stick around during her childhood. He'd visited once after she'd been born then promptly vanished. She'd asked her mother about trying to find him but, although her mum had been willing and given her all the information she knew, her search had come to nothing. Then, as the years passed, she had decided she no longer cared where he might be or what had happened to him. She had Ginny, her friends, and her job and that was all that mattered.

'Too much dwelling on the past never does one any good, does it?' Ginny blinked and patted Tia's shoulder. 'Dear me, I think I need a chocolate biscuit.' She picked up her mug of tea and fished out the tea bag before hunting out a packet of chocolate digestives.

Tia followed her example with the tea bag but refused the offer of a biscuit. She'd learned the hard way in the past that comfort eating only added to her problems. Whatever else might happen with Juliet and co, Tia had vowed never to allow herself to become 'Big Barb' ever again.

Josh stole another glance at the Franck Muller timepiece on his wrist when he thought his PA wasn't looking. There was absolutely no logical reason why Kim couldn't have met Tia and the other woman from the magazine to show them around the spa. No reason at all, except that he had been thinking about meeting Tia again ever since their first meeting. She hadn't responded to his email suggesting lunch, perhaps he would be able to talk her into a date today.

There was something about the pretty brunette that intrigued him, and it was important that this Penny woman be convinced that the spa would be ready in time for the shoot. The publicity would be invaluable and good media coverage guaranteed with all the press attention generated by the anniversary edition. He just hoped Juliet wouldn't take it into her head to turn up for the meeting too.

The charity dinner had been an absolute nightmare. Both Juliet and Sir Crispin had behaved very oddly. Surely even someone as self-absorbed and thick-skinned as Juliet would have got the message by now that he had no personal interest in her as potential girlfriend material. Yet she persisted in behaving as if they were somehow a couple, especially in front of Sir Crispin, her escort to the dinner.

Even stranger was that Sir Crispin, far from being perturbed or annoyed, seemed to be encouraging her. Josh leaned back in his office chair and swivelled round to study the view outside his window. Why would the crafty old coot want to foist Juliet on him? Over the last few months, his broker had advised purchasing shares in Hellandback on the strength of their recent purchasing power – evidenced by their securing of some very exclusive television and merchandising options and rumours within the industry that more acquisitions were on the way.

Although it had all been done via a chain of handling companies, Josh knew Sir Crispin would have got wind of his interest in the company. Not that Josh had any particular plans regarding Hellandback; they were merely one of a number of companies in his portfolio. Still, knowing how possessive Sir Crispin was of his business group, it might be enough to set him trying to find out Josh's intentions.

The strange thing was that the share prices had been extremely good – surprisingly so, considering Sir Crispin's brother-in-law Rupert Finch had made very little secret of his ambitions regarding Hellandback.

The buzzer on his desk sounded, jolting him out of his reverie. He turned his chair back round and pressed the button on the intercom.

'The ladies from *Platinum* magazine are in reception, sir.'

'Thanks, I'll be right down.'

Kim raised an eyebrow in mock surprise as he stood and retrieved his jacket from the back of his chair. 'Are you quite sure you wouldn't like me to go downstairs and look after them?'

'It's fine. It'll be a break from studying these figures.' He slipped his arms into his jacket sleeves and straightened his tie, ignoring the faint smile playing on Kim's lips.

'As you wish,' she said.

Josh frowned at her and strode out of the room. Kim had been with him right from the start when he'd arrived in the office, fresh out of university and thrust straight into running the business following his father's death. Together they had taken Oakleaf Imperial from a small hotel chain into a blue chip leisure company with diversified interests. She was more than just a PA, she was a trusted friend, adviser and confidante.

Although sometimes he felt that she took her interest in advising him on his love life a little too far. It was like having an older sister keeping an eye on his private affairs. As the elevator door pinged to let him know he had reached the ground floor, he had to admit that her advice had saved him from some messy situations previously. Even so, the press had had a field day with some of his past relationships; his picture adorning the gossip columns of the red-top papers far more often than he would have liked.

He spotted Tia and her companion straight away, despite the crowd in the lobby. The older woman was dressed in something that looked as if it might be a Vivienne Westwood original, her chestnut hair was secured in a smooth up do, and she was wearing impossibly high-heeled shoes which looked as if they might have been acquired in a fetish shop. His receptionist had seated them in the lounge area and had provided then with coffee while they waited. He was relieved to see there was no sign of Juliet.

'Tia, it's good to see you again, and you must be Miss Taylor?' He extended his hand to both women in turn.

He guessed fashion directors had to keep up with the trends even if it made them look slightly ridiculous when a style didn't really suit them. Tia, on the other hand, was wearing a classic pale-blue slip dress that slid tantalisingly upwards as she shook his hand, making his pulse beat a little faster at the length of leg she was inadvertently revealing.

Tia's companion proved to be a royal pain in the neck as they toured the spa. By the time she'd lectured him for the umpteenth time on the importance of the shoot and had asked a million stupid questions about trivial matters, he would quite happily have called it a day and told her to find someplace else for her precious feature. Except that the publicity generated would be invaluable, and Tia kept darting small encouraging glances in his direction.

Finally, the tour was over and Penny stashed her notebook and electronic organiser into her huge leather handbag.

'Well, I suppose we can make it work,' she announced grudgingly while she removed her hard hat and smoothed her hair.

'I'm sure everything will be fine,' Tia soothed.

'I'd better get back to the office, or heaven knows what else Juliet will have messed up in my absence.' Penny clasped Josh's hand once more in a surprisingly firm grip, then turned to Tia and said, 'I'll see you back in the office.'

'Nice to meet you. Please get in touch with my PA if we can be of any further assistance,' Josh responded as the older woman wobbled off out of sight on her ridiculously high heels.

Tia's full mouth curved upwards. 'I'm sorry. Penny can be rather full-on, I'm afraid.' A small dimple appeared in her cheek as she smiled and Josh sucked in a low breath.

'Excuse me for a minute, my phone is vibrating.' She delved in her bag to retrieve her mobile and turned away from him while she took the call.

He heard her murmur, 'Okay, next week; yes, that's fine. Thanks, Poppy.'

'Sorry about that. My next meeting just got rescheduled.' She grimaced as she slipped the phone back inside her bag.

'Then perhaps I can persuade you to join me for lunch today,' Josh suggested.

For a split second he thought he saw panic flash in her dark eyes.

'If your meeting is cancelled, then surely you don't

need to rush back? And it's a beautiful day; I could use a bit of a break from the office myself.'

She caught her full lower lip between white, even teeth while she gave the suggestion some thought and he found he was holding his breath while he waited for her answer.

'Thank you; I guess I *could* have a break. I'm sure my paperwork will still be waiting for me on my desk when I get back.' She gave him a smile that revealed her dimple once more and made his heart thump a little louder in his chest. He wondered how she would react if he were to bend his head and kiss her right on the tantalising hollow.

'I'll let reception know where I am.' He tore his gaze away and walked across the lobby to the desk, elation at having persuaded her to join him adding an extra spring to his step.

'Lunch in the roof garden? Very nice. Juliet Gold wasn't in that group, was she?' Kim asked when he called up to speak to her and asked her to arrange for a picnic lunch for two to be served on his private roof terrace.

'It's a nice day, I thought I'd eat outside – and for your information, no, she wasn't, thank God.'

'Hmm. Guess I'll let you off, then.' He heard her low chuckle down the line. 'My bet is that your dining companion is the attractive brunette, then? Tia?'

'Kim, sometimes you're impossible.'

The roof garden formed part of Josh's private complex at the top of the hotel. It had been one of the first things he'd planned when refurbishing the building: a private, leafy, calm space well away from the media glare and prying eyes where he could still be close to his business interests.

'Where are we going?' Tia asked as they entered the lift.

'Wait and see.' He pressed the button to take them up to the penthouse floor. They would need to get out and go through his private apartment to reach the garden.

The faint fresh scent of her perfume teased him as they travelled upwards in silence. He sensed her unease increasing in the short space of time it took to travel to the apartment, her restless fidgeting a clear indication of her nervousness. Surely his reputation with women wasn't that bad? He knew the press had carried some far-fetched articles but he hadn't thought they would be enough to worry an intelligent young woman like Tia. As they stepped out on the landing leading to his office and his private suite, she hesitated.

'I thought we would be eating in the restaurant.'

'It's such a nice day I thought you might enjoy eating outside.' He punched in the security code to his apartment and stood aside to allow her to step through first. Perhaps it had been a mistake to bring her up here. He'd thought she would enjoy the private beauty of his garden but, instead, she appeared nervous and wary of his intentions.

She looked puzzled but entered the large hallway.

'In here.' He pressed a button discreetly hidden in the cream panelling and the door to his private elevator slid open. Tia stepped inside, a questioning frown still on her face.

'Very secret service!' she quipped.

He laughed and shook his head, trying to dispel her nerves with his actions. In a matter of seconds the elevator door reopened and they were on the roof of the hotel. Tia's heels made a hollow clicking noise as she walked out along the wooden decking towards a small circular marble-topped table surrounded by potted greenery.

'Wow, definitely a Bond-type lair.'

'I was hoping you'd be impressed.' He watched as she turned on her heel to survey the terrace, peeping over the low walls that surrounded the garden.

'Maybe we should do the shoot up here,' she suggested.

He shook his head. 'I'm afraid not. This is my private space. Only a few people ever get to come here.'

She fidgeted with her bag and he was surprised to see

her hand tremble as she adjusted the strap. 'Is that something else that's supposed to impress me?'

The elevator doors reopened as he was about to reply. Two of the waiters from the restaurant emerged with a large hamper containing tableware and food, and Tia stood to one side while they quickly set the table. An awkward silence hung between them until the waiters left.

'I'm sorry. I didn't mean to make you feel uncomfortable by bringing you here.' Maybe he should have gone for something more low key. It had felt that it was important to make a good impression and sharing this private space with her had seemed like a good idea. Plus it had the advantage of being out of public view so he was unlikely to be bothered by paparazzi.

'No, it's fine. All this is very impressive. I'm flattered.' She gestured towards the garden and the table with her hand, then gave him a small smile.

He relaxed a little at her words. Perhaps this would be okay after all. 'My mission is accomplished, then.'

Tia walked back across the decking to the table and took a seat on one of the white wrought-iron chairs opposite her host. Now there was a little more space between them, her heart rate had started to settle back down. Coming up to his apartment and then out into the garden away from the hotel guests and the staff had unnerved her. It felt a little too intimate, too soon, or maybe she wasn't quite used to the lifestyle of the rich and famous, despite her time at *Platinum*.

'What can I get you to drink?' He indicated a silver bucket filled with ice at the side of the table containing soft drinks, water and white wine.

Tia swallowed, her throat suddenly dry with nerves.

'Water will be fine. I can't believe you've gone to so much trouble.' She peered at the delicate tiered stand that stood on the table, containing all kinds of nibbles and sandwiches. Secretly she wondered if she would manage to help herself to anything to eat without knocking something over. Lately her clumsiness had reached new levels, especially when she was around Juliet or Josh.

'It's no trouble at all. It keeps my chefs on their toes.' He smiled at her as he poured the water into her glass.

Tia wished her nervousness would go. The whole thing was crazy; why was she here on Josh's patio eating lunch? She was certain that at any minute she'd probably break out in hives, and that would not be a good look.

'Ice?'

'Thank you.' Drat, her voice sounded husky.

He dropped two ice cubes into her glass and placed it on the table in front of her. He sat opposite her and passed her one of the fine white china plates with a gold rim and a matching white linen napkin.

'This looks delicious. I should have meetings cancel on me more often.' Tia tentatively took a small cream cheese and salmon sandwich from the stand in front of her, praying she wouldn't knock the whole thing over.

Josh cheerfully helped himself, piling his plate high

with food. 'I must admit, I'm quite glad your meeting cancelled. It saved me a lot of trouble.'

Tia paused for a second before taking a cautious nibble of her sandwich and swallowing. 'I'm sorry? I don't follow you.' Her pulse hitched up a notch and memories of her conversation with Helen swirled around in her mind.

'After we met the other day, I really wanted to see you again and I was struggling to think of an excuse. You didn't respond to my email so I thought maybe I'd blown my chances.' He smiled at her.

'Oh.' Unable to think of a suitable response, she took another small bite of her sandwich. Was this something to do with Helen's espionage/takeover theory? Or did he mean he liked her? He had suggested lunch in the email but she hadn't felt it was up to her to take the initiative and call him. And what about Juliet?

Josh heaved a sigh and placed a half-eaten chicken drumstick down on his plate before wiping his hands on a napkin. 'I'm sorry. I've played this all wrong, haven't I?'

She forced herself to swallow and stared at him in bewilderment, as he continued. 'I really liked you when you were looking around the spa the other day with Juliet. You were so calm and practical – you even handled Juliet's nonsense well. I hoped I might get the chance to spend some more time with you.'

Tia picked up her glass of water and took a refreshing sip, hoping that by giving her hands something to do he wouldn't notice she was shaking. Being described as calm and practical made her sound boring and matronly, like a child's governess. Juliet had said she and Josh had been out to dinner together – so what was his relationship with her? She supposed there was no other way to find out, so she plunged ahead.

'I assumed you meant you wanted a business lunch date. Juliet told me you had dinner with her the other night and I know you used to date,' she said tentatively, knowing full well that he hadn't meant a business date at all in his email.

To her surprise, Josh frowned and looked puzzled before bursting into laughter.

'Amazing. That woman's powers of self-delusion are incredible.' He shook his head. 'I did have dinner with Juliet. Juliet and at least two hundred and forty-eight other people. It was a charity dinner and she was Sir Crispin's companion, not mine. I didn't even know she would be there.'

Tia replaced her glass back on the table. 'So, you and Juliet aren't dating?' Her face heated as she posed the question, some part of her aware that she was praying his answer would be in the negative.

Josh gave a tight smile. 'No, Juliet and I aren't dating.'

'I'm sorry. It's none of my business, even if you were. It's just that, well, she said you and she used to go out together and . . .' she trailed off at the twinkle of amusement in his eyes.

'Juliet and I dated in high school, years ago. We broke up as we were leaving.' He picked up his own glass of mineral water and took a sip. 'There was an incident at the school leavers' party. Juliet was always pulling pranks, and she'd pulled one on this fat girl who was one of the scholarship students. I hadn't realised till that night how cruel she could be or how ruthless. I'll never forget the look in that poor girl's eyes. I guess it hit me then what Juliet was really like and, well, things weren't the same between us after that.'

Tia's heart raced. She remembered that moment all too well; she been the fat girl victim of Juliet's prank. It was the incident that haunted her nightmares: everyone laughing at her as she'd lain on the floor bedraggled and humiliated, covered in gunk. She'd looked around the circle of faces surrounding her for help and met Josh's eyes. He'd been the only person to assist her to her feet and see if she was okay.

'I saw her a few times after we started university but she was at one end of the country and I was at the other. My father started to become ill around that time with cancer and I wasn't interested in keeping in touch with her. Apart from the odd card or call, I hadn't heard from her until she came back to England.'

Tia was glad she hadn't managed to eat much of her sandwich. She couldn't bring herself to meet Josh's gaze, scared he might look at her and recognise that frightened teenage girl with her ruined clothes and hair from the leavers' party at Longmorton High.

The gentle touch of his hand on hers startled her. 'I promise you there is nothing between Juliet and me.'

Tia forced a shrug, her senses reeling, too aware of the heat creeping from his hand into hers.

'I only wondered. She made it sound as if you were a

couple.' She raised her head to steal a peep at his face. His expression was sombre.

'Hand on my heart, I am free and single. What about you?' He caressed the base of her thumb and a shiver of delight ran up her spine.

'I'm not seeing anyone.' It was hard to believe this was happening. The electric contact of his hand on hers was scrambling her thought processes.

'So, does this mean I haven't blown it? I haven't scared you off by bringing you up here?'

Tia felt the touch of his breath on her face as he lowered his head to kiss her His lips brushed hers, soft at first, then firmer as she responded to his kiss. He tasted cold from the water he'd been sipping but delicious, too. Part of her knew that what she was doing wasn't sensible. Juliet would be livid and, if Helen got to hear of it, maybe even her job could be at risk. That logical part of her brain was swiftly silenced by the touch of Josh's hand tangling in her hair as he pulled her closer to deepen the kiss.

Everything else was lost. Tia knew only Josh, holding her, caressing her, tasting her. A small electronic ting signalling the opening of the elevator door and the sound of a discreet cough broke her concentration, alerting them to Kim's arrival. Tia moved quickly out of Josh's embrace, embarrassed at being found in such an intimate situation.

'I'm sorry to disturb your lunch, but those urgent documents you were waiting for came through. If you could sign them now I'll get them straight back ready for the French office when it reopens after lunch.' Kim advanced towards them bearing a sheaf of papers. She smiled apologetically at them.

Josh ran his hand through his hair and took the papers from Kim, a resigned expression on his face.

'I'm sorry about this, Tia, it'll only take a second.'

Tia settled back in her seat and picked up her glass. The ice cubes had melted into the remains of her water but the crystal still felt delightfully chilled against her overheated palms.

She watched from beneath lowered lashes as Josh quickly read through the documents and added his signature at the places Kim indicated. Duty done, Josh stacked the papers back together and handed them to his PA.

'Thanks, I'll get these sent off now. Nice to see you again, Tia.' She smiled at them both and strolled leisurely away back to the elevator.

Tia swallowed the last of her water. What had she been thinking, kissing Josh like that? Well, he'd been kissing her and somebody had certainly been kissing somebody. Her lips still tingled from where his mouth had been pressed to hers.

The thought brought fresh colour to her cheeks and she resisted the temptation to raise her hand to her lips to check if his kiss had somehow marked her in some way.

'I should be getting back to work. The office will wonder where I am.' She reached for her bag and delved inside for her mobile which had been switched to silent during their lunch.

Tia saw she had three missed calls, two from Saffy and one from Juliet. She grimaced and switched her ringtone back on as she got to her feet. Kissing Josh had been a big mistake. A rather lovely one, yes, but one it wouldn't be wise to repeat.

Josh stood too and her cheeks burned at the expression of puzzled amusement in his eyes at her haste to leave.

'Thank you for a lovely lunch.' She sucked in a deep breath and held out her hand for him to shake, hoping he'd take the hint that the kiss had been a lapse that wouldn't be repeated.

He raised an eyebrow at her gesture before taking her hand in his and raising it to his lips to kiss her fingers. A move that sent her good intentions awry and made her mouth dry with desire.

'Till next time.'

She licked her lips, trying to discern the meaning behind his words.

'My phone – lots of missed messages – I really have to go.' She had to get out before she did something stupid and kissed him again.

'I'll see you out.' He released her hand and, with a smile, led her to the elevator.

10

'Where have you been?' Saffy practically bowled Tia over next to the lift doors. 'I tried calling your mobile. Didn't you pick up my messages?'

'My phone was off, I was in a meeting.' She couldn't quite bring herself to meet Saffy's eyes. Her cheeks heated guiltily with the recollection of Josh's lips on hers. She'd been so dazed after leaving him that she hadn't read her messages. The entire taxi journey back to the office had passed in a kind of blissful stupor after he'd told her that he'd be in touch.

Saffy placed a hand on her arm and towed her towards the stationery cupboard. 'We need privacy,' she murmured, and Tia made an effort to keep her feet and follow.

'I got info from New York,' Saffy said eagerly, her tone conspiratorial as they hid behind the stacks of copy paper. 'There's something very fishy about Juliet being dumped here with us. Reading between the lines, they were glad to get shot of her and not just because she's an evil cow, either.'

'Where is she now? Is she in the office?' Tia didn't

particularly feel like running into her, especially as she was fresh from snogging the man Juliet still had a thing for, even if Josh had insisted that her feelings weren't reciprocated.

'She's out, I don't know where. She left me a mile-long list of jobs and scarpered. Perhaps she's seeing Josh Banks.' Saffy shrugged.

'Maybe.' Tia was pretty certain that wasn't where Juliet had gone, but then again, who could tell? It was a struggle to keep things straight right now.

'I'm telling you, there is more to this job move business than meets the eye and then there's this mystery about the photo shoot being moved from the Milano to the Broadoak. There has to be, otherwise Helen would have backed Penny.'

'That doesn't make sense, Saf. It's probably only Sir Crispin interfering again. You know what he's like. *Platinum* is his baby and if he thinks the sun shines out of Juliet's backside, then Helen would have no choice but to back Juliet instead of Penny.' Tia bit her lip guiltily at deceiving her friend, but the strange conversation she'd had with Helen appeared to be colouring everything.

'Maybe.' Saffy gripped Tia's wrist once more as she was about to walk away back to her own cubicle. 'By the way, Ravi's got some great stuff lined up. Did he tell you?'

'Not really, but he's been hinting for ages about a couple of things.'

'Well, it's all hush-hush as they'll be in the

anniversary special, but he's got tickets and backstage passes for your favourite band, The Flying Monkeys for the next concert at the O2. The best bit is, he got extra tickets from entertainment so we can go too. And they're going to be coming into the offices for an interview! Plus, guess what else he's going to do?'

Tia winced as Saffy's grip tightened in her excitement, digging into her wrist. 'Don't know.'

'He's lined up an interview with Imogen Martin! The actress, the one who whacked her pervy ex on that chatshow. She's going to be on the next dance thing on TV but it's all secret as she's only recently been signed and no one else knows. Apparently, Ravi knows Marcus, her boyfriend; the one who does that Crimestopper programme, and he's set it all up as a favour.' Saffy released her grasp on Tia's wrist.

Tia rubbed the tender skin, reddened from her friend's grip. 'Have you been working out?'

Saffy grinned. 'Oops, sorry. Got carried away; I guess I don't know my own strength. I was just so excited, I've been dying for you to get back.'

Tia took a step towards the office space. 'It all sounds great, but I definitely do have to go, Saf, I've got oodles of stuff I need to be working on. My day somehow got totally messed up with rescheduling meetings and everything.'

A puzzled expression crossed Saffy's face. 'I thought you went straight on to your next meeting after Penny came back?'

'Um, it was an informal lunch one, in place of one

that got moved.' Tia hoped Saffy couldn't see her crossing her fingers behind her back. She hated having to lie to her friend, but if she said she'd been with Josh, then she would have a whole heap of awkward questions thrown her way that she simply wasn't ready to answer.

'Oh. It's all right for some, I suppose.' Saffy frowned.

'I'll see you later; we can talk about the Flying Monkeys concert, it sounds brilliant.' Tia scuttled away to the safety of her cubicle before Saffy could ask her anything else.

Tia deposited her handbag under her desk and switched on her computer. She stared blankly at the screen as she waited for it to fire up, her mind still on Josh and the events of the morning. Functioning on autopilot, she entered her password and allowed her thoughts to drift back to when she'd been a teenager wondering what it must be like to be one of the popular girls, and to have a boyfriend. Back to when she'd envied Juliet, and she'd dreamed of what kissing Josh must be like. She'd practised kissing the threadbare face of her old teddy with her eyes shut tight, dreaming of his lips on hers. Back then she'd eavesdropped shamelessly on the conversations of other girls, the ones who had boyfriends, as they had compared notes on what made a good snog. And now, finally, after all these years, she knew.

She stared at the long list of unopened emails filling up her screen. How had she let it happen? It couldn't happen again, however much she might want it to. Tia sighed. For the short time she'd been in Josh's arms, nothing else had mattered except being with him. Now the real world was back.

How would he react if he found out she was actually Barbara, the fat girl he remembered from all those years ago? No matter how she tried to arrange the scenario in her head it was still a disaster. Then there was Juliet. She'd suffered at her hands once before and she wasn't about to give her new ammunition to fire by starting something with the man Juliet had so clearly set her sights on.

She continued to stare at the screen. It was no use. She had to get a grip, make sure she wasn't in a situation where she was alone with Josh again and pretend the whole thing had never happened. Far better to try and get excited about seeing her favourite band at the O2 with her friends than to mope around thinking about Josh Banks.

'I won't do it.' Josh glared at Kim. He kept his voice low so as not to be heard by the photographer and his assistant who were busy setting up at the far end of the room.

She stared back at him, unperturbed by his outburst. 'I don't see that you have much choice.'

Josh tossed the pencil he was holding down on his desk in disgust. 'I agreed to do an interview, nothing else.' He shot a malevolent glance at the journalist who was busy consulting with the photographer about the position of a tinsel-bedecked Christmas tree.

Kim folded her arms across the front of her neat pinstriped blouse. 'And a photo shoot. You knew it included a photo shoot.'

'It seemed reasonable to me that if they were interviewing me and taking pictures here, in my office, that they would be standard, behind the desk-type shots.' Despite his annoyance Josh was pretty sure he detected a hint of a smile on Kim's lips.

Kim unfolded her arms and picked up a notepad from his desk. She flicked back through the pages covered with neat shorthand squiggles. 'I have the notes from the telephone conversation here, the same one I copied into your email and that you agreed to. It definitely said "calendar-style shoot".' She raised an eyebrow.

'Yeah, well, I thought that meant *Business Weekly*, not *Playboy*. At no time do I recall agreeing to strip off to my boxers and pose in a bathrobe wearing a Santa hat next to a bloody Christmas tree,' he hissed, then pasted a hasty smile on his face as Ravi, the journalist, glanced towards them.

There was a definite smirk on Kim's lips now.

'Is everything okay? You are cool with this, right?' Ravi asked as he walked back towards them. He flicked a small piece of lint from immaculate cuffs.

'Oh yes, perfectly,' Kim said. 'Well, I'll just pop downstairs to collect the robe and the rest of the bits and pieces they've requested from reception.'

Josh gritted his teeth as his assistant sashayed out of the room. He'd definitely get her back for this, she was enjoying his discomfort far too much.

'They'll be ready for you in a minute.' Ravi perched himself on the arm of one of the overstuffed leather chairs near the desk and adjusted his jacket. 'Gordon is really very good. I'm sure the pictures will look fabulous.' He gave Josh an appraising look.

Josh eyed the Christmas tree with distaste and shook his head. 'I can't believe I'm going along with this.'

'You're getting off lightly, believe me. You should see the one of the rugby player holding the gift-wrapped ball.' Ravi grinned. 'Our esteemed editor assures us this feature will be very popular with the ladies.'

Josh leaned back in his seat. 'So you're not a freelancer? You're a staff writer for *Platinum*?'

Ravi raised an eyebrow, his handsome face carefully blank. 'Yes, I'm on the staff.'

Josh knew he had to tread carefully or his words could easily be misconstrued. 'I expect you know Juliet Gold and Tia Carpenter, then?' He tried to make the enquiry sound casual, as if he were merely making idle chat to fill in time while the photographer finished setting up his props.

The journalist's expression remained unreadable. 'Juliet joined the staff recently; Tia is a good friend.'

Josh effected a careless roll of his shoulder. How good a friend was Tia with Ravi? He'd assumed that the journalist was gay from his mannerisms but then again, who knew these days? 'I met them both the other day,' Josh said. 'Tia was here earlier. She's a lovely girl.'

Ravi smiled. 'Tia's cool, although she's quite reserved

till you get to know her. I don't know Juliet so well.'

Josh recalled the soft urgency of Tia's lips on his and decided she wasn't as reserved as her friend thought. Although she had managed to skip off back to her office without giving him her mobile number, so maybe Ravi had a point. 'That's a diplomatic answer. I used to know Juliet before, a long time ago.'

'Juliet said. You were at school together, boyfriend and girlfriend?'

Josh wondered why Ravi hadn't mentioned that he knew that bit of information before the interview. 'By the way, this is off the record, isn't it?'

Ravi held up his hands. 'Tape is all packed away.'

'Juliet was my girlfriend when we were at school. I hadn't seen her since we left, apart from a couple of social occasions when we were invited by people who knew both of us. That's maybe three or four times over the last ten years. Then she got back in touch a few weeks ago and ever since she's been all over me like a rash. She seems keen to pick things up where we left off, for some reason.'

'You don't sound too thrilled about it. Juliet has given everyone at the office the impression that you and she are tight again. I take it that's not exactly true?' He folded his arms and looked thoughtfully at Josh.

'Juliet is the mistress of wishful thinking. Everything she's ever wanted in life, Juliet has got. Either her father buys it for her or she steamrollers everyone into giving way.' He grimaced as he recalled exactly how many times in the past he'd witnessed Juliet's ruthlessness in action.

'Excuse me for saying so, but you don't strike me as the kind of man who'd be that easy a pushover. You have a reputation in business as being pretty tough.'

Josh sensed the journalist had chosen his words carefully. He smiled at Ravi, well aware of how he was portrayed in the media: a ruthless business tycoon who'd turned his father's ailing hotel chain around into a multimillion-pound conglomerate.

'No, I suppose I'm curious about her motives. Juliet is pretty easy on the eye so I'm sure she can't be short of male attention. Besides which, she never does anything without a good reason.'

Ravi shrugged. 'Maybe her biological clock has started ticking.'

Kim re-entered the office suite, loaded up with a navy silk bathrobe, embossed with the hotel crest and the various other items the photographer had requested.

'Looks like it's show time,' Ravi said as Kim advanced towards them.

Josh groaned.

'Here you go.' Kim held out the bundle of navy silk towards him, her lips curved in amusement.

'I'm going to be a laughing stock at the January board meeting,' Josh grumbled.

'I'm sure you'll look terrific. The readers will lap it up.' Ravi grinned.

'I'm sure your new friend Tia will be first in the queue for a copy,' Kim added slyly.

As Josh headed off to the washroom to change, he

noticed the flicker of interest in Ravi's eyes at Kim's remark. He silently resolved to have a word with his PA later when the journalist and photographic crew had gone.

Saffy was busy talking, her hands flying around in her usual animated fashion as she updated Ravi on her suspicions about Juliet. It had been a few days since Tia's meeting with Josh and now she, Ravi and Saffy were camped in the Bunch of Grapes public house a few streets away from the office. They had temporarily abandoned the Pink Pagoda after Juliet had called in a second time to join them for drinks.

Tia took a sip of her tonic water with ice and sighed. The ambience in the Bunch of Grapes left a lot to be desired. The floorboards smelt faintly from generations of spilled beer, and the faded red velveteen upholstery of the bench seats bore multitudes of stains and cigarette-burn pockmarks made before the introduction of the smoking ban. The drinks were, however, cheaper, and since Ravi was munching his way through a bag of cheese and onion crisps, it appeared that they did sell snacks.

She bit back a yawn. Left to herself, Tia would have preferred to skip the after-work drink to go straight home. She'd been putting in long hours lately, writing up copy and organising features for the forthcoming issues of the magazine. Since Ravi had been out of the office for most of the week and Saffy had been run ragged by Juliet, Tia felt obliged to go along to the pub with them to catch up when Saffy had suggested they go out.

'Are we keeping you up, darling?' Ravi asked.

'Sorry, I am a bit tired tonight,' Tia apologised, placing her glass down carefully on a dog-eared beermat.

'Been burning the candle at both ends, have we?' Ravi questioned suggestively.

She flushed as Saffy put down her glass to give Tia her full attention.

'No, I haven't been out at all except for my usual gym sessions. My social life is as cruddy as usual.' It was quite true; she'd been working late most evenings and by the time she'd got home to have supper with Ginny, she'd then spent the rest of the evening dozing in front of the television.

Josh hadn't been in touch and she couldn't quite decide if she was relieved about that or annoyed. Relieved, because it avoided any awkwardness, and annoyed, because kissing her was obviously so meaningless to him. Thinking about it now, she realised that he hadn't even bothered to ask her for her mobile number before she'd left him at the hotel that day. Not that she would have given it to him, as she only gave her number to a select group of people – otherwise she felt as though she was never off duty.

'She's gone pink,' Saffy teased.

'I've got something on my phone that'll make her go

even redder.' Ravi reached inside his jacket pocket for his mobile. Saffy immediately leaned forward in her seat to look as Ravi scrolled through various images on his phone.

Grinning with satisfaction he shooed Saffy away and passed the phone over to Tia. Her face burned as she took in the image. It had clearly been taken during a photo shoot and featured Josh wearing a navy silk robe and Santa hat next to a Christmas tree. The robe had been artfully arranged to fall open and show an expanse of his bare chest shadowing down into a tantalising narrow gap below his waist. Her pulse quickened as she looked and guilty memories of his kiss sent even more heat into her cheeks.

'Where did you get that?' She handed the mobile back to Ravi.

'Let me see.' Saffy grabbed it from Ravi's hand. She studied the image, her eyes widening. 'Nice,' she said appreciatively.

Ravi grinned. 'I thought you'd like it. I did his twelve Christmas crackers interview the other day. He certainly had nice things to say about you, Tia.'

She picked her glass up and sought refuge in a cooling gulp of tonic water. 'That was kind of him.' She kept her voice as bland as possible and wondered what exactly Josh had said to Ravi. Surely he wouldn't have said anything about them kissing?

'He wasn't so complimentary about dear Jools. In fact, I got the distinct impression that she was rather a pain in the bum.'

'Isn't she just?' Saffy muttered with feeling.

'He seemed to think, rather like Saffy, that she's up to something.'

'That's a definite; the woman is as wily as a fox, if you ask me. There's something very fishy about her getting that job, and now she's chasing Josh Banks? Weird, I mean he's certainly a good catch but something isn't quite right.' Saffy frowned.

'He also seemed to think you and he had met somewhere before,' Ravi continued, fixing his gaze on Tia.

'It's hardly likely. I mean we don't exactly move in the same circles. I guess if he's been to a gala or something he might have passed me on the stairs or somewhere, I suppose.' Tia wondered if her nose would grow like Pinocchio's if she kept on lying. She resisted the urge to reach up and check for herself.

Ravi arched an eyebrow. 'I don't think passing on the stairs was quite what he meant. He seemed sure he knew you. By the way, he asked me for your digits but I didn't think I should pass them on without checking with you first. He has your email address, hasn't he, darling? And he could always call you at the office – unless, of course, he wanted them for something more personal.'

'Oh, is he keen on you?' Saffy's face lit up.

'No, I don't think so. Though he does have something of a reputation with women.' Tia dropped her gaze, suddenly acutely uncomfortable with the direction of the conversation. It would be so awful if Josh realised who she really was. Even so, she couldn't help feeling a little cheered that he had asked for her number after all.

'So, he didn't ask you directly for your digits?' Saffy looked at Tia.

Tia shook her head. 'I had to leave quite quickly after the meeting I went to with Penny, so perhaps he forgot. I expect it's simply to do with the big shoot at the spa. Ravi's just trying to stir things up as usual.' She forced herself to smile and look unconcerned.

'Oh, pity. He's quite a hotty.' Saffy continued to look at Ravi's phone, scrolling on to another image. 'Wow, and who is this guy?'

Tia caught a quick glimpse of a muscular naked man holding something that looked like a rugby ball in Christmas wrapping paper in front of his groin. A dull red flush stained Ravi's cheekbones. 'That's another one of the Christmas crackers, and he's my dinner date for tonight.' He took the phone back from Saffy.

'Typical, all the best-looking ones are either gay or taken.' Saffy winked at Tia.

'I didn't know he was gay,' Tia mused. She knew Ravi had said the player was a member of the national rugby squad and she was sure it would have been in the press.

Ravi returned his mobile to his jacket pocket. 'Well. He asked me on a date, and I'm guessing it wasn't merely for my sparkling repartee.'

Tia smiled and shook her head. 'Well, have fun and don't do anything we wouldn't do.'

'In Saffy's case, that means I can do absolutely anything I like, then,' Ravi chortled while Saffy gave him a disapproving glare.

*

Tia's mobile rang as she unlocked her front door. She wrestled the key from the lock and then retrieved her phone from her bag before it could ring off. A mobile number she didn't recognise was on the screen and her heart gave a wild flutter as she wondered if it might be Josh.

'Hello.'

'Tia, its Juliet.' Juliet's clipped public school tones sounded in her ear.

'Um, hi.' Tia hadn't seen much of Juliet all week, apart from the second unwanted appearance in the Pink Pagoda, and had been quite happy to avoid her. She speculated on how Juliet had managed to get her mobile number since Tia certainly hadn't given it to her.

'I called at the Pink Pagoda to see if I could catch up with you there but I must have missed you all.'

Tia stepped inside the hall and closed the front door, keeping her mobile pressed to her ear. 'Was it something urgent you needed to see me about?' She tried to think whether there was anything she should have done that Juliet should have been aware of.

Juliet laughed her tinkly laugh that never failed to set Tia's teeth on edge. 'It was about tonight, of course.'

'Tonight?' Okay, she'd obviously missed something. What was happening tonight?

'Didn't you get Helen's messages? There's a special charity event on tonight. Helen said she'd emailed you and sent you a text. She should have been attending with Penny but apparently something's cropped up and they can't make it, so you and I have been delegated to attend instead.' Juliet sounded faintly annoyed. Tia wondered if it was because she'd been asked to attend the event or if it was because she'd been ordered to go with Tia.

'No, I haven't received anything. Where is it and what's it in aid of? Is it formal or what?' Tia dropped her handbag on to the side table in the hall and hunted for a pad and pen to take down the details. The last thing in the world she felt like doing right now was having to glam up to go to some boring event, especially if Juliet was to be her companion.

'It's some stupid charity event. Sir Crispin has organised it and it's important that *Platinum* magazine is represented. It's a black tie formal at the Royale. It starts in a little over an hour. You do have something formal you can wear, don't you?'

Tia gritted her teeth. 'Of course. Why? Did you want to borrow something?' How dare Juliet imply that she might not have the right kind of clothes for a formal event. She knew implying that Juliet might not have the appropriate wardrobe was a case of living dangerously. As a senior figure in the fashion world Juliet had to look on trend at all times, especially at occasions where all eyes would be on her.

'Don't be ridiculous! I'll meet you at the Royale in an hour,' Juliet snapped and rang off before Tia could say anything else.

Tia glanced at her watch. This would leave her with a fraction over thirty minutes to grab a shower, reapply her make-up and do something with her hair before heading back out of the door again to meet Juliet. A very *annoyed*

Juliet, at that, after Tia's snappy retort about the dress.

As she made her way upstairs her stomach growled, reminding her that she hadn't had anything to eat since lunchtime. The house seemed to be empty: there was no heavy rock music blasting from the kitchen or scents of paint wafting around the stairwell, so Ginny must have gone out.

Her mobile beeped twice in quick succession, signalling the arrival of text messages. Sure enough, there was one message from Helen commanding her presence at the Royale for the Excellence in Publishing Awards to Charity and another from Ginny saying she had popped out to the supermarket to buy gin and toilet paper.

Tia ordered a taxi then sent a quick message to Ginny telling her about her change of plans for the evening before sending another message to Helen confirming that she'd be able to attend the event at the Royale. She dropped her mobile down on to her bed and headed for the bathroom.

By the time she returned clad in her bathrobe and with her wet hair swathed in a towel, her mobile had started to ring. This time it was Helen.

'Miss Carpenter, I'm so sorry this is such short notice. Penny has injured her ankle and I'm at A and E with her now. She fell off those bloody heels of hers on the stairs at work. Keep an eye on Miss Gold, see whom she talks to, and if she's especially familiar with anyone. Sir Crispin will be there, so be discreet.'

'Helen!' Tia started to protest that she wasn't about to act as a spy, but she wasn't sure Helen could hear her.

The line had become so crackly at Helen's end that all she could hear was a lot of incoherent background noise. She waited a few seconds to see if the reception improved, only for the connection to disappear.

'Marvellous!' Tia tossed the phone back on the bed and went to dry her hair. Luckily her short, sleek bob only took a few minutes to style, affording her time to touch up her make-up for a more sophisticated evening look. She changed the neat studs in her ears for long diamante droppers before opening her wardrobe.

Despite her bravado with Juliet, she wasn't too sure what to wear. She had a choice of three formal gowns, all of which had seen service before at various prestigious work-related events. Two were distinctly wintry in style and not quite right for a bright, warm summer's evening. That left her third choice, an ice-blue chiffon dress that always made her feel like Sleeping Beauty, except that this dress was strapless and plunging at the back.

She glanced at her watch once more; there wasn't time to dilly-dally about, the taxi would be arriving in a few minutes. She zipped herself into the dress, slipped on her high-heeled strappy silver sandals, picked up her phone and evening purse, and headed downstairs. No doubt Juliet would have something disparaging to say about her appearance. The dress was several seasons old and definitely not as cutting edge as the one Juliet would undoubtedly be wearing, but at least it flattered her tiny waist and dark hair.

'So, Cinders, you shall go to the ball,' Tia muttered as she changed the contents of her handbags over at the foot of the stairs and waited for her taxi. She frowned at her reflection in the hall mirror as she checked her lipstick. 'I don't suppose I'll find a handsome prince there, though. Sir Crispin hardly fits that particular bill.'

J uliet wasn't in the foyer when Tia arrived at the hotel.
She checked her appearance in front of the cloakroom
mirror, taking a few minutes to steady her nerves before
setting off in search of her colleague. It felt weird to be
actively looking for Juliet at a social event. In the past Tia
had spent most of her time trying to avoid Juliet and her
gang.

She forced herself to nod and smile to acquaintances
amongst the staff from other magazines as she entered
the function room. As she gave her name to the maître d',
she resisted the urge to shudder at memories of the last
time she'd dressed up for a night out with Juliet around.

Sir Crispin was already seated and holding court
when she arrived at the large, circular table. Juliet was
seated a few chairs from Sir Crispin, next to a pretty girl
with an elaborate hairdo. Tia believed she caught a faint
frown of displeasure on Juliet's face as Tia took the place
indicated for her, although with the Botox, it was hard to
be sure. Juliet had departed from her trademark black
and was wearing a gold Versace dress, definitely from
this season's collection.

'Miss Carpenter!' Sir Crispin proclaimed, breaking off his conversation with what looked like a group of accountants and their wives. 'How very good to see you. You're looking as charming as ever.' He turned his attention back to the other guests with an overtly gracious smile. 'Tia is our beauty editor at *Platinum*,' he announced, then resumed his conversation without bothering to introduce his companions to her.

Tia, rather surprised that Sir Crispin had actually recognised her, poured herself a glass of water from the jug on the table and settled in her seat to look around the room. The long windows opening on to the garden terrace were ajar, allowing some fresh evening air into the room. There were quite a few faces there that she recognised: celebrities, TV personalities and staff from other publications among them.

She'd known about the event for ages, it was an annual bash, where various publications all patted themselves on the back and charities received funding and had their profiles boosted. However, since it was usually Helen and Penny who normally attended, it had fallen off her radar.

Sir Crispin was still holding forth to the group on her right. Tia looked at the slender young woman next to Juliet wearing the very expensive dress and the fancy hairdo and wondered if she was Sir Crispin's companion for the evening. The two seats immediately next to Tia were empty and she tried to guess who else might be attending. Hopefully, it wouldn't be more accountants or marketing executives.

'I didn't think you were going to make it,' Juliet said.

'I had to wait for a taxi,' Tia answered coolly, ignoring the peevish note in Juliet's voice.

She took a sip of water and allowed the surrounding hum of conversation to wash over her while she studied the printed programme which lay on the table in front of her, listing the evening's schedule.

Her stomach grumbled in protest when she saw that dinner was still thirty minutes away. She placed the programme back down on the white damask tablecloth and continued to gaze around the room, amusing herself by trying to identify the celebrities at the different tables.

Happily preoccupied, she automatically turned to smile a welcome as the vacant seat next to her was pulled out for the late arrival.

'Tia, what a nice surprise.' Josh slipped into the seat next to her.

Her face heated as she was conscious of Juliet watching them from her position a few seats away.

'I didn't know you would be here,' she murmured. She smiled and said hello to Kim, who took the other vacant chair.

'I wasn't expecting to see you, either, but I'm so pleased that I have.'

He smiled and Tia felt her colour deepen at the twinkle in his eyes.

'Josh, darling, I didn't know you would be joining us. Tia won't mind swapping seats so we can sit together,' Juliet called to him, half rising from her chair.

Tia felt a gentle pressure on her leg from Josh's hand

keeping her in her seat. 'I think Tia is fine where she is, we'd better not disturb the seating plan,' Josh called back.

Juliet resumed her seat, barely bothering to hide her displeasure. She cast a murderous glance at Tia when Josh wasn't looking.

'Please don't offer to move. I don't think I can get through three hours of Sir Crispin's hospitality if I have to endure Juliet as well,' Josh muttered.

Tia hesitated, caught between a rock and a hard place.

As if sensing her dilemma, Josh smiled at her. 'Pretty please, with sugar on top. You wouldn't be so heartless.'

'I have to work with Juliet.' A thrill of excitement rushed through Tia, even as she felt a little bit guilty about not changing seats. She was all too aware that Josh had kept his hand on the top of her leg, the warmth of his touch reaching her skin through the layers of chiffon.

'Sir Crispin should give you a medal.'

Tia bit back a giggle as a white-gloved waiter placed a plate containing her starter in front of her. Embarrassingly, her stomach gave an audible gurgle of appreciation as the delicious scent of the clear soup reached her nose. She pressed her hand against her stomach in an effort to silence it and hoped Josh hadn't noticed amidst the general noise and bustle in the dining room.

'You can have my bread if you want,' he offered, seeing she had eaten hers already, sending fresh spurts of colour into Tia's cheeks. So much for hoping he wouldn't notice.

'Thank you. I wasn't expecting to come here tonight. Juliet and I are standing in for Penny and Helen, and it's been a long time since lunch.' She picked up her spoon and hoped she wouldn't embarrass herself any further by spilling it down her dress.

'You're looking very beautiful.' He moved his hand from her leg to slip his bread roll discreetly on to her plate.

Tia wondered if she could possibly turn any redder.

'Thank you.'

She was aware of Juliet eyeing her suspiciously, probably wondering why Josh's head was so close to hers and what he might be saying to give her face such a beetroot colour. She wished she was better at taking compliments but somehow she still expected them to come with a string attached, even after all this time.

'What brings you here?' she asked.

'I'm patron of one of the charities receiving a cheque tonight and *Platinum* are sponsoring my particular charity, hence my enjoyment of Sir Crispin's hospitality.' Josh lowered his voice so that the others at the table couldn't hear. 'Although I suspect that for some reason he doesn't actually like me.'

Tia concentrated on her soup for a moment and tried to think of an appropriate response. She didn't want to act as Helen's spy, but what if some of what she'd been told was true? It also wasn't helpful having Josh sitting so close to her murmuring in her ear. Her whole body was alert to his proximity and it was becoming increasingly difficult for her to think clearly.

'Why do you think he doesn't like you?' She popped a piece of bread into her mouth and waited for his answer.

Josh placed his spoon down in his empty soup bowl. 'I'm not sure – except, of course, he does prefer to be the main player in any arena. Perhaps he sees me as some kind of threat.'

Tia swallowed her bread. 'But you aren't a threat, are you? In business, I mean?' She was glad her cheeks were already pink as it saved her from looking so guilty at trying to snoop into something that wasn't any of her business.

Josh gave a low chuckle. 'Hardly. I guess Crispin and I are probably on the same side, as I've diversified a bit lately and bought some shares in Hellandback. I would have thought it was better that I had them instead of Rupert Finch.'

Tia waited until the waiter had removed their empty dishes. 'Maybe he's scared you'll take over.'

Josh laughed out loud, causing a few people to turn and look in his direction, including Juliet.

'I don't think so. I've no desire to become a media magnate.'

Tia breathed a low sigh of relief. It seemed Helen had been wrong on that score, then. Josh turned away from her for a moment to listen to something Kim was saying. Tia took a moment to catch her breath and calm herself down with a sip of water. She tried not to look in Juliet's direction, fully aware that her card had been well and truly marked now as far as her colleague was concerned.

'I wondered when I would get to see you again. You ran off the other day when things started to get interesting and like an idiot I forgot I hadn't got your mobile number.' Josh turned his attention back to her just as the main course was served.

'You have my email address.' Tia picked up her cutlery. If Josh wanted to get hold of her, it wasn't difficult. He could have emailed her or rung her at the office. She wondered if he was only bothering to flirt with her now to annoy Juliet or simply to pass the time.

The idea depressed and rather killed her appetite for the delicious chicken à la king.

'I tried to get your number from your friend Ravi.'

Tia recalled the images of Josh on Ravi's mobile and heat curled low in her stomach. 'You could have called the office.'

'I'm always cautious about personal calls to a workplace – especially when that workplace is a magazine.'

Tia gave a tiny shrug and forced herself to nibble at her dinner. 'You really don't have to make excuses. If you wanted to contact me, that's fine, and if you didn't, I wasn't languishing about, waiting for you to contact me.'

She smiled and tried to remind herself that she hadn't especially wanted him to contact her. Hadn't she decided it would make her life way too complicated if he were to ask her out on a date, anyway?

Josh gave her a quizzical look. 'I did email you, as I definitely did want to see you again, but you're right. I should try harder.'

Tia made a mental note to check her spam folder for

Josh's email but she wasn't certain that she wanted Josh to try harder to persuade her to go out with him.

Josh finished his dinner and continued to watch Tia when he thought she wasn't looking. Most of the women he knew who would have made a comment like that would have done it provocatively, expecting him to chase after them. Yet, in the way Tia had spoken, there had been no hint of expectation. It had been a simple statement of fact. Damn it, he wished she *had* languished by the phone, even if only a little bit.

He knew Kim had observed their whole exchange, even if she hadn't caught exactly what had been said. He was also very aware of Juliet in her gold gown watching his every move. There was something strange going on there and he didn't trust her.

Sir Crispin caught his eye as he glanced around the table and Josh found himself being drawn into a discussion on marketing. Not that he was expected to contribute much, it was more that he was expected to listen to Sir Crispin as he held forth on one of his hobby horses. As the older man continued to drone on, Josh decided he would infinitely prefer to spend his time talking to Tia.

However, Tia had turned her attention to the middle-aged man sitting on the other side of her, who, as far as he could tell, was conducting a riveting conversation on accounting. He leaned back in his chair and stifled a sigh.

'Don't you dare say anything,' he murmured out of

the side of his mouth to Kim when Sir Crispin's attention had been momentarily distracted by the arrival of his dessert.

'Wouldn't dream of it,' Kim responded, smiling.

Josh wished he wasn't so aware of Tia sitting next to him. He'd noticed her as soon as he'd neared the table, her pastel chiffon dress catching his eye in a sea of black tie and garish dresses. The dress revealed the smooth skin of her shoulders and as she leaned forward, he could see the slightly raised line of her spine. She laughed at something the man in glasses said to her and he found his grip tightening round the stem of his wine glass.

For a wonderful, delicious second he wondered what it would be like to take Tia somewhere private, away from the hustle and bustle of the dining room with the hum of chatter and clink of cutlery on china plates. To have her to himself in a quiet room, just the two of them alone, where he could unzip her dress and allow it to fall to the floor so he could caress her creamy skin. She glanced up and caught his eye. Colour suffused her pretty face and he wondered if she could read his mind.

With the emptied dessert plates cleared away and the coffee cups and petits fours in place, the master of ceremonies called the room to order for the speeches and presentations to begin. Tia adjusted her chair to gain a clearer view of the podium, manoeuvring so that her back was towards him and he could no longer see her expressive face so clearly.

Josh dutifully applauded the first speech without paying much attention to the ceremony. He was too busy wondering why he felt so affronted by Tia's coolness towards him. He would definitely have to try much harder if he wanted more than a business relationship with her, that was for certain. A smile tugged at the corners of his mouth; chasing Tia could prove to be a lot of fun.

13

The line of trophies on the podium table grew steadily shorter as one by one the various proud recipients went up to collect their award and shake hands with whichever celebrity had been drafted in to present it. Josh concentrated on the smooth curve at the nape of Tia's neck and waited for his turn to mount the podium to collect the cheque for his charity.

'And now the special award for services rendered to the publishing industry. A rare lifetime achievement award to Sir Crispin Stanford-Hope.'

Josh watched as Sir Crispin rose to his feet, graciously nodding his head in acknowledgement to the assembled crowds as they applauded.

Kim leaned forward. 'Doesn't Sir Crispin sponsor most of this event?'

'Yes,' Josh answered as Sir Crispin made his way to the podium to receive a large silver and glass trophy.

'Then doesn't that mean technically he's giving an award to himself?' Kim asked.

'I think so.' Josh knew Tia had heard their exchange from the way her spine had stiffened. He willed her to turn her head so that he could talk to her but instead she kept her gaze fixed firmly on the podium where Sir Crispin had begun his speech. He couldn't resist inching his chair forward and slightly to the side so that he could see her profile more clearly, then he drapped his arm casually over the corner of her chair as if engrossed in Sir Crispin's speech.

The light pink colour in her cheeks deepened but she still kept her eyes fixed on the podium. 'What are you doing?' she hissed out of the corner of her mouth.

'Listening to Sir Crispin.' He tried to keep the amusement out of his tone as her eyes sparked with indignation. 'I could move my arm but then everyone would wonder what you'd said.'

Her mouth compressed into a straight line as she dutifully applauded Sir Crispin as he exited the stage brandishing his award like an FA Cup winner. Josh smiled to himself and admired the faint scattering of freckles on the top of Tia's shoulder.

The master of ceremonies took over once more and Josh dragged his attention reluctantly back to the podium.

'It now falls to the chair of the fundraising committee, Mr Rupert Finch, to present the cheques to this year's designated charities.'

Josh had met Rupert Finch before on a couple of other occasions. There had been rumours circulating lately that his media group, Prime Productions, was gearing up to expand. Josh had asked his broker to look into the group when he'd decided to diversify his business but there had been something about Rupert that he hadn't liked. It was hard to believe that he and Sir Crispin were brothers-in-law. There was certainly no love lost between them and their rivalry was legendary.

There was nothing definite that he could put his finger on about why he distrusted Rupert Finch, but he'd learned over the last few years to trust his instincts as much as his business sense and the man set his inner alarm sensor sounding.

Rupert Finch approached the microphone. A tall urbane figure with a distinctive thatch of silver hair, he was regularly featured on the business pages and the gossip columns. Josh wondered if he'd tried to veto Sir Crispin's lifetime achievement award. Hostilities between the two men had intensified even further following Sir Crispin's elevation to the peerage a few years earlier.

Josh heard his name announced amidst thunderous applause and stood to make his way to the stage. Unable to resist the temptation he allowed his fingers to drift briefly across Tia's bare shoulder as he walked away.

The soft touch of Josh's fingers on her skin as he left to collect his award sent a shiver of heat through Tia's body. She licked lips that had suddenly dried as he walked up to the microphone on the podium to accept the cheque from Rupert Finch. The bright footlights along the front of the small stage appeared to throw Josh into bright relief as the official photographers all grabbed their pictures.

Tia stopped clapping and rested her hands in her lap,

aware she was trembling. Josh posed with Rupert and the cheque, his professional smile fixed in place. Sir Crispin arrived back at the table with his trophy while Josh began his brief speech, thanking the sponsors and advertisers for their support.

Distracted by the murmur of congratulatory conversation from her companions at the table and Sir Crispin ordering champagne for the group, Tia took her gaze from the stage and encountered Juliet's frosty expression.

Applause rang out all around her and she realised that Josh had finished speaking. Juliet continued to glare while the toast master gave the closing remarks and invited them all to drink to the generosity of the sponsors. Tia stood along with the rest of the room and fumbled for her glass which had magically been filled with champagne during Josh's speech.

'Here.' Josh reached her glass before her.

His fingers tangled with hers around the slender stem of the glass and the liquid contents wobbled dangerously in her grasp.

'Careful,' he steadied the glass, 'it's good stuff, better drunk than spilled.' He released her fingers and she took a hasty sip of champagne.

She resumed her seat, wondering what would happen next. The ceremonies appeared to be over and people were beginning to circulate around the room. Outside on the terrace in the dusk the lit ends of cigarettes appeared like orange fireflies as the smokers indulged their habit.

Kim had vanished and Josh retook his seat next to Tia.

'Josh, darling, congratulations. Loved your speech.' Juliet positioned herself in the narrow gap between Josh and Tia.

Faced with a view of Juliet's long, elegant back, Tia edged her chair away slightly and wondered if she could use the opportunity to escape. The whole situation made her uncomfortable and there was no way she was about to become another one of his conquests – however tempted she might be.

Gathering her bag and lacy Pashmina, she stood and prepared to make her way out on to the terrace past the smokers before Josh could get away from Juliet. She had barely managed more than a few steps before Sir Crispin appeared in front of her.

'Miss Carpenter, Tia, my dear, accompany me on to the terrace.'

It wasn't so much a question but a command and Tia found herself being steered firmly through the crowds and out on to the garden terrace. The air was cool after the crowded room inside and she shivered a little as she pulled her fine lace Pashmina over her bare arms.

The smokers appeared to have been shepherded away to a designated area of the terrace, leaving behind the faintly acrid smell of smoke to mingle with the scented roses which grew against the trellis work on the outside of the building. Through the windows Tia could see the bright lights inside with gorgeously dressed women mingling like exotic butterflies against the black dinner jackets of their male companions. The faint strains of dance music drifted out on the summer night air.

'Splendid evening.' Sir Crispin strolled over to the stone balustrade at the edge of the terrace where there was no one else around. Tia followed somewhat hesitantly a step behind him.

'Yes. Congratulations on your award, Sir Crispin.' Her supper tumbled in her stomach and she wondered why he'd brought her outside.

'Young Banks appears to be quite keen on you.' Sir Crispin turned to face her.

Tia stared at him, unable to think of a suitable response.

'Good work. Using feminine wiles, eh?' He winked and Tia wondered how much champagne he'd drunk. If he weren't her employer and such a powerful man in the industry, she would have given him a sharp answer and gone back inside.

'I hardly know him, Sir Crispin. We've only met a few times for the shoot for the anniversary edition.' She kept her tone cool even though her legs were shaking beneath her.

'Humph, Helen told you what I suspect?' He raised a bushy eyebrow.

Tia nodded. 'But, I really don't think—'

'I don't pay you to think, young lady. Just keep your eyes and ears open, that's all. I'm not asking you to do anything you might feel uncomfortable about.'

Tia longed to point out that the whole idea made her

uncomfortable and surely all he needed to do to end the charade was to challenge Josh with his suspicions.

Sir Crispin patted the top pocket of his dinner jacket and produced a cigar. 'I want to get to the bottom of this funny business. Banks is mixed up in it – that I do know. I'm not sure who else. Miss Gold appears to have some ideas.'

'I don't know that I can—'

'Just keep a weather watch on the pair of them. Helen seems to think Miss Gold is playing some kind of double game although I'd put money on my bloody brother-in-law Rupert being involved in it somewhere.'

'But, Sir Crispin—'

'Ah Banks, come to take the air?' Sir Crispin raised his voice and Tia turned to see Josh walking through the open French doors towards them.

'I came to see where the prettiest girl in the room had disappeared to.' Josh stopped next to her. He'd unfastened his bow tie to leave it loose around his neck and unbuttoned the top button of his shirt. Tia wondered how he'd managed to shake off Juliet.

'Thought you might be sussing out the opposition in the old hospitality business.' Sir Crispin bit the end off his cigar and spat it over the edge of the balustrade.

'Well, maybe a little. I think you'd do the same, Sir Crispin, if you were in my shoes.'

'Maybe, my boy, maybe,' Sir Crispin acknowledged. 'I'd better move before the smoking police come and harass me. Fellow can't even enjoy a good cigar in peace these days.' He ambled off down the terrace still grumbling as one of the waiters appeared at his side to point the way.

'I thought you were talking to Juliet?' Tia moved her Pashmina a little higher up her arms.

'I was being talked *at* by Juliet. Luckily for me a fashion editor from another magazine came over to speak to her so I left Kim guarding my exit and came to look for you.'

'Oh.' Her breath hitched in her throat as Josh straightened her Pashmina, his fingertips grazing the delicate inner flesh of her arms.

'Are you cold?' His eyes met hers and she shook her head. Her pulse hammered in her throat as he bent his head to brush his lips against hers.

She felt him hesitate for a split second as if gauging her reaction before sliding his arms round her waist and deepening the kiss. His hands were warm against the exposed skin of her back. He tasted of coffee and mint chocolate petits fours.

Her hands seemed to make their own way to the nape of his neck to stroke the soft slight curl of his hair. Enveloped by the friendly darkness she was temporarily oblivious to her surroundings. Only a sudden cool breeze on the sensitised skin of her arms and back reminded her that they were on the terrace.

Tia stepped back out of his arms. 'We shouldn't be doing this, it's madness. I ought to go.'

'I'll take you home.' Josh stared at her and she wondered if the slightly dazed expression she saw on his face was mirrored on her own.

Tia's heart thumped against her ribs as she gathered her wrap and her wits. 'No, it's fine. I can call a cab.' She wasn't sure if she could take being in the confines of a car alone with Josh, not now, while her senses were still reeling from his kiss.

She turned on her heel and began to walk back across the stone slabs towards the brilliantly lit interior of the hotel. What had she been thinking? Hadn't she decided it would be better if she didn't get close to Josh? Her life was complicated enough without risking her hard-won new identity. Then there was Juliet. Her stomach lurched, Juliet already hated her, if she'd seen them outside on the terrace then Tia would be a dead woman. Even worse, Sir Crispin had asked her to keep an eye on Josh, not to kiss him.

'Tia, wait. Please let me take you home. The theatres are turning out at this time, it'll take them ages to get you a taxi.' Josh caught up with her in the lobby after she'd battled her way throught the crowd. Thankfully there had been no sign of Juliet.

'No, it's fine, honestly. You should stay and enjoy the rest of the party.' Tia looked around for the doorman but Josh had already asked for his car to be brought round.

'Don't be silly, my car will be out front in a couple of minutes.' He caught hold of her hands, forcing her to halt.

Tia sensed people were beginning to look in their direction. 'Okay.' She gave in, unwilling to attract more attention.

The doorman re-entered the lobby and passed Josh his car keys. 'Your vehicle is out front, sir. Have a good evening.' He touched his top hat as Josh slipped him a tip.

Tia slid into the front passenger seat of the shiny black limousine as the valet held it open for her. She reached for her seatbelt, glancing back at the hotel as she did so, only to catch a glimpse of Juliet's furious expression as Josh pulled the car away from the curb.

14

'This is very kind of you but I could have taken a taxi.' Tia settled back in her seat, her heart still thumping as she gave Josh her address. The look of pure hatred Juliet had given her as they left the hotel had sent shivers of fear down her spine. Tia had seen that exact same look on Juliet's face before. Two days before the ill-fated leavers' party at school when she'd spotted her with that tube of glue outside Mrs Johnson's office.

She sucked in a breath and closed her eyes, struggling to regain control. That was behind her now. She wasn't Barbara any more. Juliet had no power over her.

'Tia, are you okay?' Josh's voice, warm with concern, snapped her back to reality.

'I'm fine, just tired. It's been a long day and I wasn't expecting to be out this evening. Normally I'd be curled up in bed by now.' She opened her eyes to see him grinning mischievously at her last remark.

'It's okay, I won't go there, although I did like the image it conjured up in my mind.' He slowed the car as the traffic built up, bringing them to a halt behind one of the city's numerous black cabs.

Tia shook her head in mock despair. 'If you think the idea of me in my night attire with my face covered in the latest gloop that I'm testing out is sexy, then you are a sad boy.'

'Hey, in my defence, no one mentioned gloop,' Josh protested, sliding the car neatly into a gap between two buses as the heavy traffic began to move once more.

'I'm a beauty editor; there's always gloop.'

Josh shot her a glance as the traffic ground to a halt once more. 'Is that what Sir Crispin wanted, out on the terrace? To talk gloop?'

She fidgeted in her seat, uncomfortable with the sudden turn of conversation. When she spoke, she kept her tone light. 'He *is* my boss. It was simply a few things about the anniversary edition.'

'It's not something I'd have taken a beautiful woman out on to a moonlit terrace to discuss.'

She watched him out of the corner of her eye, trying to discern what he was thinking while he concentrated on the traffic.

'Well, you know Sir Crispin . . .' Tia gave a little shrug. She wasn't cut out for the espionage business.

'Yes, indeed I do,' Josh replied and took the turn to steer them away from the worst of the traffic and into the less busy back streets.

She wasn't sure what to make of his last remark so she remained silent. Could Josh have something to do with what had been happening with the share prices after all? She didn't fully understand all this business of buying and selling shares, or what it had to do with Sir Crispin's control of the company, much less why he suspected Josh.

All the more reason to stop seeing Josh except on a purely professional basis. Once the shoot was done and the magazine edition put to bed, that would be that. She wouldn't have any excuse to see him again. As she took another peek at the man sitting beside her she didn't feel quite so happy about that idea.

She pushed her concerns to the back of her mind and concentrated on directing Josh through the streets surrounding her house. Finally he stopped the car and turned off the engine outside the neat Edwardian terraced house she shared with Ginny. A light still showed in the front room and Tia guessed her god-mother had waited up for her to come home.

'So, this is where you live?' Josh peered at the house.

'Yes.'

'Mmm, you're such a woman of mystery that I half expected some secret underground lair, or an apartment at Kensington Palace.'

'I'm not mysterious. Private maybe, but not mysterious.' She hesitated, wondering if she should ask him in for coffee. It seemed rude not to, and Ginny was still up, so there wouldn't be any likelihood of repeating the kissing incident on the terrace.

'Well, no one wanted to give me your mobile number. *You* haven't given me your number. You kiss me and then disappear. I think that's mysterious.'

Tia tried to judge if he was smiling in the half-light of the car interior. 'I suppose you'd better come in for coffee and meet Ginny. Maybe then you'll see there's no mystery. I'm simply a very private person.'

'I thought you'd never ask.' He kissed her cheek and leapt out of the car to come around, opening her door for her.

Tia led the way along the short narrow path leading to her front door. The skin on her cheek still tingled from where his lips had brushed her face. She was conscious of his presence right behind her as they entered the hallway and wondered if she'd made a mistake inviting him in.

'Ginny, I'm home.' She opened the door to the lounge and glanced in. The reading lamp was on and a newspaper lay spread open on the seat next to a pair of glasses, but the room was empty.

'She must be in the kitchen.'

Tia led Josh to the end of the hall and into the bright airy kitchen. Ginny was at the sink with her back towards them as she filled the kettle.

'I saw the car pull up and thought I'd pop the kettle on.' Her godmother turned with the kettle in her hand.

'Ginny, this is Josh Banks. Josh, this is Ginny Carpenter, my godmother.'

Tia could have sworn she saw Ginny's complexion pale for a second but then she seemed to gather herself.

'Nice to meet you.' She placed the kettle down and offered her hand for Josh to shake.

Josh accepted the outstretched hand. 'It's good to meet you, too. Tia's told me a little about you.'

He'd met this woman before, he knew it. She'd recognised him too, judging from the way she'd reacted when Tia introduced him.

'I'll leave you two alone, mine's a tea when the kettle boils, Tia dear.' The older woman slipped out of the kitchen.

Tia collected the mugs and set them down on the counter, while Josh tried to recall where he'd met Ginny before. Somewhere else, a long time ago. She hadn't had grey hair then, and she'd been plumper.

'Tea or coffee?' Tia asked.

'What? Oh, um, coffee, please.' He forced himself to concentrate on the present.

'Penny for your thoughts?' Tia teased, as she spooned coffee granules into the mugs.

'Nothing very interesting. Like you, I'm a little tired. Has your godmother lived in this area long?' He disliked not being entirely open with Tia but the irritating fragment of memory lurking at the back of his mind held a clue to something. Something important to do with Tia and that eerie sense of familiarity he got whenever he met her.

'She's lived in London for years but she only moved into this house a couple of years ago.'

Josh took a seat opposite Tia while she waited for the kettle to boil. 'So she's always lived in London?' He knew he must sound stupid but he knew he remembered Ginny from somewhere else and it wasn't in this setting.

Tia smiled politely, a faint crease of bewilderment furrowing her brow. 'Yes.'

The kettle came to the boil.

'Shall I take that for you?' Josh offered as Tia picked up Ginny's mug of tea and placed it on a small tray along with a couple of biscuits. Maybe if he saw Ginny again, it would help him to recall where he'd seen her before, or perhaps he could ask her.

'No, don't get up. I'll be back in a minute.' Tia smiled once more and slipped out into the hall carrying the tray. In the distance he heard the faint murmur of female voices before Tia returned, closing the door behind her.

'Ginny's asked if you'll excuse her. She's very tired so she's heading off to bed. She's not been feeling very well for the last couple of days. I think she's overdone it with the DIY.' Tia took a seat on the shiny chrome bar stool opposite him. The crystals on the voluminous pastel chiffon skirt of her dress sparkled under the overhead lighting as she kicked off her dainty high-heeled silver sandals and stretched out her toes. 'That's better.'

'Feet ache?' Her toenails were perfectly manicured and painted with a dark plum colour. He must have it bad if the sight of her bare toes turned him on.

'Definitely, it's been a very long day.' She stifled a yawn, covering her mouth with her hand. 'Sorry.'

He wondered if she had been instructed to make him leave. 'It's a shame your godmother's gone to bed. She seemed familiar. I'm sure I've met her somewhere before.' He knew Ginny was avoiding him for some reason, and he wished he knew why.

'Ginny?' Tia laughed. 'It's unlikely, not unless you're

into home decorating too and met her in the aisles of the paint and tile warehouse.'

Josh took a small sip of his coffee. Tia's astonished reaction certainly appeared to be genuine. Nonetheless, he knew he'd met Ginny before and Ginny had known it too.

'The atmosphere won't be very pleasant at the office tomorrow. Juliet didn't look happy when we left the hotel and I don't know if she saw us together out on the terrace.' Her pretty elfin face pinked as she spoke.

Josh placed his mug down carefully on the counter. 'What, you mean when we were kissing?'

The colour deepened on Tia's cheeks as she frowned down at her coffee, and Josh bit back a smile. He enjoyed teasing her a little. He reached across to take her hand in his. 'I told you before, don't worry about Juliet. I know she can be pretty nasty if she doesn't get her own way, but it seems to me that you are more than capable of dealing with her.'

Tia lifted her gaze and the expression in her soft dark eyes made his heart skip a beat. 'Thanks for the vote of confidence.'

The weight of her small hand in his felt curiously right, as if she belonged. For some reason he realised Tia was terrified of Juliet. He sensed that whatever lay behind it went deeper than any kind of rivalry for his affections. His ego wasn't so huge that he could believe that.

'You can always tip iced water on her again.' He attempted to lighten the mood.

Tia forced a faint smile. 'I don't think that would be a good idea.'

Her eyes met his and he swallowed the lump that had suddenly formed in his throat. There was something about Tia's delicate vulnerability combined with a sense of déjà vu that continued to bother him.

She lowered her gaze once more and extracted her fingers from his grip. 'I don't want to be an ungracious hostess, but I really do need to get some sleep.'

Reluctantly he eased himself up from the stool and took a final swallow of coffee. 'You're right, I should be getting off home. I'd better go and grovel to Kim for abandoning her to Juliet's tender mercies.'

Tia stood too, tiny in her bare feet. 'Thank you for bringing me home.'

She walked with him along the hallway to the front door, her skirts swishing softly as she moved.

'Well, thanks again.' She cracked the front door open quietly and waited for him to leave.

A small white and grey moth blundered into the hall through the open door, beating its wings against the yellow light of the small lamp on the table at the foot of the stairs.

'I don't suppose I can persuade you to give me your number?' He reached inside his jacket for his phone. He knew she would refuse but thought it was worth a try.

She shook her head. 'You can get me at my desk.'

'I'll be in touch.' Unable to resist, he dipped his head to kiss her lips.

He felt her sigh softly as he kissed her. Her eyes

appeared dark and mysterious in the soft light of the hall as he lifted his head.

'Goodnight, Josh.'

He heard the door click shut behind him and she was gone.

Tia waited in the hall until she heard Josh start up his car before heading upstairs. She tapped on Ginny's door and looked in when she heard her call her name.

'I thought I'd come and say goodnight. Are you okay? You looked very pale downstairs.' Tia entered Ginny's room and crossed over to the bed.

Ginny lay propped up against a pile of pillows, her book lay unopened on her lap. She moved the book aside and patted the coverlet. 'Darling, come and sit down.'

Tia sat on the edge of the bed. 'Is something wrong? Do you feel ill?'

Something was wrong, she knew it.

'I'm all right, truly. Tia, there's something I have to tell you. I should have told you a long time ago but at the time I thought I was doing the right thing.' Ginny swept a hand through her hair and Tia noticed she was trembling.

'I don't understand.' Fear settled in Tia's stomach like a cold lead weight. She'd never seen Ginny look so serious.

'I never thought this would happen. If I had thought for just one minute . . .' Ginny bit her lip and saw the older woman was struggling to keep back tears.

'Gin, what's wrong? What is it? Is it something to do

with Josh?' As soon as she spoke, Tia knew she was right.

Ginny nodded and pulled a tissue from the box standing on the small side table next to her bed.

'He recognised me.'

Tia shook her head in disbelief. 'He said he thought he knew you. But how?'

'He came to see you once before, at home – when you were Barbara.'

15

Tia froze for a moment, struggling to understand her godmother's confession.

'Came to see me? When? Where?' The blood roared in her ears and she was glad she was seated on the bed; otherwise she knew she would have fallen to the floor. The coffee she'd so recently swallowed rose from her stomach leaving the burning sensation of bile at the back of her throat. Josh had been to see her and Ginny had never said anything. She wasn't sure which of the two things was the most incredible.

A tear escaped and ran down Ginny's cheek. 'I thought I was doing the right thing. It was after that awful leavers' party.'

Tia pressed the back of her hand against her mouth to keep back the low moan that threatened to escape. A tidal wave of memories washed over her, sucking her under.

'You'd gone out to the chemist to fetch another prescription for your mum,' Ginny began, her face wet with tears. 'The doorbell went and I thought it might be the district nurse so I went to answer it.'

Tia wanted to be sick. The events of that day had been buried at the back of her mind for so many years, and yet it was all too easy to dredge them to the fore again.

'After the state you came home in the night before, and with your mum so poorly, I was angry and upset. I'd been up all night helping you get that stuff out of your hair and we'd kept it all from your mother.' Ginny broke off for a moment with an anguished sob.

Tia screwed her eyes shut tight as the pain of the remembrance gripped her.

Ginny blew her nose on her tissue and carried on, her voice thick with emotion. 'It was Josh Banks, he'd cycled round. I didn't know why he'd come, all I knew was that somehow he'd been involved with what had been happening to you. He was Juliet's boyfriend, after all. He asked if you were all right.'

Ginny stopped once more to pluck a fresh tissue from the box. She dabbed her eyes and drew in a shaky breath before continuing.

'I didn't know if he was genuinely concerned about you or if he'd just come to gloat so he could report back to her. I let him have it with both barrels, exactly how I felt about the whole thing.'

'What happened?' Tia reached for the tissues and pulled out a handful. Her tears fell like scalding rain down her cheeks as she tried to compose herself. 'What did he say?' All this time she'd believed that Josh hadn't known what Juliet and her gang had planned. His reaction that night, the shock and compassion in his eyes, had been genuine. She had been certain of it, and had clung to that belief like a life raft in the days and weeks that had followed. He wouldn't have gone to her home to gloat.

Ginny sniffed. 'He stood there and took it. He didn't say a word. I ranted on about your mother being terminally ill and worthless privileged kids who looked down on hard-working scholarship students. He stood and took it all then went and got back on his bike and left.'

Tia groaned. 'Why didn't you tell me?' Her whole world was crumbling around her. First the reappearance of Juliet, and now this latest revelation. By now Josh would have put the pieces together and figured out her real identity. All the hard work she'd put in eradicating her past would be for nothing. She'd be labelled 'Big Barb' once more.

'I meant to, but then your mum got worse and you were still so fragile from the whole thing. It wasn't till after you'd moved here and you started to tell me more about what had gone on that I realised I shouldn't have said what I did to him. I thought if I told you, then it would be raking up all the bad memories for you. You seemed to be so much happier in your new life and I never, ever dreamed I'd ever see him again or that he would be able to connect me to you.'

Deep in her heart Tia knew Ginny had a point but for her godmother to have kept quiet for so long felt like a dreadful betrayal. She scrubbed at her cheeks disregarding the mess she must be making of her skin.

'He said he thought he knew you. He'll work out that I used to be Barbara – I know he will – and then what?' Tia clasped her hands together in a bid to stop herself from shaking. She wanted to scream. What had she ever done that was so terrible that her life was about to be destroyed for the second time?

Ginny sighed and reached out to cover Tia's trembling fingers with her hand. 'Then we'll deal with that if and when it happens. You haven't done anything wrong or dishonest, you simply changed your name by deed poll and gave yourself a fresh start.'

'What if Juliet finds out? It'll be all around the *Platinum* offices in no time. She already dislikes me and now, after tonight, especially if she saw what happened on the terrace—'

'What happened on the terrace?' Ginny asked.

'Josh kissed me.' Well, that would be one problem solved. He wouldn't want to kiss her again, not when he figured out that Tia was really big Barb, tub of lard, the fat, freaky girl from school.

'I didn't realise the two of you had become quite so close. I should have guessed when he brought you home tonight.' Ginny released her hands.

'I've tried not to get close to him, believe me.' Tia shrugged, misery settling over her like a cold grey cloud.

Ginny set her pile of crumpled tissues down on the nightstand. 'But you still have a thing for him, don't you? Even now, after all this time. I'm so sorry, Tia.'

'What's done is done. I suppose I'll have to wait and see what happens.' She picked disconsolately at one of the tiny crystals on the skirt of her dress.

'You could go and see him,' Ginny suggested, her red-rimmed eyes hopeful. 'Talk to him, see what he says.'

Tia swallowed, bemused. Talk to Josh and do what? Fling herself on his mercy? What must he think of her? She had kept quiet about her connection to him and Juliet even when he'd said he thought he knew her. At the very least it was a lie by omission. Her mind raced over all the possibilities. He probably thought she was a nutcase. What if he told Juliet? What would Saffy and Ravi think if they found out she'd lied to them all this time?

Each thought brought a fresh stab of pain. She would have to resign, leave the magazine and go and work on a cosmetics counter somewhere.

Ginny turned back the covers of her bed and stood up.

'I'm going to fix us another drink, I think we need one or neither of us will get much sleep tonight.' She placed her hands gently on Tia's shoulders. 'Go and change out of your dress, I'll bring you up some milk and brandy.'

Tia made her way along the landing to her room. Her work clothes lay draped across the small chair in the corner of the room where she'd discarded them in her haste to change. Her handbag rested on the dresser, the contents spilling out on the shiny polished surface in an untidy heap.

She carefully unzipped her dress and slid it on to its padded hanger before pulling on her sleep vest and shorts. She sat at her dressing table and surveyed her tear-streaked face. Her eyelids were red and puffy while streaks of black mascara mingled with the remains of her blusher and foundation. She tore a hank of cotton wool from the large pack on the dresser, applied her cleansing lotion and began to methodically remove the remnants of her make-up.

If only she could expunge her past as efficiently as she could remove her make-up. She had to calm down, everything would work out – it had to.

Kim replaced the telephone on the receiver and looked enquiringly at Josh.

'Tia Carpenter is here to see you.'

He guessed Kim must be wondering exactly what had happened after he'd left her at the hotel to take Tia home. She'd already let him know that Juliet had been none too happy with his departure from the dinner.

Ever since he'd left Tia at her home he'd wondered what he would say to her the next time they met. Meeting a face from his past at her house had shaken him more than he cared to admit. He'd lain awake until the small hours of the morning trying to put the pieces of the puzzle together once he'd realised exactly where and when he'd last seen Ginny.

'Do you want me to go down and meet her?' Kim persisted.

'No. I'll go myself.' He closed the window on the computer. He hadn't been able to concentrate on the information in front of him anyway. It crossed his mind that Tia or Barbara (or whatever her name was) might not be too happy with the contents of the email Sir Crispin's company had just sent. Unless of course that was the reason she was here.

Kim's perfectly groomed eyebrows arched a little in surprise as he raised his arms above his head to stretch before getting up from his chair.

'I take it things went well between the two of you last night?' she asked as he passed her desk.

He wasn't sure that was the phrase he would have chosen. 'Let's just say the night was full of surprises.' And it seemed that the surprises weren't over yet, if Tia had presented herself down in the hotel lobby.

He pressed the button to take the lift down to the reception area, still trying to reconcile his memories of Barbara with Tia as she appeared today. The idea that they were one and the same person simply blew him away.

He remembered going to Barbara's house the day after the party, prompted by guilt and the awful hurt he'd seen in her eyes that night. He'd suggested to Juliet that she might go with him to see if Barbara was all right, only to be met by an incredulous gasp and a peal of laughter. Suggesting she apologise would have been a waste of breath.

Memories of the night of the leavers' party rushed back into his mind like fragments from a highly coloured film. One of the teachers, attracted by all the commotion, had collected Barbara from the girls' toilets where she'd been attempting to clean the worst of the mess from her clothes and hair. He could still recall the smell of the gunk that Juliet had used in her booby trap, odorous and sticky like three-day-old dead fish.

Naturally Juliet and her crowd had been conspic-
uously absent by then. Barbara had been taken home by
a member of staff and he'd never seen her again. He
wasn't sure any more quite what had prompted him to
track down Barbara's address and go round. Except the
terrible, destroyed expression in her eyes when he'd
helped her to her feet that night and led her away from
the laughing crowd to the girls' toilets had haunted him.
He'd felt even worse when he'd learned via the school
gossip that one of the reasons Barbara had been tricked
into going into the caretaker's cupboard was somehow
connected with him.

The elevator doors pinged open. He saw Tia straight
away, sitting on the edge of one of the button-backed
leather sofas. Dressed in a plain ivory dress with her feet
and knees together, and her bag on her lap, she looked
like an errant schoolgirl waiting to see the headmaster.

With her sleek chestnut bob, slender figure and
classic oval face she bore no physical resemblance
whatsoever to the girl he'd known as Barbara. Barbara
had been a fat girl with frizzy blond hair, crooked teeth
and glasses. A girl who'd been in his art class and English
lessons, a girl he hardly noticed except when she'd lent
him a pen or dropped her books.

Tia gave a visible start as his gaze locked with hers
across the busy lobby. He was wrong on one score,
though; her eyes hadn't changed except that they were
no longer hidden by the ugly, old-fashioned glasses she'd
worn when she was Barbara. She stood and he noticed as
he approached that her knuckles were white where she

had a tight grip on the handle of her bag.

'Thank you for seeing me. Is there somewhere private where we could talk?' Her request came out at barely above a whisper.

'We can go up to my apartment.' He wondered what she would have to say for herself. Damn it, he wasn't even sure what to call her any more. They crossed the lobby to the elevators in silence, side by side. Tia kept her eyes fixed firmly on the floor as the lift slowly ascended to the top of the hotel.

He studied her covertly in the mirrored walls of the elevator looking for something that should have given him a clue earlier that she wasn't who she claimed to be. Nothing, from the neat pearl studs in her earlobes to the black designer shoes on her feet, gave any indication that she wasn't Tia Carpenter, beauty editor from *Platinum* magazine.

Tension radiated from her as he unlocked the door to his apartment. He stood aside to allow her to enter before leading the way through to the lounge.

'Take a seat.' He indicated the matching cream leather sofas that stood on either side of the fireplace.

'Thank you.' She perched on the edge of the one nearest to the door as if ready to flee at any moment. In the bright summer sunshine pouring in through the windows he spied the dark smudges of fatigue on her face which had almost been successfully concealed with cosmetics.

'Would you like a drink?'

She shook her head.

'I'm sorry, I don't know what to call you any more. Is it Tia or Barbara?'

She flinched slightly as he said the name Barbara and he felt an unexpected pang of sympathy. It must have taken a lot of courage for her to come to the hotel and ask to see him.

'It's Tia.' She lifted her chin and gazed at him with defiant eyes as if daring him to correct her.

'I think maybe I need a drink.' He left her sitting in the lounge while he grabbed a bottle of lager from the fridge in the kitchen.

On his return he found she had moved from her position on the sofa to stand next to the large picture window that looked down on the front of the hotel and the park across the street, her neat figure silhouetted against the light. He took a swallow of his beer as she swung around to face him.

'I shouldn't have come. It's just, I wanted to explain.' Her expression held a mute appeal.

Josh dropped down on to the sofa and took another swig of his beer. His original irrational anger at her deception fought with a natural curiosity to hear whatever explanation she might give. For such a huge change to have taken place in her appearance it had to be quite a story.

'I'm listening.'

16

Tia eyed him warily from her position by the window and wished she could stop her legs from shaking. The milk and brandy Ginny had given her the previous night had been strong enough to knock out a horse, yet she'd still remained awake for most of the night.

Josh continued to watch her, sipping occasionally from the open top of the bottle of larger. His pose suggested he was amenable and open to hearing what she had to say but she knew he must be angry that she hadn't told him earlier who she really was. Especially after he'd kept telling her that he thought he'd met her before.

'You were right when you said that you thought you knew Ginny, and when you said you thought you knew me from somewhere.' Her words came out with a wobble but she drew a deep breath and pressed on. 'I didn't know that you'd met Ginny until last night, after you'd gone.' Her courage began to crack under his blank blue gaze, and she licked her lips.

'Go on.' A small shift of his shoulders indicated his interest.

'There was no reason for me to tell you about my past. I'm Tia now. The Barbara part of my life is closed and done with, and has been for the last ten years. I thought that our only meeting would be at the shoot for the magazine and that would be it. You'd never see me again.' She sank down on to a chair next to the window and waited for his response. It was done now, out in the open, for better or worse.

'Why didn't you tell me you knew me? Didn't you trust me, or was it something that old loon, Sir Crispin, put you up to? He seems to have a bee in his bonnet about the Hellandback shares at the moment.' His tone was deceptively cool but Tia could tell from the spark in his eyes that she needed to choose her words with care.

'I didn't tell you because I don't tell anyone. Like I said, that part of my life is over, done, finished with and I didn't expect to see you again once the shoot was completed. I didn't know if you and Juliet were dating again or how close you both still were. As for Sir Crispin, he only knows me as Tia, he wouldn't know or care that I knew either of you before.' Why had he thought Sir Crispin might be using her? Had he been up to something fishy with Juliet to do with the share prices and a possible hostile takeover? If that was the case, then Helen was right to be wary, suggesting that Juliet might be playing a double game.

'You look so different, I wouldn't have recognised you as Barbara if it hadn't been for Ginny. Did you have surgery?'

It was a fair question, she supposed, but it still stung. Had she really been so ugly that he thought she'd needed to go under the knife? She drew another wobbly breath to try and steady her nerves.

'When my mother died, I was too upset to eat. The weight started to fall off me and Ginny encouraged me to exercise more. I went on a diet, changed my hairstyle and got contact lenses. Apart from some dental work I didn't do anything else. I suppose losing so much weight was enough to change my appearance.'

Josh leaned forward and placed his lager bottle on the floor at the side of the sofa before leaning back again. 'Why the name change?' His tone gave her no clue as to his thoughts.

Tia sighed, 'Would *you* want to keep a name that had made you deeply unhappy? You *do* remember what they used to call me at school?' Despite her best efforts her voice cracked and she had to blink to keep tears from falling.

She watched his face as realisation dawned there.

'Changing names was Ginny's idea. At first it was suggested in fun but then, when I thought about it, I liked the idea. It drew a line under my past.' She opened her bag and fumbled for a tissue.

Josh swept a hand through his hair. 'I'd been thinking all kinds of things. I wondered if you were under some kind of witness protection programme, you know, as if you'd informed on the Mafia or something.' He gave a dry chuckle and shook his head in bewilderment.

Tia couldn't help smiling a little despite her

unhappiness. 'Sorry, nothing so exciting, only a fat girl giving herself a makeover.'

'I can't believe you're Barbara.'

His close scrutiny made her shift uncomfortably on her seat as she blew her nose.

'Who else knows about this?'

'No one, only Ginny, and now you.' Panic gave an edge to her voice.

'Unbelievable.' He continued to stare at her as if seeing her for the first time.

'You won't tell anyone?' Her voice faltered. An early morning meeting had meant that she hadn't yet been into the office so she still had to encounter Juliet.

He shrugged and her heart beat an anxious tattoo against her ribcage.

'Why would I? It's up to you if you wanted to change your name and how you look. It's not illegal, as far as I know. It's hard to believe I used to see you everyday for years and didn't recognise you.' He shook his head.

A wave of relief flooded through her and she half rose from her seat.

'I don't think you ever took that much notice of me. You were busy with Juliet.'

Her secret was still safe and once the pictures were done for the magazine she wouldn't see him again. She tried to ignore the hollow, sore feeling deep inside generated by knowing it was almost over. Everything they'd shared before was meaningless, based on a falsehood, that she had been someone else. There was no way he would be interested in her now, not now that he knew she was 'Big Barb'.

'Josh Banks, the teenage hormone years.' He smiled apologetically and she knew he was remembering the past.

'I expect Penny will be in touch with you about the photo shoot.' She edged towards the door, anxious to leave.

'Won't you stay and have some lunch?' Josh stood too, his level gaze still fixed on her face.

'No, I have to go. I need to get back to the office. I just wanted to see you to tell you.'

He crossed towards her and the room seemed to grow smaller. 'It's okay, I understand.'

'Um, I don't suppose we'll meet again unless I see you at the shoot.' She held her hand out for him to shake, the movement feeling strangely formal after everything that had passed between them.

He clasped her hand and the touch of his fingers on her skin made her breath hitch in her throat at the electricity between them.

'I take it you haven't spoken to anyone at your office, then, today?' His eyes held a hint of suppressed amusement. He still had her hand in his.

'No, I had an early meeting and my phone is out of charge.' A bad feeling grew in the pit of her stomach. She knew she should have charged her phone last night but with all the upset it had slipped her mind.

'Ah.'

Blast the man, he was smiling openly now. 'What's so funny?' she demanded.

'Sir Crispin has done a deal with a TV channel. He's using one of his film units to make a programme about *Platinum*'s anniversary and the run-up to the big day. He's sending a crew to film the shoot here at the spa. You, me, Penny and Juliet are to be on tape as part of the programme.'

Tia stared at him for a moment, temporarily rendered speechless. She'd genuinely thought her life couldn't get any more complicated but now here was Fate hurling yet another curve ball in her direction. Damn, Helen had probably known this was in the pipeline and hadn't passed the message on.

Josh gently squeezed her fingers. 'Hello, Earth to Tia.'

'You are joking, aren't you?' He had to be kidding. She usually avoided even having her picture taken and now she was supposed to be filmed? And with Juliet?

'I thought you knew.'

She eased her fingers free from his hold. She had to leave and figure out what to do. 'No, no, I didn't. I guess I *really* should get back to work.'

Josh escorted her the short distance from his apartment to the elevator.

'I guess I'll see you again soon.'

She couldn't decide from his expression how he felt about seeing her again. Certainly she didn't expect him to still be interested in her now. Yet, there was still that strange undercurrent running between them, or maybe that was wishful thinking on her part. He hadn't asked for her phone number this time.

'I expect so.' The elevator doors opened and she quickly stepped inside to press the button for the ground floor.

The doors slid shut and her last view of Josh was of him raising his hand in a farewell gesture. Alone in the lift, Tia slumped against the cool metallic wall. She hoped she could trust him to keep his word and not give her away to Juliet. The elevator pinged once more, announcing her arrival in the lobby, and she straightened herself up to leave the hotel. Whatever happened next she was determined she would never be the victim again.

Saffy commandeered her as soon as she entered the office, taking hold of her arm in an iron grip and steering her off to a quiet spot out of immediate sight.

'Okay, spill!' she demanded, releasing her.

'What about?' Tia rubbed her arm when Saffy released her. With so much happening lately she wasn't quite sure what her friend wanted to know.

'Everything! A little bird told me that you and the Bitch Queen went to the awards last night instead of Penny and Helen and a certain beauty editor was seen locking lips with Josh Banks on the terrace. Next thing I hear is that the said beauty editor – my bestest best friend – is going to be starring in a TV programme with none other than Mr Josh-snogger-on-the-terrace-Banks. Juliet is storming around the place in such a foul mood even the cactus on her windowsill has wilted, you are missing and everyone keeps asking me stuff and my so-called bestest best friend hasn't given me the goss.' Saffy folded her arms and tapped one stiletto-clad foot on the carpet.

'Yes, I went to the awards. Penny fell off her shoes on the stairs and ended up in casualty so she had to drop out.'

'And?' Saffy arched her pencilled-in eyebrows and continued to tap her foot with barely concealed impatience.

'Yes, Josh kissed me but it didn't *mean* anything. We'd had a drink, you know how it is.' Tia did her best to sound nonchalant and off-hand.

'Humph, you were seen leaving with him, in his car.'

'He took me home to save me from calling a cab.' Tia could feel her face heating under Saffy's eagle-eyed scrutiny.

'Right, course he did. I bet he came in for "coffee".' Saffy unfolded her arms and made air-quotes to emphasise the word 'coffee'.

'Nothing happened!' Tia protested.

Saffy placed her hands on her hips. 'Tia, this is me, Saffy. You can tell me,' she wheedled.

Tia sighed. 'Cross my heart and hope to die, nothing happened. He dropped me off, came into the house, sat in my kitchen and drank a quick coffee and left. End of story.'

'Okay, have it your way. I heard that you two were so busy playing tonsil tennis on the terrace that you were oblivious to everybody and everything else and yet you expect me to believe he didn't rip your clothes off and shag you senseless once you were on your own?'

Tia laughed out loud at the expression of disbelief on Saffy's face. 'Well, it's true. He didn't and, what's more, he's never likely to. It was simply one of those heat-of-the-moment kisses fuelled by too much champagne on my part, that's all.'

Saffy frowned. 'For heaven's sake, Tia. You kiss a gorgeous and rich bloke like Josh Branks, have him take you home and then you don't do the horizontal tango. I'm disappointed in you.'

'Yeah, well, I'm sorry. I'll try harder next time.' She crossed her fingers behind her back to offset the lie. There was probably as much chance as a snowball in hell of Josh wanting to rip her clothes off after this morning's revelations. He probably thought she wore a corset to hold her blubber in.

'Maybe you'll get the chance to get it on together when you're filming at the spa. The mood Juliet's in, I daren't ask if I'm going on that little outing. Pity. I always wanted to be on TV and after everything you told me about the spa, I'd love to see inside,' Saffy sighed.

'Shame you have the perfect face for radio, darling.' Ravi appeared at Saffy's elbow in time to catch her last remark and earned himself a dig in the ribs from her elbow as a result.

'And as for you, you floozy.' He wiggled his eyebrows suggestively at Tia as he thrust a newspaper at her, folded back to the showbiz diary column.

Tia read it with her heart in her mouth, Saffy leaning over her shoulder to read it as well:

Is pretty beauty editor, Tia Carpenter, from Platinum magazine, hotelier and eligible bachelor Josh Bank's latest fling? It was rumoured that Mr Banks had been seeing the new-in-town fashion editor and socialite Juliet Gold, from the same magazine, but at last night's prestigious press industry charity awards dinner he appeared to have transferred his affections from fashion to beauty.

'Ooh,' Saffy murmured, 'you had so better avoid Juliet.'

Tia thrust the paper back at Ravi. 'Wonderful. I think my day is just about complete.'

Tia crept into her cubicle and hoped she could avoid Juliet's notice long enough to skim through her emails and make good her escape. The fates were definitely against her.

'I wondered when you planned to show your face after that shameless exhibition last night.' Juliet might have kept her voice low but Tia was certain everyone in the nearby cubicles had their ears pressed to the partition walls to hear what was going on.

'I had meetings this morning.' Tia kept her gaze fixed on her screen.

'You think you are so smart, don't you? Well, trust me on this: by the time I'm finished with you, you'll wish you'd accepted my offer of friendship and stayed away from Josh Banks.'

The naked venom in Juliet's voice made Tia's pulse race in fear. 'Please don't be so childish. I've done nothing wrong. And for your information, I'm not dating Josh. He merely gave me a lift home to save me from calling a cab.'

'Yes, after you flung yourself at him out on the terrace

in front of everyone in the industry like the little slapper that you are!' Juliet's voice rose with anger. 'It's even made the gossip columns. Well, get this, lady, as far as I'm concerned the gloves are off. Don't get too attached to either Josh or your job because in a few months' time you won't have either of them.'

'Are you threatening me?'

'Not threatening – promising!' Juliet hissed.

Tia froze, unable to respond. Her emotions roiled in a mixture of fear and anger as Juliet slammed out of the cubicle. Damn, she'd thought she would be better at dealing with Juliet now that they weren't teenagers any more. She covered her face with her hands, angry with herself that Juliet still had the power to scare her even after all this time.

'It's okay, babe, you can turn round now; she vanished up her own backside.' Ravi placed a gentle hand on her shoulder.

'Oh, Rav, what am I going to do?' First the confession to Josh, and now the scene with Juliet – what a day, she thought.

Ravi enveloped her in a bear hug. 'It'll be okay. We've got your back, darling.'

Tia wished she could be as confident as she breathed in the familiar reassuring scent of her friend's expensive cologne. She felt shaky and uncertain, and Juliet's nastiness had left her feeling miserably like her old self again.

'I don't get it.' Saffy stared gloomily into her shot glass at the bar of the Pink Pagoda.

'What don't you get?' Ravi took a sip of his chilled white wine and discreetly checked the time on his gold wristwatch.

Tia fiddled with the unwanted gin and tonic that her friends had insisted she have and waited for Saffy to reply.

'Well, if Josh Banks was so busy exchanging saliva with you on the terrace that he didn't care who could see you, then how come he's not interested in you now?' She turned her attention to Tia. 'I mean, is he one of those guys who blows hot and cold, or do you think he might have been using you to get at Juliet?'

'I don't know. It was one of those mad moments. Warm night, nice champagne.' Tia shrugged and tried to look nonchalant. 'I don't think he wanted to make Juliet jealous.'

'Darling, I don't think it would be to make her jealous, more to make her leave him alone,' Ravi suggested. 'Let's face it, that woman is really not quite sane and desperate times call for desperate measures.'

'He was desperate so he kissed me?' Tia gave him a playful push. A few years earlier a comment like Ravi's would have sent her scurrying for a mirror, convinced that the joking sentiment was true. Perhaps she had come further than she thought.

'No, you know perfectly well what I mean. If he kissed an attractive, beautiful woman like yourself, then she would get the message that he wasn't interested in a Botoxed bitch like her.' Ravi rolled his eyes and took another sip of his wine. 'Anyway, fascinating as all this is, I have to dash.' He jumped down from his bar stool.

'Hot date?' Tia asked.

'That would be telling, darlings. Have fun and Saffy, don't get drunk.' He swallowed the rest of his wine in a couple of large gulps and, after gathering up his leather shoulder bag, he made his way out of the bar.

Saffy downed her shot. 'Do you want another gin?'

Tia shook her head, 'No, I'm good, thanks.'

Saffy signalled the bartender and ordered another shot. 'Working with Juliet is doing my head in. At this rate I'll be a bloody alcoholic by the time the anniversary edition is put to bed. She keeps vanishing without telling me where she's going. I'm writing up my copy and hers and she's messed up so many things. And now, of course, she's practically growing devil horns and a tail she's in such a foul temper.'

'I know, I'm sorry, Saff.'

Saffy handed a five-pound note to the bartender and shook her head. 'It's not your fault. I'm thinking of looking for another job.'

Tia stared at her. 'No, you can't. I don't think Juliet is going to stick around for long. Helen doesn't like her and I thought it was only a temporary arrangement until after the anniversary edition was finished.'

'I wouldn't rely too much on Helen, and Juliet behaves as if she's a permanent fixture.'

Tia bit her lip. Saffy had a point. Helen wasn't the most reliable of people and if Sir Crispin decided Juliet was staying, there would be no getting rid of her.

She left Saffy still drinking in the Pink Pagoda and made her way home on the Tube. The air underground was hotter and stickier than usual, redolent with the stale smell of sweaty, overheated bodies.

The house was unusually silent when she let herself into the relative coolness of the hall. A faint breeze coming from the direction of the kitchen led her towards the rear of the house. The back door stood open, allowing the evening sunshine to light up the tiles on the kitchen floor. Ginny was clearly visible at the end of the garden attacking an overgrown bush with a pair of secateurs.

She spotted Tia in the doorway and waved before making her way slowly along the narrow path through the various plants and shrubs growing in the borders on either side.

'How did it go?' Ginny swept a stray lock of hair from her forehead, mopping her brow with the back of her hand as she did so. Her eyes were anxious and she had dark circles which Tia knew were from lack of sleep.

'With Josh? Or with Juliet?' Tia stepped out on to the tiny stone patio and took a seat at the small wrought-iron table they kept outside the back door. The red brick wall of the house and the pale pink slabs beneath her feet seemed to radiate heat. Ginny flopped on to the chair opposite her and fanned herself with her hand.

'Either of them, both of them. I've been on tenterhooks all day and your darned phone was off when I tried to text you.'

'Flat battery or I would have called.'

Guilt needled her while she filled her godmother in on her meeting with Josh. She should have checked her phone and called Ginny once she was back at the office.

'Oh Tia, I'm so sorry. Are you all right? It must have been awful for you.'

'It was okay. I don't think he'll be wanting to kiss me again in a hurry, though.' Tia flashed a rueful smile.

Ginny sighed, relaxing back on her seat. 'I'm sorry about that too.' She gave her a small smile in return.

'I don't know what came over me. Summer madness!'

'A handsome man, champagne, moonlight . . . I've had those moments myself.' Ginny's eyes twinkled.

'Like I said, I'm not expecting a repeat, not now he knows that I'm big, fat Barb.' Tia tried to make her comment sound light and carefree but she knew she wasn't fooling Ginny.

She would never have confessed it to anyone, not even her beloved godmother, but she'd always nursed a secret fantasy that one day she and Josh would meet again. In her fantasy it had been a lot like the incident on the terrace. She would be wearing a beautiful dress and Josh would gaze into her eyes and recognise her as the girl she'd used to be before declaring his previously unspoken undying secret love for her.

At least the dress and the kiss had been right, even if the recognising her and declaring undying secret love bit hadn't gone quite so well. That was the problem with fairytales, they were best kept as just that.

'What about Juliet?' Ginny asked, her pleasant face creasing with fresh anxiety.

Tia blew out a breath. 'I don't know. When she attacked me today I froze up. Ravi came to my rescue.'

'Do you think you should tell Ravi and Saffy who you are and what happened to you before when you were at school?' Ginny's voice was gentle.

Tia picked at a loose flake of paint on the tabletop with her fingernail. 'I don't think it's a good idea.' Everything was happening too fast.

'They're your friends, they'd understand,' Ginny urged.

Tia looked up to meet her godmother's mild gaze. 'Supposing they don't? Ravi and Saffy are the first real friends I've ever had. All through college I didn't really mix with anyone or get very close to them. If I tell Rav and Saffy and they don't get it, then I'd have no one again, just like before. I might as well still be Barbara.' The ache in her chest grew deeper, squeezing her heart so tight it physically hurt her to breathe.

'Tia, if they're the friends you think they are, then they will understand. I'm sure of it.'

'I know, but I'm not sure that I'm ready to take that chance.' Why had Juliet had to come back into her life? Why?

Josh paced restlessly up and down across the terrace of his rooftop garden. Up above the city there was a slight and welcome breeze cooling his skin as he walked. Spread out below him the lights of the city were flickering into life as the sun moved lower, painting the sky with streaks of pink and gold.

Ever since he'd said goodbye to Tia at lunchtime he'd been unable to focus on any of his daily tasks. He paused to lean on the metal handrail and took in the view of the parkland beyond the hotel. There was no doubt about it, she had managed to get under his skin in a way no woman had managed before. The question was did he want to do anything about it?

He had tried to recall his memories of Barbara and reconcile them with Tia as she was today. The only thing he could remember with any clarity was Barbara's eyes. Even then she'd had beautiful eyes. They were the colour of old sherry with flecks of amber and green, fringed with long dark lashes. When she'd looked at him this morning, pleading with him to understand, he'd felt as if she could see into his very soul.

The intercom on the wall buzzed, rudely interrupting his thoughts. His first instinct was to ignore it; he wasn't expecting anyone and he'd asked not to be disturbed. It buzzed again and he pressed the response button ready to reprimand the person on the other end.

The receptionist's voice sounded discreet and a little worried as she explained the situation.

Josh sighed. 'I'll come down.'

Juliet was in the lobby and demanding to see him.

She must have been persistent to get past the receptionists who were adept at fielding casual enquiries. He gave a last lingering look at the panorama below and, with a sense of foreboding deep in his belly, pushed the button to call the elevator.

She was waiting for him near the reception desk, her

tall slim figure dressed in the usual black designer outfit, blond hair swept back in a neat chignon and Gucci sunglasses firmly in place.

'Is there something I can do for you, Juliet?' He stood a little away from her and dug his hands into the pockets of his trousers. Whatever her reasons for coming to see him were, he was sure they weren't good.

'Josh, darling.' She crossed the gap between them in a few easy steps to plant a kiss on his cheek. He could smell the heavy, rich scent of her perfume. 'Why don't we go through to the bar and you can buy me a drink? And maybe I can tell you what I can do for you.'

'Jools, I'm pretty sure there really isn't anything you can do for me.' Except maybe take off those stupid glasses, he thought to himself.

She stroked a finger down his cheek, removing any trace of her bright pink lipstick that she might have left there. 'Oh, but I'm sure there is. I have a business proposition that might interest you.'

'Really.' He made no move to follow her into the bar. Every nerve told him to go in the opposite direction, and quickly.

She smiled. 'Really. This is the kind of proposition that could have big money attached to it. Don't you think the least you could do is come and have a drink and hear me out? For old times' sake.'

The phrase seemed grotesque coming from Juliet after his conversation with Tia that morning about what old times had meant to her. He was tempted to tell his former girlfriend to go to hell before he returned to his apartment.

Except that there was still the wretched photo shoot to complete, and now, it seemed, thanks to Sir Crispin, a documentary as well. Either way, they were much too good as promotional events for him to pass up, even if it did mean having to put up with Juliet for a while longer. There was also Tia to consider; he wanted to see her again.

'Well, are you interested or not?' Juliet asked. He sensed she was struggling to curb her irritation.

Josh hesitated for a moment longer before reluctantly following Juliet into the bar area. He might as well listen to whatever it was she wanted to say. He might even find out why Sir Crispin had been behaving so strangely towards him. All the same, his gut was advising him to steer well away.

18

Ravi and Saffy had their heads together next to the water cooler when Tia arrived at the office the next day. The buzz of their conversation came to an abrupt halt as she approached.

'What's up?' The flushed excitement on Saffy's face combined with the sudden silence upon Tia's arrival was all that was needed to put a charge in the air.

'This is a bit awkward.' Ravi kept his voice low.

'What is?' Tia helped herself to a beaker of water to take back to her desk.

'Ravi saw Josh with Juliet last night.' Saffy clapped her hand over her mouth as if frightened more gossip would slip out.

Ravi glared at her.

'Well, thank you, little Miss Tactful.'

'Watch out, you're spilling the water!' Saffy scooted out of the way as Tia accidentally slopped some of her drink on to the floor, barely missing Saffy's Jimmy Choo-clad feet.

Tia stood the now half-empty beaker down on a nearby table. 'Josh was with Juliet? When? Where?' She felt slightly sick. He'd sworn he wanted nothing to do with Juliet. Had he been lying to her all along? Even worse, he knew her real identity now, could she believe him when he'd said he wouldn't tell Juliet?

'I was at the Broadoak last night waiting for my date in the bar. The one that leads off the reception area, and then Juliet walked in with Josh Banks. They didn't see me as I was in one of those little wood-panelled booths they have in there, but they were definitely there together and it looked like a planned meeting to me.' Ravi reached out to touch her arm. 'I'm sorry, darling, I intended to break it more gently but gobby big-mouth over there let the cat out of the bag.'

Tia snatched her water up once more. 'It's okay, no big deal. I was surprised, that's all.'

'We don't know what went on, though. I mean they weren't snogging or all over each other, were they?' Saffy returned Ravi's glare with a warning glance.

'No, but they were together.'

'But not *together* together,' Saffy persisted.

Ravi moved his shoulders in an 'I give up' gesture of surrender. 'No, I don't know if they were *together* together. They were just . . . together.'

Tia didn't want to get drawn into the debate. 'Okay, I've got to get some work done. All the messing around lately with the shoot planning and everything means I've had my eye off the ball. I have to get my list of complementary subscriptions submitted to marketing or I'm toast.'

She knew that once Saffy and Ravi started arguing

they could carry on for ages. It didn't matter, anyway. Josh had been meeting Juliet – fact. What his or her motives were wasn't any of her business, even if it did sting when she thought of them together. She simply had to hope that he'd kept his word about not disclosing her true identity.

She took her seat at her computer and tipped the water from her cup on to the potted palm that lived on her desk. The plant looked as battle-scarred and limp as she felt. Even as she tried to push Ravi and Saffy's argument into the recesses of her brain the thought kept recurring that maybe this was the start. This was exactly what Juliet had threatened her with yesterday.

She pulled up her file of free subscription recipients on the computer and checked off the names. Heads of the beauty houses, leading salons and VIP movers and shakers. These were some of the people who supplied her with insider gossip, samples and tips to provide copy for her columns. If any of the people on her list failed to receive their free issue of the magazine then Tia knew big trouble would follow and she was already a day late. She printed off the list along with authorisation dockets and signed them off. Poppy could run them straight down to the sales and marketing department when she took the outgoing post.

The phone at her elbow buzzed and she dropped the list on to the tray of work for the intern before taking the call.

'Miss Carpenter, meeting in my office, now.'

Tia mumbled an affirmation and gathered up her

notebook. She hoped Helen wasn't going to start questioning her about the events at the awards dinner. Her tone certainly hadn't given anything away, although she must have seen the gossip column write-up.

Much to her relief there was no sign of Juliet as she crossed the floor to Helen's office. She rapped on the door and entered at her boss's invitation.

'Take a seat.' Helen gestured vaguely at the empty chairs in front of her desk before leaning back in her seat to study Tia.

Tia perched on the edge of the chair nearest the door and opened her notebook. Her fingers slipped a little on the pen and she tightened her grip ready to make notes, conscious of Helen's unmoving steely grey gaze.

'Now, as you know, Penny will be away from the office for a while with a badly injured ankle, thanks to her escapade on the stairs. I'm not going to say much about the awards dinner although it was brought to my attention the fact that your conduct had received a mention in the press.' Helen paused and sighed.

Tia was pretty sure she knew who had shown Helen the article in the gossip column. At a guess she was blonde, had the latest designer clothes and the initial J.

'I have to tell you, though, that I do have a few concerns about the wisdom of your conduct. I trust there won't be a repeat of that incident?'

'No, there won't. I'm sorry Helen.' Tia felt pretty safe in guaranteeing she wouldn't be kissing Josh in public or in private anytime soon.

'With Penny being out of action for a few days and the

shoot coming up at the Spa, I don't want any mistakes. This is the main feature and carries the theme for the issue. As you are the second most senior member of staff involved with this project, I expect *you* to assume some of Penny's responsibilities. Miss Gold hasn't been in England long enough to take on the task although she will be assisting you. I presume you saw the email about the film crew?'

Tia swallowed and nodded. At least Helen considered her to be senior to Juliet. It was small comfort but better than nothing.

'This documentary is quite a big deal. The last time something like this got made, it was about *Vogue*. Obviously Sir Crispin expects this to be much bigger than that in terms of viewing figures, especially as the anniversary is hugely important to him. *Platinum* is the cornerstone on which he built Hellandback, hence his continued personal interest.' Helen rolled her eyes at that idea as if she wished he'd stop being so interested and allow her to do her job.

'I'm sure everything will be fine.' Tia hoped her attempt at confidence was more persuasive than it felt.

Helen's expression indicated that she didn't appear convinced. 'I know you're stretched at the moment with Anna still being away, but Juliet is very experienced and should be able to take a lot of the load and her department staff can support yours.'

'Thank you.' Helen had to be joking if she believed Juliet would do any work.

'One more thing: please use some discretion in future

with your personal relationships, especially where Mr Banks is concerned. It wouldn't reflect well on the magazine to have any kind of repeat of the shenanigans of the awards caught on film.' Helen looked meaningfully at her.

Tia flushed and mumbled a reply. Clearly the kissing incident had caused more of a storm than she'd realised.

Assuming she was dismissed, she scuttled out of Helen's office to collapse into her seat with a sigh of relief, once back in the safety of her own cubicle. She dropped her notebook on the desk and noticed that Poppy had collected the tray with her letters and list. That was one heap of work out of the way at least.

Thanks to Penny's accident it looked as if her workload was about to double for the next few weeks. Thankfully Penny's assistant would be able to handle the arrangements with the photographers, models and stylists as Penny was normally ultra-organised. The biggest problem would be working with Juliet and having a film crew around during the shoot. Not to mention having Josh there too.

She picked up one of the long-lasting lipsticks that littered the top of her desk and started to fiddle with the tube.

'Focus, Tia. You can do this,' she muttered to herself, replacing the lipstick on the desk before opening up a new document to write her copy on 'How to Keep Your Lips Luscious and Kissable'.

*

Kim stood in front of Josh, one hand on her hip and an exasperated expression on her face.

'Would you like to sign these now?' She flourished a sheaf of papers at him with her free hand and Josh realised she must have asked him the same question more than once, judging by her tone.

'Yeah, sure, sorry Kim.'

She placed the documents neatly in front of him. 'Is everything all right? You seem a little distracted today.'

'I've a lot on my mind at the moment.' He bent his head to sign the papers, taking care not to meet her gaze.

'Hmm, that's not like you.'

'Could you set up a meeting with Rupert Finch in the next few days?'

'I can try. Is it urgent, or shall I just find a slot in your diary?' Her tone was nonchalant but he knew Kim like the back of his own hand. She wasn't fooling him for a second.

'I think sooner rather than later, please.' He sensed her hesitating. 'Here you go.' He handed her the signed documents and waited for her to leave.

'Rupert Finch?' She thumbed the papers in her hand, clearly hoping he'd expand on why he wanted to meet a man he couldn't stand.

'Rupert Finch,' he said and turned his attention back to his computer screen, ignoring Kim's sigh.

'Okay, Rupert Finch it is,' she muttered as she made her way back across the office to her own desk.

It might be a huge mistake setting up a meeting with a man he distrusted, but from his conversation the previous evening with Juliet he knew he had to uncover more about Finch's intentions. It wasn't so much what Juliet had said, but rather what she had hinted at instead which had intrigued him.

He wasn't certain what Juliet's role was in the proceedings. She certainly had appeared to be more than simply a messenger for Rupert Finch. He stared at his screen without seeing a single word of the report on the display. He'd never met anyone with an ego quite the size of Juliet's. There were only so many ways you could make it clear to someone that you weren't interested in them.

Even after he'd kissed Tia on the terrace after the awards ceremony, Juliet still couldn't seem to accept that is was Tia he was interested in and not her. Not that he'd had any ulterior motive in his mind at all when he'd kissed Tia. He'd been oblivious to everyone and every-thing when he'd been out there under the moonlit sky with the scent of the climbing roses mingling with the soft, delicate fragrance of her skin.

A newspaper lay on the corner of his desk with an item in the gossip column ringed in red. He wondered if Tia had seen it. Kim had spotted it and marked it out for his attention. There was no doubt that Juliet would have read it. She had always been an avid reader of those kinds of things. He was also pretty certain that a girl who didn't even like sharing her mobile number wouldn't be very pleased at finding her name plastered across the tabloids.

Josh closed his eyes. Maybe he was losing the plot.

Lately it felt as if he'd spent far too much time thinking about women and not enough time taking care of business. Usually he was pretty single-minded when it came to running his affairs, both business and personal. Since Tia had entered, or should that be re-entered, his life, everything had gone crazy. He shook his head to clear his thoughts and then opened his eyes. He needed to stay sharp if he intended tangling with Rupert Finch.

19

Tia quickly discovered that her new duties during Penny's enforced absence included keeping tabs on the building progress at the spa, liaising with the film crew and co-ordinating the models, photographer and everything else necessary to make the shoot a success.

Juliet was conspicuous only by her absence. She seemed to neatly avoid every piece of work Tia attempted to give her by fielding it to Saffy or merely being 'too busy' to have it completed on time. Fortunately, Saffy, Ravi, Penny's assistant and Poppy, Tia's intern, all pulled together to help take up the slack. Josh's PA, Kim, also proved to be worth her weight in gold, sending Tia regular bulletins on progress with the building works and preparing key areas ready for the shoot.

At least keeping busy helped to keep Tia's mind off Josh. Kim had told her he, too, was working long hours to ensure everything continued to proceed smoothly at his end. He'd also been travelling abroad to some of his other hotels. She wondered if his long hours included finding time to see Juliet or if, as Saffy kept insisting,

Ravi had been mistaken with what he saw.

Finally a date was set for the film crew to begin the preliminary shots. Kim told her they planned to film Josh in his office and some background footage at the site first. Tia already knew they intended to visit the *Platinum* offices. They planned to film the monthly editorial team meeting and to garner background film of the day-to-day running of the magazine.

'I bet Juliet shows up for that one,' Ravi muttered when Tia broke the news as they sat at their favourite spot in the Pink Pagoda.

Saffy nodded her agreement. 'Oh yeah, and she'll probably try to hog all the camera time to make it look like she's done all the work, lazy cow.'

'Where does she keep swanning off to?' Ravi asked, helping himself to a handful of peanuts from the fresh tray that the barman had placed in front of them.

'No idea. She lists them as meetings on the shared diary but she never seems to have anything much to show for them and never says who they're with.' Saffy took a sip of her fruit juice and pulled a face. 'This would taste so much better with vodka in it.'

'You're cutting down on the booze, darling, before your liver stops working,' Ravi reminded her. 'Have a peanut.'

'So where is she going?' Tia toyed with her white wine.

'You should follow her, Rav. Do one of your investigative pieces,' Saffy suggested.

'That's not a bad idea. There is definitely something

going on, and wouldn't it be lovely to get some dirt on her royal smugness.' He tossed a peanut into the air and caught it in his mouth.

'Well, I'm sick of getting her work dumped on me all the time. With this extra work to do it's not on, I'm absolutely knackered,' Saffy said. 'I've tried talking to Helen about it but she just blanks me out.'

'The film crew are coming on Monday, so we know darling Jools won't bunk off then. That only leaves tomorrow. Has she got any blanks in her diary then, Saff?' Tia asked.

'Yep, she's out from ten-thirty till three o'clock, so it's either a stupendously long lunch or she's off on one of her mystery journeys.'

Ravi grinned. 'I guess I'll try and tag along after her, then.'

Tia smiled back at him. She hoped he wouldn't return to the office and say that Juliet had gone to meet up with Josh. That would be too shattering. At least so far, even if he hadn't shown any further interest in Juliet, it appeared he had kept his word about not disclosing her real identity to her.

It had been almost four weeks now since she'd last seen him. Four weeks since her confession, and not a word. Kim told her he had been very busy and she had commented that he seemed distracted. Sometimes Tia had received the impression that the PA thought Tia might have something to do with his distraction. How or why that should be the case she had no idea, especially as he'd still made no attempt to contact her. Although without her mobile number he would have had to contact her via the magazine.

'Great, go for it. I hope it's something juicy. If it turns out she's just getting pedicures or visiting her plastic surgeon for a Botox top-up, I will be *so* disappointed.' Saffy took another gulp of orange juice and gave a little shudder as she swallowed.

'Your Uncle Ravi will get on the case, so drink your vitamin C, it's good for you.' He gave Saffy a little nudge with his elbow, causing her to turn her head and glare at him.

'And how's your love life going, Tia? Heard anything from the delicious Mr Banks? Or is he still on the naughty list since I saw him meeting Juliet?'

Tia forced herself to smile at her friend. 'Oh, for heaven's sake! It was just one kiss, that's all. I'm quite sure Josh probably has a whole string of women he can date; that kiss was weeks ago. Why would he bother with me? It's much better we keep a professional relationship anyway, especially with the film crew around when we do the spa shoot.'

Ravi exchanged a meaningful glance with Saffy. 'Oh yes, do let's be professional, darling and, as you say, that kiss was *so* last year. It's only that Saff and I have noticed you've been a bit moony lately, I'd hate to think you had a broken heart. What you need is a good night on the razz. Tell you what, why don't we hit the clubs on Saturday night?'

Saffy perked up a little at this suggestion. 'I'm game.'

'Sure, why not?' Tia couldn't think of an objection

other than that she didn't really enjoy clubbing much. She'd never been much of a dancer and the clubs with the hordes of pretty girls in skimpy dresses and seemingly sophisticated drinking habits always made her feel out of place and self-conscious. Still, it was better than staying at home, mooning about, as Ravi had suggested. Maybe she would meet someone, and he could help her to move on from her past and Josh.

'Fabulous, we'll set something up. Now, what are we going to do about dear Jools?' Ravi asked.

'I'll tip you off when Juliet leaves the office tomorrow. If she takes a taxi, you can follow her on your scooter and if she walks, which, let's face it, is pretty unlikely, then you can shadow her,' Saffy said.

'What if she sees him?' Tia asked.

'Darling, I'm supposed to be out and about, remember, getting stories, meeting people.' He rubbed his fingertips together to get rid of the peanut dust. 'Anyway, I must love you and leave you, I'm meeting my man for an early supper.' He winked at them and left.

'Do you think he's serious about this new bloke?' Saffy asked as Ravi vanished out on to the street.

'Looks that way, doesn't it?' Tia finished the last of her wine.

'Lucky for some, eh?' Saffy pushed the remainder of her orange juice away.

'Maybe we'll get lucky on Saturday.'

Saffy giggled. 'Knowing Ravi, he'll want us to go to one of the gay clubs and a fat chance we'll have there of pulling somebody.'

Tia joined in with her friend's laughter. 'I know, but at least the music will be good.'

Tia waited a full hour for Juliet to arrive at work late, and watched as she swept into her area with scant acknowledgement of any of the other staff.

Some time later, the phone on her desk buzzed, indicating an internal call, and Tia snatched up the receiver.

'Okay, she's gone and Ravi is following her. He's going to text me with updates.' Saffy sounded breathless with anticipation.

Nervous excitement bubbled in Tia's stomach. 'We're all crazy, you know that, don't you?'

'I know, but it's driving me nuts not knowing what she's up to. At least we'll have an answer,' Saffy reasoned with a giggle.

'So long as Ravi is okay.'

'He'll be fine. He used to work for *The News of the World*; I'll let you know when I hear from him.'

Tia replaced the receiver with a flash of unease about the whole plan. It had been one thing sitting in the Pink Pagoda and joking about following Juliet, but quite another now that they'd actually put the idea into practice.

Her phone soon buzzed with another internal call.

'Miss Carpenter, my office, now.' It was Helen, but this time there was no mistaking the frost in her voice.

Tia collected her notepad and hurried across to Helen's office, wondering what had gone wrong.

Helen was pacing up and down beside her desk as Tia entered. As soon as Tia stepped through the door, Helen thrust a piece of paper at her. 'I've just received this!'

Bewildered, Tia took the paper and examined it. Her blood ran cold as she scanned the few curt lines of complaint.

'I don't understand.' She looked at Helen.

'It seems one of our major advertisers has not received their complimentary subscription this month. There doesn't appear to be much to misunderstand; this is one of *your* clients.'

'But I did the list a few weeks ago; it was signed off and passed to my intern to give to circulation and sales.'

'Well, something has gone wrong. I checked with circulation this morning and they say they got a list from you but it was to stop all your current subscriptions as you were revamping your list.' Helen's back was stiff with anger as she wheeled around to face Tia.

'But I didn't, I printed off my usual list and signed it off. I haven't any need to revamp my list. I keep it up to date.' Tia felt sick. This was awful, if what Helen was saying was true, then none of her connections would have received their issues.

'Well, I suggest you get on the phone and do some serious fence-mending. I'm not happy with this at all, Miss Carpenter. I expect better from my senior staff. Please consider this a warning to get your act together.'

Tia's vision was blurred by unshed tears of anger as she escaped from Helen's office. She didn't have to puzzle very hard to work out who was behind the sabotage of her list. Clearly, Juliet must have taken the list from the basket of work she'd left for the intern and substituted a list of her own with entirely different directions. The trick was plainly Juliet's handiwork, but proving it would be another matter entirely.

She would have to confront her about it but first she had to sort out the damage and hope it wasn't too late to smooth things over.

It was mid-afternoon by the time she had finished emailing and phoning all the contacts from her list to apologise. She had reset the subscriptions, and arranged for copies of the magazine to be couriered to everyone along with small bouquets and chocolates for her biggest names.

It wasn't until her stomach growled with hunger that she realised she'd missed her lunch and she hadn't heard anything from Saffy. Picking up her bag she decided to pop out to the nearby sandwich bar to grab something to eat. There was no sign of Saffy in the fashion department and Ravi's desk was still empty as she hurried to the elevator.

The air outside on the street felt muggy as she made her way through the congested pavements to the small sandwich bar which served most of the neighbouring offices and the local taxi rank. She debated taking a seat at one of the small metal tables outside and eating her lunch there, but the sky had turned an ominous grey. Instead, she opted for collecting a coffee to go and a ham and cheese panini to eat back at her desk.

She couldn't resist pausing to take a large bite as

she left the sandwich shop, hoping it would halt the rumblings in her stomach. Walking with her head bowed, she concentrated on juggling her cup of coffee and stowing her lunch back in its bag. An unexpected tap on her shoulder made her jump.

'Can I help you carry something?' Josh asked.

Her heart gave a leap as she looked into his dark blue eyes. 'No, it's okay, I'm fine. I didn't see you, where did you come from?'

He took the polystyrene coffee container from her so that she could rewrap her panini. 'I've just come out of a meeting in the building over there.' He indicated one of the nearby blocks with his free hand. 'I'd forgotten it was so close to your offices, or I would have called you to see if you were free for coffee or something.'

She held up the sandwich bag. 'This is my lunch break, I've been so busy I missed it.'

His gaze locked with hers, making her pulse skip. 'I understand the busy part. It's been crazy for me too.' He made no move to return her take-out cup of coffee.

'Yes, well, I think we both have the film crews around on Monday and then we're all set for the shoot and filming on Tuesday.' She held out her hand ready to take her cup back.

'I guess I'll see you on Tuesday, then, unless you're free this Saturday night?'

Tia swallowed and shook her head. 'I'm sorry. I'm afraid I've already made plans.' Her warning from Helen about seeing too much of Josh didn't do as much to alleviate her feelings of regret as she might have expected. Although her regret was touched with a little annoyance that he seemed to think he could simply snap his fingers and she'd be free when he hadn't made any kind of effort to get in touch with her over the last few weeks. Although in fairness, Kim had said he'd been away for some of that time.

'I don't suppose you've reconsidered about giving me your mobile number?'

She shook her head. His fingers touched against hers as he returned her coffee. She couldn't tell if he was annoyed by her refusal to go out with him or share her number.

'See you Tuesday, then.' He lowered his head and pressed his lips briefly, but firmly, to hers before striding away towards the taxi rank before she could recover from the surprise.

Her pulse still racing, Tia re-entered her office building. So much for not allowing Josh to affect her emotions again. Damn the man, after almost four weeks with neither sight nor sound of him she'd convinced herself that her feelings for him had diminished. Preoccupied with her thoughts, she'd barely made it upstairs when she spotted Saffy signalling frantically to her across the office.

'Can't talk now, Juliet is back,' she hissed as soon as Tia was in earshot. 'Meet me in the Pink Pagoda after work.' Saffy scuttled back into her department, leaving a befuddled Tia behind.

Tia walked slowly back to her cubicle wondering what exactly had happened. She noticed Ravi still hadn't returned to his desk and she hoped nothing had gone wrong. She checked her emails and the voicemail on her mobile but there was nothing. It looked as if she would have to wait until after work to find out what Ravi had uncovered. She barely had time to take a slurp of coffee and a bite of her sandwich before Helen summoned her to her office once more.

She was relieved to find that this time the meeting was a team briefing regarding the planned filming on Monday. Juliet, Penny's assistant and Saffy had all been called too. The atmosphere in the room was hostile to say the least. Penny's assistant clearly felt she should have been organising things by the way she tutted every time someone made a suggestion; Helen was still cross with Tia, only speaking to her when absolutely necessary; Juliet disliked everyone and made barbed comments hinting at their incompetence at every opportunity; and Saffy and Tia disliked Juliet. It took an hour and a half before Helen closed the meeting and dismissed them all back to their departments. By then Tia's coffee was stone cold and her Panini no longer appetising.

She placed the remains of her lunch in the bin next to her desk. Her stomach still felt empty and she wished she hadn't resisted the temptation at the sandwich bar to buy a bar of chocolate to go with her sandwich. She could have used a confectionery pick-me-up.

'Helen said to give you these.' Juliet appeared at her side to drop a bundle of papers haphazardly on to Tia's desk. 'You look rather frazzled today. I do hope the pressure isn't getting too much?' Her icy tone implied she couldn't care less one way or the other about Tia's well-being.

'Not at all. I find it stimulating.' Tia forced herself to smile sweetly.

'Oh good. I heard what happened with the complimentary subs, by the way. You should be more careful, that could have caused you a lot of problems.' To anyone listening in it would have sounded as if Juliet really cared about the mix-up with the subscriptions.

Tia squared her shoulders. She was under no illusions about the real meaning behind Juliet's words. She wondered if she should start checking her seat for superglue before she sat down. 'I think we *both* know that *I* wasn't the person responsible for that particular problem. Fortunately, I have an excellent understanding with my contacts so it was simple to sort out.'

Juliet's eyes sparked with annoyance. 'Really? Well, that was lucky, wasn't it? I'm surprised Helen didn't take something like that more seriously, but then she does lack leadership qualities.'

'I've always found Helen to be very fair,' Tia replied in a mild tone. Helen was fairer than some of her previous employers, even if she was rather formal with her staff. '*Platinum* owes most of its market share to Helen's expertise.'

'Perhaps some new blood in the office will shake things up a little. People who actually do know what they're doing,' Juliet mused, her eyes narrowing as she waited for Tia's response.

'I wasn't aware that we were getting any new staff.'

Juliet's mouth curved upwards in a thin, spiteful smile. 'Oh, there are always staff changes at any organisation. It doesn't do for anyone to get too comfortable in their roles. Especially if the people in those roles start making mistakes.' Her smile broadened slightly. 'But, better not say too much. Enjoy your weekend – well, as much as that's possible when you're you.' She sailed out of Tia's cubicle almost knocking Poppy over as she left.

As soon as she'd gone, Tia pressed her palms together to stop the trembling in her hands.

'Is everything all right?' The young intern hesitated at the entrance of the cubicle, a bundle of files tucked under her arm and an anxious frown on her face.

'Great,' Tia reassured her and wondered if she would get hit by lightning for telling so many fibs in one day.

'Was there a problem the other week over the subscriptions?' Poppy asked.

Her grey eyes were anxious behind her narrow-framed glasses.

'Nothing that couldn't be sorted out,' Tia reassured her.

'I'm really sorry. I think it might be my fault. It's just that Juliet offered to take the lists down with her things, so I gave the slips to her,' the intern ventured.

Tia thought that explained how Juliet had obtained the list. 'It's fine, there was a bit of a mix-up, but it's sorted now. However, if she offers to do any more favours for us like that, come and let me know. She's a touch absent-minded, so I like to keep tabs on things.'

Poppy appeared relieved by her explanation and offered to get her a fresh cup of coffee and some chocolate from the machine on the next floor. Tia accepted and the young intern went away, her usual happy countenance restored.

When she'd finally finished reviewing all the work from Helen and gone through the files Poppy had given her, it was well after her usual finishing time. She'd been glad of the fresh coffee and the *Twix* that Poppy had given her as a peace offering for her error in allowing Juliet access to the subscription list.

By the time she finally arrived at the Pink Pagoda there were already three 'hurry up' texts on her mobile. She spotted Saffy's magenta hair in the group at the bar and made her way towards her.

'I thought you were never going to get here,' Saffy grumbled as Tia slipped on to the bar stool next to her.

'What's happened? Where's Ravi? I thought he'd be here by now.' Tia dumped her handbag down on the bar and fumbled inside for her purse. She'd certainly earned a glass of wine today.

'I've been trying to get to you all day, but first you got hauled off by Helen, then I got bogged down with all the work Juliet hadn't done. I thought I'd catch you when you got back, but then dear Juliet reappeared and we had that shitty meeting! Ugh, what a day.' Saffy shook her head and took a swallow of what looked like Coke.

Tia accepted her own glass of wine from the bartender and took a large gulp. 'So, where's Ravi? And what happened?'

Saffy gave an excited wiggle on her stool. 'He set off after Juliet. She got in a cab and he followed on his moped. He sent me a text when she got out at a coffee bar.'

'A coffee bar?' Tia couldn't help feeling a little disappointed. After the big build up she'd been expecting something more exciting.

'Shut up and listen!' Saffy ordered. 'It wasn't so much where she was, it was who she was meeting!' Her eyes sparkled.

Tia's spirits sank and she prayed Saffy wasn't about to say Josh. 'Come on, then, spit it out!'

'Rupert Finch!' Saffy hissed. 'There, now are you interested?'

Tia gaped at her. It made sense that if Juliet were in cahoots with anyone else it would be Rupert Finch, but then where did Josh fit in to all this? And what was in it for Juliet?

'It gets better!' Saffy continued. 'Ravi managed to sneak inside after he'd parked the scooter. He could only get glimpses as he had to make sure he wasn't seen, but they were doing more than just talking. He saw Juliet kiss him and they were holding hands. Apparently they were all over one another like a rash.'

Tia blinked. 'Seriously? But he's old enough to be her father.'

'And, get this, after about twenty minutes they left together and Ravi followed them. They checked into a hotel right around the corner from the coffee bar! Juliet has been bunking off to shag Rupert Finch!'

'No!' Tia struggled to grasp what Saffy had told her. If it were true, and she had no reason to doubt her friend, then what was Juliet doing with Josh? The whole thing was fantastic.

'It's true. Honestly, Ravi said there was no doubt about what was going on. Apparently, that old creep Finch was touching up her bum while they were checking in so they were hardly heading up to a bedroom for a business meeting.'

Tia shook her head in amazement and swallowed some more of her wine. 'I can't believe it. But we all thought she was seeing Josh.'

Saffy snorted. 'It seems pretty obvious to me. She's shagging old Finch to get the proverbial bunk up the executive ladder, though the circulation figures on his mags aren't a patch on *Platinum*'s, and she's seeing Josh Banks for some decent sex, not to mention his cash.'

Tia placed her empty glass back down on the bar and signalled for a refill. 'I'm trying to get my head round it all.'

'Tell me about it! The breathtaking deception of the woman is huge!' Saffy took another sip of her drink and pulled a sour face. 'Ugh, I think this tastes worse than orange juice. I knew that woman had wangled her way into my job for a reason. It looks as if she's out to screw everyone and I don't just mean Josh Banks and Rupert Finch. I reckon she's after Helen's job, though if Sir Crispin finds out, the balloon will definitely go up.'

'How?' Tia recalled Juliet's words a few hours ago and her hints about shake-ups and new blood. At the time she'd thought Juliet was simply trying to intimidate her into leaving.

'Don't you see? She's not sleeping with Finch for fun, surely!' Saffy gave a melodramatic shudder. 'But if she's feeding him insider info and he's using it to get his hands on more of *Platinum*'s shares, he could use his leverage with the shareholders to get rid of Helen and install

Juliet. You know how much he hates Sir Crispin.'

'You think that's what she's doing?' Saffy's idea certainly made sense.

Her friend rolled her eyes. 'Of course! Plus, if she gets her claws into Josh as well, she gets two bites of the cherry, doesn't she? If Finch doesn't get her what she wants then she can work on Josh. God, she's a crafty cow! No wonder she doesn't have time to do any actual work in the office.'

Tia picked up her fresh glass of wine and wished she'd ordered something stronger. 'What can we do about it, though?'

'Sir Crispin sacked her predecessor, remember, when he found she'd had lunch with Finch. Well, several lunches, or maybe those weren't only lunches either. Trudie was soon sent packing.' Saffy paused, giggling softly. 'Maybe Finch makes a habit of sleeping with *Platinum*'s fashion editors.'

'Perhaps you had a lucky escape, then.' Tia joined in with Saffy's giggles. 'I don't know, what a shocking idea. I never noticed anything between them at the awards dinner.'

Saffy pulled a face. 'Well, you wouldn't have, would you? You were too busy sticking your tongue down Josh Banks's throat to watch what Juliet and Finchy were doing. And don't forget Sir Crispin was there. Rupert would have been on his best behaviour if he thought word might get back to his old lady about Jools.'

Tia ignored the jibe. 'What does Ravi think? And you still haven't said where he is.'

Saffy clutched at Tia's arm. 'No. I didn't tell you, did I? I didn't get a chance to say much to Ravi. I had a quick call from him after he left Finch with Juliet at the hotel. He was on his way to see someone else then he intended coming back to the office. Just before you got back he sent me a text to say something had come up and he'd meet us tomorrow night at Sash, the nightclub he took me to last month. He said he might have something more to tell us then.'

'He's expecting us to wait till then?' Tia pulled out her phone to send a text.

'Don't bother. I've sent him loads of texts already, he's not answering.' Saffy shook her head as Tia started to thumb the keys.

'Crap. What do you think he's planning?' Tia dropped the phone back in her bag.

'No idea. I tried asking but he wouldn't say. God, I hate people who hide things.'

Heat fired into Tia's cheeks. 'He's probably got a good reason.' Guilt prickled at her over the secret she had hidden from Ravi and Saffy.

'Don't you find that people who keep secrets or who won't tell you things always justify it by saying they have a good reason, even when half the time they don't? They just like having a secret, it makes them feel important,' Saffy sighed.

'I don't know. I suppose they think they have a good reason, though.' Tia didn't think keeping her past a secret made her important.

Saffy swallowed the last of her drink with a shudder.

'Ugh, I'm glad we don't keep any secrets from each other.'

Tia acknowledged her comment with a nod and a heavy heart. She wondered if now would be a good time to confide in Saffy about her hidden identity. Then again, perhaps Saffy might react badly if she knew that Tia had kept her in the dark for such a long time, especially after what she'd just said on the subject of secrets.

'Listen, I'd better go or I'll miss my connection. Meet you at Sash tomorrow night. I'll text you with a time and where I'll be; we can grab a drink at a bar first before we go in.' Saffy hopped off her stool and headed for the door.

Tia cradled the last of her wine and watched her go. Perhaps her reasons for changing her identity would seem stupid to Saffy. It wouldn't be everyone's first response to the kind of things that had happened to her, but at the time it had seemed as if it were the answer to a prayer. To escape being Big Barb and all the misery and unhappiness of the past like a caterpillar shedding its cocoon and emerging as a butterfly, had felt like a stroke of genius or a dream come true.

Would Saffy and Ravi have wanted to be her friends if she'd still been Barbara with the frizzy hair and dodgy fashion sense? She knew she should give them more credit but she couldn't keep down the old insecurities. 'The biggest loser in Loserville,' Juliet had dubbed her. She knew she should give them more credit but her old insecurities still raged. If Juliet got her way now, that's where she would be again while her high school nemesis assumed her position as leader of the pack once more.

She had to hope that whatever Ravi had in mind was going to work – and quickly – or she would be starting the autumn in the dole queue looking for another job with her life in ruins.

21

The evening air was clammy and oppressive as she slowly made her way home. In the distance thunder rumbled ominously and she wished the storm would break to cool everything down.

Ginny was in the lounge, lying on the sofa and fanning herself with a large hand-painted Japanese paper fan that she usually kept on display in her bedroom.

'Is everything all right?' Tia rushed to her side alarmed by her sickly appearance.

'I'm fine, honestly, but it's so hot today. I was out in the garden and I felt a little woozy so I thought I'd better come in here and lie down for a while.' Ginny appeared pale despite the heat in the small room.

'Can I get you a drink?' She wondered if she should call a doctor. It wasn't like Ginny to be unwell.

'No, I'm fine, honestly, just a little twinge in my chest. Come and sit down, tell me about your day.' Ginny patted a space on the cushioned seat of the sofa.

Normally, Tia would have told her about Ravi following Juliet, the problem with the complimentary subscriptions, everything. Now, though, looking at

Ginny's pallid face beaded with dewy droplets of sweat, she didn't want her godmother to get upset.

'Oh, there was nothing worth mentioning today. Ginny, you really don't look well.' She took hold of Ginny's wrist and checked her pulse to discover it was thready and racing. 'I'm calling the doctor.'

Tia hurried into the hall and pressed the buttons on the phone with shaking fingers, ignoring Ginny's faint call of protest. Her godmother was clearly seriously unwell. Fortunately, she caught the doctor as she was leaving the surgery for the evening. Within fifteen minutes the doctor was in the house and ringing for an ambulance to take Ginny to the hospital for observation.

'Will she be okay?' Tia asked her as soon as they were out of Ginny's earshot.

'I think she'll be fine but we do need to run some tests on her heart, the ambulance should be here in a few minutes. I'll stay here with her, but you might want to run and grab some things for her to take with her as she'll definitely have to stay overnight,' the doctor suggested.

Tia hurried off to do as she had said, tears stinging her eyes while she packed a small bag with nightwear and cosmetics. Doctors and hospitals always reminded her of her mother's illness. She couldn't bear it if anything bad were to happen to Ginny, too. The doctor was opening the front door to allow the ambulancemen access to the house as she arrived back in the hall.

She accompanied Ginny to the hospital and struggled to subdue any evidence of her concern while her godmother was installed in the coronary care unit.

'Really, so much fuss over a few little aches. I feel better already,' Ginny protested as Tia unpacked the contents of the overnight bag into the locker next to Ginny's bed.

'You need to have tests done. Doctor Morgan thought you might have had an angina attack or something.' Tia closed the locker door.

Ginny sighed and frowned at the machine beeping away next to her. 'Angina, phooey, I think it's this oppressive weather that's made me feel a bit odd. I hope they don't leave R2D2 here attached to me all night and this blooming oxygen mask. A good night's sleep is probably all I need to put me right.'

Tia smiled, relieved that her godmother felt well enough to be grumbling and cracking jokes. 'It's to keep track of your heart rate. You have to keep it on for about an hour, that's what the nurse said.'

'Hmm, I will be fine, Tia, I promise. I'm sorry if I scared you.' Ginny caught hold of her hand and gave her fingers a reassuring squeeze.

'Just make sure you *are* fine, and please try to behave yourself. I'll be back to see you in the morning.' Tia smiled at Ginny, her spirits lifted by the welcome sight of a little colour returning to her godmother's cheeks.

'Hopefully they'll see sense and let me out in the morning,' Ginny muttered, adjusting the green plastic oxygen mask which the nurses had strapped to her face. 'Don't worry about me! Now, get off home and get some rest. I don't like the thought of you being out at night in a strange area.'

It was dark by the time she had walked from the hospital to the tube station to get a connection back to the house. Thunder continued to growl menacingly in the distance and her clothes clung stickily to her back in the heat. Her stomach clenched at the thought of anything terrible happening to her godmother. Ginny was all she had left now. Tia's mother had been an orphan and she had given up on finding her father since his disappearance soon after she was born. Apart from Ginny she had no one else in the world.

The storm, which had been threatening all evening, finally broke as she emerged from the tube station to walk the last half-mile or so home. Large, cold raindrops spattered down, quickly soaking through her clothes and wetting her hair. The scent of damp earth filled the air as she bowed her head and hurried on through the storm, wishing she had taken a coat.

'Where are the flipping buses and taxis when you need them?' she muttered, flinching as lightning cracked overhead. She'd always hated storms.

A large black car pulled up to the kerb, spraying her sodden legs with more muddy water. She'd already lifted her head to curse the driver before she realised it was Josh.

'Need a lift?' His warm grin was a welcome greeting.

She opened the door and climbed gratefully into the front passenger seat. Water from her wet clothes collected in pools on the cream leather upholstery.

'I'm sorry. Your seat will be soaked.' She swept her soggy fringe back out of her eyes.

He shrugged, a gesture of sheer nonchalance. 'I don't think it will be half as wet as you. What brings you out in this weather?'

Tia explained about Ginny while he drove the short distance to her home. Fatigue and worry overwhelming her as she explained what had happened.

'I'm sorry about Ginny,' he said, pulling the car up in front of her house. 'Are you okay? You look absolutely exhausted.'

The concern on his face triggered the tears she'd been holding back all day. Suddenly, everything felt too much for her to bear.

'I've had a totally crap day and now poor Ginny is ill.' She fumbled for a tissue in her pocket only to discover that in the rain it had turned to pulp.

'Find your key. Come on, let's get you inside.' Josh produced a folding umbrella from the pocket of the driver's door and held it protectively over her as they hurried along the path and into the house.

'Go upstairs and get out of your wet clothes, I'll put the kettle on.' He gave her a gentle nudge in the small of her back to point her towards the stairs.

'But . . .' she started to protest, but he simply shook his head and walked off towards the kitchen.

By the time Tia appeared in the kitchen a few minutes later he'd located the mugs and the tea bags. With her dark hair swathed in a pale pink, fluffy towel and her slender frame ensconced in an equally fluffy matching dressing gown, she looked frail and tired. Her face was bare of her usual make-up and dark shadows lay under her beautiful eyes.

'I made you a mug of tea.' He proffered her the drink. From the drawn look on her face her day must have been truly awful even before her godmother's illness. He'd thought she'd looked weary when he'd met her by the sandwich bar but clearly now she was exhausted.

'Thanks.' She took the mug from his hand and sipped. 'Oh, I needed this.'

Lightning flashed once more outside the kitchen window and the kitchen lights flickered as the thunder crashed hard on its heels.

'I think the storm is right overhead now.' Josh picked up his own drink to take a sip. His vantage point opposite Tia afforded a tantalising glimpse where the dressing gown had fallen slightly open at the neck. Soft shadows converged along delicate, creamy skin, drawing his gaze.

She glanced nervously at the kitchen window, seemingly unaware of where his focus lay. 'I've never liked thunderstorms,' she began quietly. 'When I was a little girl one brought down a big tree at the bottom of our garden. It just missed the house when it fell and ever since I've been a bit jumpy, especially if the bangs are very loud.'

'I'm sure you're quite safe here. I didn't notice any big trees near this house.' He tried not to stare at her cleavage even as he wondered if she had any clothes on under the fleecy robe. He couldn't remember the last time he'd felt so nervous around a woman, probably not since his teens, way back before Juliet, when he'd tried to kiss Laura Beckford in the back row of the local cinema.

'What brought you out to my neighbourhood on a night like this?' Tia asked.

'Kim stayed late, as we had a lot to finish up, so I offered to run her home.' He placed his drink down carefully on the table. He couldn't quite bring himself to meet her eyes for a moment.

'She lives out here?' Tia queried, a puzzled crease appearing in the centre of her forehead.

'Not exactly. Okay, I dropped her off at her place and then came over here trying to think of some excuse to knock on your door so I could see you again.' He might as well confess the truth, even if it did make him sound as gawky and awkward as he felt. Bumping into Tia earlier that day had been all the trigger he'd required to try to see her again.

He'd picked his phone up to call the magazine and toyed with sending her an email a thousand times over the last few weeks whenever he'd been back from business trips and in the country. Only his uncertainty about how involved she might be in the situation with Rupert Finch and Sir Crispin had prevented him. If Juliet was on Rupert's team then maybe Sir Crispin had enlisted Tia.

Tia's cheeks grew pink and he noticed the colour extended into the shady area of her cleavage. Lightning flashed again, illuminating the kitchen. A loud bang followed on its heels and Tia jumped down from her stool, spilling some of her tea on to the table as she put the mug down. She almost dropped it, her hands were shaking so badly and he could see from her face that she was terrified.

Without thinking he stood and wrapped his arms around her, gathering her to him. She quivered as the storm released another thunderbolt and clung on to him, sending the towel covering her wet hair tumbling on to the floor. The rain-wet scent of her skin and delicate trace of her perfume filled his nostrils, speeding his pulse as she pressed her body close to his.

He raised his hand to smooth her damp hair, cradling her head as she leaned, trembling, against his chest. 'It's okay,' he murmured, 'most storms just make a lot of noise.'

Another clap of thunder followed his words and he felt her flinch. 'I'm sorry,' she began, her voice muffled against him. 'You must think me such a big baby.'

He kissed her damp hair in reassurance. 'No, I'd never think that of you. You've been through too much for me to ever think you were a coward.'

She lifted her head, her eyes wide with surprise, and his mouth found hers. He touched and tasted her with his tongue finding the aftermath of her warm, sweet tea and something else that was uniquely Tia.

The soft fleecy fabric of her dressing gown loosened under his hands as he held her. Unable to resist he slipped his hand beneath the robe seeking her warmth. His kiss deepened as he explored her silky skin, discovering to his delight that she was, indeed, naked beneath the gown.

Her kisses grew more urgent as he stroked her curves and hollows. When he cupped her buttocks with his hands she moaned softly against his mouth. Her fingers fumbled with the catch on the front of his trousers and he moved his hand to stroke her between her legs.

He barely noticed the rain lashing against the kitchen window as she tugged his shirt free from his trousers and pressed her bare breasts against his chest, her small pink nipples hard and pebbled with desire. His lips blazed a trail from her mouth downward until he had one of those small, rosy tips in his mouth.

A small squeak of pleasure escaped from her as she freed him from the rest of his clothes so her hands could explore his body at will. The touch of her fingers against his skin was driving him crazy. He backed her against the edge of the table, desperate to be closer to her, to take her and make her his. If he didn't take her soon, it would be too late.

She clung to his neck as he lifted her on to the table top and parted her legs to push inside her, feeling her shudder with pleasure as he moved. He couldn't remember the last time it had felt like this, so hot and urgent. She moved with him, gripping him with her legs, urging them both on to the point of no return, until she collapsed against him with a final cry.

He stood for a moment, his legs shaking as his heart slowed its thudding to a more normal rate. Tia's head rested against his shoulder – her expression hidden from his view.

What the hell had they just done?

22

Outside the window the storm had settled down into steady, driving rain punctuated by the distant rumble of retreating thunder. Josh's heart rate slowed, steadying beneath the spread of her fingertips on his chest. Tia's own pulse was still racing as the air began to cool around her heated flesh.

She closed her eyes for a second, savouring the hard masculine feel of his body against hers, skin to skin. The subtle scent of his cologne mixed with male pheromones tugged at her senses. Slowly she opened her eyes and lifted her head to look at him. His breathing became less ragged as his gaze locked with hers before he kissed her tenderly on the lips once more.

The edge of the table bit into the back of her thighs as Josh helped her down. She still couldn't quite believe what they'd done. This was so unlike her, to be wild and spontaneous. All of her past, and rather limited, sexual experiences had taken place in bed, usually with the lights off.

She collected her robe from the floor and shrugged into it while Josh zipped himself back into his trousers.

As she tugged her belt into a knot he took her in his arms again, making her breath quicken.

'This wasn't quite how I envisaged my first time with you would be,' he murmured, his voice warm against her ear.

Tia had a flashback to some of the more graphic daydreams she'd had about Josh when they'd been at school together. The memories sent a fresh rush of colour into her cheeks. She hadn't envisaged ever doing something so wild with him either, even though she'd certainly had lots of other ideas.

'No, I've never done anything quite like that before,' she confessed.

He stroked her cheek with a long, lean finger. 'I promise next time will be better.'

Desire heated within her at the thought of a next time, tempered only by slight annoyance at his certainty that she would want to repeat the experience. She fanned her fingers out once more against his bare chest, noting with pleasure the small hitch in his pulse caused by her touch.

'Hmm, we'll have to see about that.' She couldn't resist a small smile as his pupils dilated slightly at her words.

'It's been a long time since I got so carried away by the moment. You realise we didn't um, use any protection?' A flicker of anxiety showed briefly in his eyes.

'It's okay. I'm covered.' She stepped back out of his embrace, harsh reality bursting her romantic bubble. Fortunately, she was on the pill but even so, it had been stupid of them both to take a risk.

She folded her arms across her chest and walked the few steps to where her mug of tea stood, cold and forgotten. Out of the corner of her eye she watched Josh collect his shirt from the floor. He slipped his arms into the sleeves and began to fasten the buttons. It certainly looked as if the fun was over for the evening. She wondered how he would react if she were to suggest that he stay for the rest of the night. Would he be delighted or make polite excuses to get away?

A delicious and dangerous heat rose in her stomach at the idea of Josh staying overnight and sleeping in her bed. She picked up her mug from the table, idly cradling it between her hands as she tried to find the right words to ask him to stay. It was stupid to feel so embarrassed and tongue-tied after everything they'd just done together.

He crossed to the sink, clearing away his own mug and washing his hands while her mind raced through a horde of possible phrases.

'You know, you could always stay over. That is, if you wanted to?' Damn, that sounded lame. Tia waited for his response, her feet fidgety with anxiety.

He turned around, leaning back against the sink as he dried his hands. His dark blue eyes seemed to look right through her and she struggled to resist the urge to pull her robe more tightly around her body.

'Believe me, I really wish I could, but there's some other place I have to be tonight.'

Sure, he sounded regretful, but words were easy. Surely there was no reason why he couldn't stay, not if he wanted to. Anger mixed with bitter disappointment filled her. The unspoken message was clear; he'd already obtained what he'd come for and then some. He probably hadn't expected her to offer herself on a plate, so to speak, on the kitchen table.

'Then I'd better not keep you.' She strode over to the door leading to the hall and opened it.

'Tia, I genuinely do have to go. I don't want to, I'd much rather be here with you.' He surveyed her with a level gaze, a slightly puzzled expression on his face.

'It's fine. I need to get some sleep. I'll have to go to the hospital tomorrow and I've a hot date tomorrow night at Sash.' She feigned a yawn. He didn't need to know her date was with Ravi and Saffy. This way at least she would keep some dignity even if it meant he left thinking she was the worst kind of tart. Then again, after having sex with him on the kitchen table he probably thought that of her anyway.

He collected his keys and phone from the countertop where he'd left them. She could tell from the look on his face there were messages on his phone demanding his attention and she wondered who they were from.

'I guess I'll see you at the photo shoot on Tuesday, then.' His voice was cool now and his icy expression made her shiver.

She didn't answer immediately, fearful of betraying her true feelings. He followed her along the hall to the front door.

'See you next week.' She opened the door and stood aside, waiting for him to leave.

For a brief moment she thought he was about to say something else as he stepped outside, or even kiss her once more. Instead, his lips compressed into a tight, thin line and he gave her a brief nod of farewell.

With that, Josh strode off down the rain-drenched path and Tia closed the door firmly, blocking him from her sight.

Despite the noise from the retreating storm, Josh heard the door click shut. He resisted the urge to turn around and go back. Instead, he kept his head bowed under the driving rain and made his way to the car.

Once inside he shook the rain from his hair and glanced back at Tia's house. No light shone in the downstairs windows, everything appeared closed and empty.

'Damn.' He slapped the steering wheel in frustration.

He was pretty sure Tia had been lying when she'd claimed to have a hot date for tomorrow night. Even so he was surprised to find himself riled at the thought that she might be seeing someone else. He gave her house one last look and pulled away from the kerb.

The traffic lights were on red at the end of the street, affording him the opportunity to extract his mobile phone from his pocket to check the messages he'd seen waiting. A quick look before the lights changed to green told him he had several missed calls. He swore under his breath, already guessing who most of them were from. He should have been at his mother's home by now and she was probably trying to find out where he'd got to.

He should have told Tia why he couldn't stay. It wasn't as if he had anything to hide. The truth was, he'd grown so used to keeping his own counsel that he found it hard to trust anyone with details of his private life. He'd been burned too many times in the past when women he'd been dating had shared confidences with the press and he'd ended up reading intimate details about his private life in the gossip columns.

Things had moved so fast with Tia, and yet he still felt cautious. He'd didn't think she was the kind of woman who sought press attention. She seemed to keep her life pretty private. After all, he hadn't known about her past life as Barbara until recently. Even so, the strength of his feelings for her disturbed him more than he cared to admit. God, he hadn't lost control of himself the way he just had with her tonight since he'd been about seventeen. Trust things to happen tonight, the one time he had a commitment he absolutely couldn't break.

He pulled up outside the hotel and hurried through to his apartment, ignoring the message being waved at him by the receptionist on the lobby desk. Whatever it was he'd pick it up on his way back out, after he'd showered, changed and collected his overnight bag.

A look of relief spread across the receptionist's face when Josh reappeared in the lobby some fifteen minutes later.

'Mr Banks, I've several messages for you!'

Josh hefted his bag on to his shoulder and took the sheet of paper from the young man behind the desk.

'Okay, thanks.' He scanned the sheet. Two messages from his mother, asking where he was. One from the journalist he'd met at the Christmas Cracker shoot for *Platinum*, asking him to ring him, and one from Juliet, asking if he'd be at his apartment that evening.

He tore off the strip with the journalist's message and tucked it in the back pocket of his jeans before handing the rest of the sheet back to the receptionist.

'Please call my mother and tell her I'm on my way. Also, ring Miss Gold and tell her I'm unavailable – permanently.'

The receptionist coloured at being entrusted with a personal task, stammering his assurances that he'd deal with it as Josh made his way to his car. A drive down the motorway into Kent and a night at his family home awaited him.

Tia lay back amongst the bubbles in her bath and closed her eyes. She breathed in the soft scent of rose petals, trying to persuade her mind to empty and her body to relax. Instead, pictures of Josh's expression as he'd left the house kept forcing their way to the front of her thoughts.

'Insufferable, annoying man.' She snapped her eyes open and sat up, sending the soapsuds swirling around her.

Let him go off and do whatever it was he claimed he had to do! One thing was certain, no matter how good the sex had been with him, if he thought she would be up for a repeat, then he would be sadly disappointed. She reached for the soap and began to work up a lather along her arms and legs. There was no way she was going to end up on his booty call list.

She rinsed off the lather and stepped out of the bath, wrapping herself in one of the large cotton bathsheets that Ginny kept on a rail in the bathroom. The towelling brushed softly against her damp skin as she made her way back to her bedroom. Her mobile phone buzzed on her night-stand as she entered the room. Praying it wasn't a message from the hospital to say Ginny was worse, she hurried over to look at the screen.

Relief that it wasn't a message from the hospital turned into anger when she read the text.

'Thought you'd like to know. Don't bother trying to contact Josh this wkend, he's with me.'

She didn't need to check to see who the sender might be. It could only be Juliet.

Tia sank down on the edge of the bed, still staring at the message on the screen. Was that where he had to be tonight? With her? What was Juliet playing at? Was she sleeping with Rupert Finch or with Josh? Josh had said he wasn't involved with Juliet but Ravi had seen him with her. Maybe it was simply one of Juliet's malicious tricks. It wouldn't be out of character for her to do something like that, but the timing coming right after what had happened a short while ago certainly seemed fortuitous.

Tia pressed the delete button and dropped her phone back on to the table next to the bed. Perhaps she'd have a better idea of what was actually going on when she spoke to Ravi. In the meantime, one thing she knew for sure was that Josh Banks was definitely not going to work his way into her knickers a second time.

23

Ginny was in a belligerent mood later the following afternoon when Tia arrived at her bedside bearing gifts of grapes and a bottle of fruit juice.

'Honestly, I can't believe they won't let me come home. So much fuss, it's ridiculous. I feel tons better now.'

'Well, they said your heart tracing wasn't quite right so they need to keep you a little longer.' Tia sat on the chair next to Ginny's bed, relieved to see she no longer wore the oxygen mask from the previous night. 'It's better to be safe than sorry, I suppose.'

'I suppose so,' Ginny grumbled.

'You'll be out of here soon enough,' Tia reassured her, pleased to see her godmother looking much better for her night in hospital, even if she hadn't enjoyed her stay.

'I thought about you last night, during that terrible storm.' A worried frown furrowed Ginny's forehead.

'I was okay, really.' Tia pretended to tidy Ginny's locker, hoping her godmother wouldn't notice her heightened colour.

'I know how much you hate thunder.'

'Honestly, I was fine. By the way, I'm meeting Ravi and Saffy later on for a bit of a night out,' she added, changing the subject before Ginny could comment any further.

'Oh that's nice, you should go out more often. You could ask Saffy to stay over with you if you don't want to be by yourself,' Ginny suggested.

Tia kept her face averted and arranged the grapes she'd brought in a bowl she'd found on the bedside table. 'Maybe. I'm all right by myself, though, and I'm sure they'll let you home tomorrow if you're good.'

Ginny stuck her tongue out in response and Tia laughed.

After staying until the end of visiting hours, she went home to change into club wear. Saffy had texted her telling her to meet her at Smithy's, a small bar she knew near to the club so that they could go in together. There was no word from Ravi on what he had planned.

By the time she arrived at the bar what little enthusiasm she'd managed to scrape up for the night out had almost evaporated. She would much rather have spent the evening in front of the TV munching Maltesers and feeling sorry for herself. Saffy was already at the bar, resplendent in an electric-blue sequinned mini-dress and vivid heels which matched her hair colour.

'Oh goodie, you're here at last. What are you drinking?' Saffy asked.

'A soft drink please. It's so warm out there, if I start on the alcohol too early I'll be nodding off no matter how loud the music might be.'

Saffy shook her head and snagged the bartender's attention to order a lemonade.

'How's Ginny?' she asked, turning her attention back to Tia.

'Fed up and wanting to come home. The hospital did say they might let her out tomorrow if her heart trace has settled down. She did look much better, though.' Tia accepted her drink, tilting it towards Saffy in acknowledgement. 'Cheers! I'll get the next one.'

Saffy tipped a shot of something into a pint glass containing fizzy liquid before chugging it down.

She gave a delicate burp. 'That's better!' Saffy grinned at Tia's grimace. 'Hey, I've been good all week and the drinks will be more expensive in the club.'

'What is that stuff?' Tia eyed Saffy's glass cautiously.

'Cherry bomb – Red Bull and cherry vodka. You should give it a go.' Saffy ran the tip of her tongue over her lips and flashed a wicked smile.

'You're incorrigible. Any word from Ravi?' Tia sipped her lemonade thinking she'd made a decidedly boring selection.

'Nothing.' Saffy opened her handbag to retrieve a tiny compact mirror. 'He is such a big tease.' She checked her hair in the mirror, and fluffed up her spiky fringe. 'He'd better show up tonight, and he'd better have some good stuff to tell us.' She covered her mouth with her hand and gave another belch. 'Oops, pardon me. Too much fizz too fast.'

Tia smoothed the short skirt of her red silk dress, as tiny butterflies flapped queasily in her stomach.

'Maybe we should go,' she suggested, placing her almost full glass on the bar. 'There'll probably be a queue.'

'Queue, schmoo!' Saffy flapped a dismissive hand. 'I know one of the door men. Do you remember Zack? Ravi's ex? Well, guess who's working the doors tonight?'

Tia followed Saffy out of the bar and into the street wishing she had drunk something stronger than lemonade after all. She had a feeling she was going to need it.

Sure enough, a small crowd of clubbers were blocking the pavement in front of the entrance to the club. Two large men in evening suits stood on either side of the doorway monitoring the line while people slowly filed in between them for appraisal and admittance inside.

'Come on!' Saffy grabbed Tia's hand and steered her through the throng to the entrance.

'Cooee! Zack!' Saffy waved her free hand in the air to attract the attention of the pony-tailed doorman on the left.

Tia felt the eyes of a dozen annoyed clubbers burning into her back as Saffy merrily queue-jumped her way to the front of the line.

'Saffy! You look hot, babe.' A broad smile split the man's face. 'Go on in, Ravi arrived a while ago, he's in the chill spot.'

Tia slunk inside the club hard on her friend's high heels.

'See, told you it'd be fine.' Saffy smiled. 'I wish the

entrance fee wasn't quite so steep, though – I mean, twenty-five quid!' she muttered digging inside her purse for her money.

Tia nodded agreement, blowing out a breath at the admission fee as she handed over her own money.

'Now I know why I didn't come with you last time.'

Saffy shook her head. 'No, you didn't come here with us last time because Helen dumped that pile of work on you at the last minute, remember?'

Tia followed Saffy down a curving flight of stairs with walls covered in tiny multicoloured glitter tiles on either side. It was like being trapped inside a giant disco ball.

'Where are we going?'

'The club's on three floors. This is the basement and "chill zone". The music is quieter down here and there's table service for your drinks.' Saffy's voice was barely audible above the wall of techno beat that met them as they entered.

The chill zone was full of people sitting on the large squashy sofas and standing in groups. The walls had the same mirror-tiled mosaic effect as the stairs and subdued blue lighting swept across the room making it hard to see until her eyes adjusted.

'I thought you said this was the chill zone?' Tia asked, catching up to stand at Saffy's side as they looked around the crowded room for Ravi.

'It is. You haven't been upstairs yet.'

The heavy weight of a male arm dropped across Tia's shoulders making her jump. 'Ladies! Welcome to Sash.'

Ravi grinned at them, draping his other arm around Saffy.

'You gave me a fright,' Saffy admonished him, wriggling free.

He laughed out loud. 'Come on, we've a table over at the back. We can sit and have a drink before we hit the dance floor.'

'I hope you've got goss and a plan to get rid of that evil cow, Juliet.' Saffy glared at him, her hands on her hips.

Ravi tapped the side of his nose knowingly. 'Come and have a drinky-poo, darling, and I'll tell all.'

Ravi's boyfriend was seated on one of the low leather sofas waiting for them on the far side of the room. He looked exactly like the image on Ravi's mobile except that now, of course, he had his clothes on.

'Tia, Saffy, this is James. James, these luscious ladies are my bosom friends, Saffy and Tia.'

Tia took a seat next to Saffy, opposite James and Ravi. They had barely sat down before a skinny waitress wearing a tight pink mini-dress, white apron and too much make-up came over to take their drinks order. Before Tia or Saffy could say anything Ravi ordered a large pitcher of sangria to share between the four of them.

'Who the hell drinks sangria in a nightclub?' Saffy asked, her face aghast.

'You do now, darling,' Ravi responded as James took his hand.

Saffy rolled her eyes. 'Well, come on then, tell us all

the juicy deets about Miss Po-face Juliet's bit of naughtiness. Then I might, just *might*, forgive you for ordering such a naff awful drink.' She wriggled forward to the edge of the couch, her heavily-mascaraed eyes wide with anticipation.

Tia bit her lip and moved a little nearer so she could hear Ravi better above the steady beat of the music. She wasn't sure how much she wanted to hear about Juliet's escapades, especially after the text she'd received from her the previous night.

The waitress returned with the jug of sangria and four glasses before Ravi could begin his story. He paid and waited for her to leave before leaning in towards Saffy and Tia.

'Well, I followed Juliet to an Italian coffee bar over in Kensington. I watched her go inside, then I parked the scooter, bought a paper and watched her from the outdoor tables. At first I couldn't see who she was with.' He paused to pour himself a drink from the jug and took a sip.

'Go on, then,' Saffy urged.

'It took me a minute for my vision to adjust to looking through the smoked glass. I didn't want to risk sitting inside in case she saw me.'

'I can imagine you sitting there behind your paper like James Bond,' James interspersed, oblivious to the look he received from Saffy for interrupting the story.

Ravi smiled at his boyfriend before continuing. 'Luckily she sat with her back to the window so I could see the bloke she was meeting. I mean, there's no mistaking Rupert Finch!'

'You told me this bit already. Then what?' Saffy demanded.

Tia's pulse picked up speed as Ravi took up the story again. She helped herself to a glass of sangria and took a small sip to steady her nerves.

'I saw him stroke her face and then he kissed her. It was a real smacker, on the lips, looking for a lost bit of chewing gum job, so it definitely wasn't an "all-business" meeting. That was the first shocker. They must have been talking and feeling one another up like a couple of teenagers for about ten to fifteen minutes before they left the café, hand-in-hand. I hid behind the paper until they'd turned the corner, then I set off after them to see where they were heading.' He paused for another gulp from his glass and, no doubt, for a touch of dramatic effect.

'Will you hurry up and finish this bloody story before the club shuts.' Saffy poured a drink from the jug and chugged it down, grimacing as she reached the bottom of the glass. James stared at her with a faintly horrified expression on his face.

'I'm getting there,' Ravi protested. 'Anyway, I followed them and saw them go into one of those trendy little boutique hotels. I watched them collect a key from the desk and head off up the stairs. I waited until I was sure they weren't likely to come back down, then I went and had a word with the receptionist.'

James gave Ravi an admiring look. 'You would be so good in the secret service.'

'It turns out that they've been meeting there several

times a week.' Ravi arched a meaningful eyebrow.

'I thought Rupert Finch was married to Sir Crispin's sister?' Tia said.

'He is, to one Mrs Celestine Finch, and yes, she's Sir Crispin's older sister. She's the one who brought most of the money to the partnership. He's in his early sixties but Mrs F is shaking seventy and apparently she's a right one. That's why they've never divorced although he's had several flings. As soon as she thinks they might get serious she yanks on his reins and it's bye-bye, bit on the side. That's one of the reasons Sir Crispin hates him. That, and of course the way Finchy keeps trying to muscle in on Hellandback,' Ravi explained, topping up his glass with sangria and pouring some for James.

'I'm surprised Juliet risked being seen after Sir Crispin sacked Trudie for fraternising with the enemy, and she only had *lunch* with him.' Saffy pounced on the jug as soon as Ravi set it down and refilled her glass, clearly having overcome her objections to his choice of beverage.

'It gets better, darling. I went off and did some digging. Tia, sweetie, didn't you mention something being hokey with the shares and Helen behaving oddly? It seems you were on to something. According to my man in the City, there are rumours that Rupert Finch has been acquiring shares in Hellandback through a third party. It's all very complicated as there are all kinds of rumours and rules, et cetera, in place, but from what I can see it's true. Sir Crispin landed himself in the financial doodah a while ago with some bad property decisions and that Mexican film thing that went tits up. Anyway, he had to flog quite a few assets and some of his holdings to stay afloat. Mrs F has shares in Hellandback but darling Rupert apparently fancied holding some in his own right too.'

'I thought Josh had some of those shares.' Tia frowned, trying to understand what Ravi was implying. If it was what she thought it was, then Juliet's hints about new blood and Helen's job could well be justified.

'He has. I wasn't sure how many, or why Juliet was so keen to jump him as well as Rupert. I mean, he's obviously better-looking, but even so, she's a pretty cold fish is our Jools. It turns out that he has quite a chunk. If Rupert could persuade him to sell to him, then he could put them together with his portion and his old lady's and effectively seize control of Hellandback.' Ravi took another sip of his drink as the implications of what he had suggested began to sink in.

'Or, alternatively, if Josh sold to Juliet, then she could join up with Finchy and run Hellandback. That could be why she's trying to cosy up to him,' he added.

Tia and Saffy stared at him. Neither suggestion sounded good.

'Oh, crap!' Saffy said.

24

'You mean to say that Rupert Finch, if he gets to buy Josh's shares, might have enough clout with the shareholders to oust Sir Crispin and take control of *Platinum*?' Tia tried to get her mind to grapple with the problem. Thank goodness she'd only had lemonade and a few sips of sangria.

'Exactly.' Ravi nodded.

'And presumably Juliet would be installed as editor of the magazine? You think that's why she's embroiled in all of this?' Saffy asked, her voice loaded with apprehension.

Ravi nodded again and swirled the ice and fruit pieces in his drink round and round.

'Bloody hell! Can't we just tip Mrs F the wink about her old man getting his leg over with Juliet and nip the whole thing in the bud?' Saffy looked morosely at the now empty jug of sangria.

'I don't think it's going to be that simple,' Tia said. She debated telling them about her conversations with Helen and Sir Crispin. Only her promise to Helen stopped her.

'Then we have to stop Finch from getting his hands

on the shares.' Saffy looked at Ravi. 'If he doesn't buy Josh's shares it'll be okay, won't it? I mean, he can't get more from anywhere else, can he?'

'Not in the volume he needs, I don't think. Well, that's if the chap I know in the City was telling the truth.' Ravi frowned and placed his glass down on the table.

'Wow, it's like MI5 or something.' James sipped his drink and gazed admiringly at Ravi.

Saffy turned, her face alight with excitement. 'Then you could talk to him, Tia.'

'Talk to whom?' For a moment Tia thought her friend meant Ravi's unknown informant, then realised Saffy was talking about Josh.

'You know, the bloke who had his tongue down your throat at the big awards do? The one you'll be seeing next week when we film that bloody photo shoot?' Saffy clicked her tongue in exasperation. 'Josh, you ninny!'

'Why would he listen to me? Even supposing he wanted to, which he won't, as we had a bit of a bust-up. I don't even know that he's talking to me. Anyway, this is all about business and Josh is ruthless when it comes to profit and loss. Plus, he's seeing Juliet as well.'

'Ravi didn't see him snogging Juliet, only meeting her. Oh God, you have to stop him from selling his shares to her.' Saffy clutched at Tia's arm. 'We have to do something. Can you imagine working for Juliet? I'd rather go work on a market stall than work for her.'

'She was with him last night.' Tia shrugged. Clearly Saffy was convinced that she held some kind of magic sway over Josh. Maybe if she was more like Juliet and prepared to use sex to try and get her own way she might stand a chance but, since that was definitely not on the cards, then Saffy was barking up the wrong tree.

'How do you know where Juliet was last night?' Saffy stared round-eyed at her.

Tia swallowed. 'She texted me to say she was with Josh. She wanted to gloat.'

Ravi arched a brow and Saffy was, for once, lost for words.

'I don't even know the woman, but I have to say she sounds a complete cow.' James helped himself to another slurp of his drink, breaking the awkward moment.

'Maybe I shouldn't have asked Josh to join us here tonight, then.' Ravi got to his feet, looking at someone behind Tia.

'Tell me you didn't.'

She knew straight away from the apologetic look on his face that he wasn't fooling. Saffy gave her a supportive squeeze on her arm before twisting round on the couch to see if Josh was indeed approaching. Tia stayed where she was for a second, struggling to compose herself. Emotionally she was a mess, she had no idea how he would react to her or if Ravi had said she would be there. Belatedly, she realised he did know she would be there. She'd told him herself when she claimed she had a hot date.

She fixed a tight, polite smile to her face and turned to greet him, hoping her friends wouldn't be able to tell how awkward she felt. At first her view was blocked by Ravi who had walked out to shake his hand and lead him back to their table, giving her a valuable few seconds' reprieve before she faced him.

'You know Tia, of course. This is Saffy, another colleague from *Platinum*, and my friend, James.' Ravi made the introductions and resumed his seat, scooting up closer to James so that there was room for Josh on the sofa.

Tia lifted her chin and forced herself to look Josh in the eyes. He looked good. No, he looked better than good, he even managed to make Ravi look a little dowdy. He'd obviously had no difficulty in obtaining entry to the club and she was surprised they hadn't tried to corral him in the VIP area. His deep blue eyes met hers as if he knew what she was thinking and her breath caught at the back of her throat.

The corner of his mouth quirked upwards and she knew he was remembering the last time he'd seen her. Her skimpy silk dress suddenly felt much too short and too revealing. She averted her gaze, pretending to fuss with the fruit in her drink and wished her skin would cool down.

The skinny waitress in the pink dress returned and collected the empty jug and Saffy's glass on to her tray.

Ravi gave Josh an enquiring look and, apparently happy with his response, promptly ordered another jug of sangria.

'Good God, I feel as if I'm in bloody Benidorm; all we need is a straw donkey,' Saffy groaned.

'Oh stop whingeing! You're quick enough to drink your share. Buy your own, if you don't like it.' Ravi pulled a face, making James snort with laughter at Saffy's look of outrage.

'I'm going for a pee,' Saffy anounced, struggling to her feet.

Tia hesitated for a moment, wondering if she should go with her, but knowing how long Saffy usually took in the bathroom, she decided to stay where she was.

'Darling Saffy, she's always so very direct,' Ravi murmured.

The waitress returned with a fresh jug of sangria. Josh picked it up and filled his glass before he topped up Ravi's and James's drinks.

'Tia?' He held the jug over her almost-empty glass.

'Thank you.' She forced the words out.

Her tongue felt as if it were glued to the roof of her mouth. Why had he come tonight? How could anyone seriously think that she, or any of the little group sitting around the table, could possibly influence Josh about a share sale? Maybe they should simply tell Sir Crispin what they knew. He'd probably fire Juliet so at least she'd be out of the way in the short term. Then again, Sir Crispin thought Juliet was wonderful, and she was so slippery he probably wouldn't believe them.

Josh filled her glass, placed the jug back down on the table and stretched his long legs out to the side, leaning back on the sofa as if he were enjoying a leisurely night out with company. Tia wished she'd gone to the toilets with Saffy. At least then she could have escaped his keen gaze.

Ravi and James were busy staring into one another's

eyes and exchanging snatches of whispered conversation. Tia fidgeted uncomfortably in her seat and tried to think of a suitable neutral subject to discuss with Josh. Anything, to break the awkward silence stretching out between them like an invisible wall, would suffice.

The difficulty being that even a normally safe neutral topic such as the weather was infused with problems. If she remarked on the heat it might trigger a reference to the storm and she didn't want to bring that subject up under any circumstances. She could hardly ask after his health and since he'd filled the glasses she couldn't even offer him a drink.

'Did he stand you up?' Josh broke the silence first.

Tia's brain was a complete blank. 'Sorry?'

'Your hot date. Did he stand you up?'

Tia glared at him. 'Why did you come tonight?' She wasn't in the mood to appreciate his twisted sense of humour. He knew full well that she hadn't got a date and that she'd made up the lie on the spur of the moment to save face. Now he was rubbing her nose in it with his hot date comment.

Josh shrugged, and crossed his stretched-out legs at the ankles. 'Ravi asked me.'

Like that was a satisfactory answer! She wondered what Ravi had said to Josh to get him to come. Had they discussed Juliet and the shares? Did Josh know about Juliet and Rupert Finch? Much more importantly, did he care?

Tia settled back in her seat and folded her arms. She wasn't going to say another thing. Hopefully Saffy would reappear from the toilets soon and rescue her. She avoided looking at Josh, casting her gaze around the room to fake an interest in the people around them.

She kept busy, pretending to be fascinated by a girl who appeared to be wearing a dress manufactured out of black bin bags and Bacofoil. It wasn't until the sofa cushion next to her dipped under his weight, that she realised Josh had changed seats to sit next to her.

'Something interesting over there?' His breath tickled, warm on her ear.

Tia shrugged and deliberately tilted her shoulder slightly to make it clear she wasn't interested in talking to him.

Ravi broke off from his conversation with James to lean towards her. 'We're popping up to the next floor to see what's happening. If you hang on here for Saffy, we'll be back in a min.'

He and James strolled away towards the stairs leaving her alone with Josh.

'Well, what shall we talk about now?' Josh asked. He draped one arm casually along the back of the sofa behind her neck.

'I don't know. Do we have anything much to talk about?' She shifted slightly on her seat, placing more distance between them, every cell in her body on red alert at his proximity.

The corners of his mouth twitched upwards, riling her still further.

'I'd have thought so, after last night. We didn't exactly get much of a chance to talk afterwards.'

Tia's face heated and she tucked a stray lock of hair behind her ear to hide her embarrassment. 'I expect Juliet didn't want to be kept waiting any longer. I'm surprised you're not with her tonight,' she suggested, aware that she sounded waspish.

He frowned. 'I don't know anything about Juliet. It was my mother's house that I needed to get to. Yesterday was the anniversary of my dad's death and Mum likes me to go down and stay the night at home. It's something I've always done, and she counts on me being there. I thought I'd made it clear that whatever was between Juliet and me finished years ago.'

Tia risked another glance at his face. She couldn't help feeling touched that he cared about his mother enough to keep her company on what had to be a horrid day for her. She remembered meeting Josh's mother once. It had been at one of the school functions, Juliet had been showing parents to their seats, while Tia, and a boy called Barry, who had a flatulence problem, had been relegated to the kitchen to wash up the dirty teacups from the refreshments at the interval.

She knew how awful she felt herself whenever the anniversary of her own mother's death rolled around. Even after all these years it still hurt and, like Josh's mum, she had her own routine of remembrance. Josh certainly sounded sincere, but it didn't explain Ravi spotting him meeting Juliet a few weeks earlier in the hotel bar.

Saffy reappeared out of the crowd and flopped down on the opposite sofa before she could ask Josh anything else.

'Oh my God, you should see the queue in the loo. These bloody bodyshaper knickers are cutting my arse in half and I was dying for a pee.' Saffy helped herself to another glass of sangria, knocking it back with a satisfied sigh.

'Ravi and James went upstairs to check out what was going on up there,' Josh said. Tia could hear suppressed laughter in his voice.

'Oh cool, there's a fab dance area up there with brilliant lights, and we can look for VIPs.' Saffy grabbed her bag and bounced up off the sofa again. 'Are you guys coming?'

'Be there in a few minutes,' Josh answered before Tia had a chance to speak.

Saffy flashed Tia a knowing smile and a wink before heading off to look for James and Ravi amongst the dancers on the next floor.

'Maybe we should go too.' Tia picked up her bag ready to follow her friend.

'Wait.' Josh caught her hand in his. 'What made you think I was leaving you to meet Juliet?'

His hand felt pleasantly warm and heavy as he wrapped his fingers around hers. She tried to ignore the traitorous heat that flared low in her belly at his touch and remember why she couldn't trust him.

'She texted me, not long after you'd left, telling me you were with her. You'd had messages on your phone when you were at my house and Ravi saw you with her a little while ago at the hotel.' Tia tried to sound nonchalant, as if none of the things she'd said were a very big deal, even though they were. At least, they were to her. She couldn't be certain about how Josh felt.

'The messages on my phone were from my mother, she was worried because I was late. I couldn't stay with you last night and, believe me, you have no idea how much I wanted to, but I'd promised I'd go and spend the night at my mother's. We talk about Dad, look through old photo albums and raise a glass in his memory. I've gone every year since he died, and I spent this morning with her at the cemetery placing flowers on the grave.' His expression was sombre as he spoke and Tia knew he was telling the truth.

'I'm sorry about your dad. I didn't know.' She could understand how Josh's mother felt. Tia still visited her own mother's grave every month to refresh the flowers and tell her what was going on in her life.

'There was a message waiting for me when I got back to the hotel after I left you. Juliet wanted to meet me at my apartment. I got the receptionist to blow her off. She must have assumed I'd been with you and thought she'd cause trouble.'

'And the meeting with her at the hotel a few weeks ago? Ravi thought you were together.'

Josh frowned as if trying to recall the meeting. 'She turned up one night demanding to see me. I went down and met her in the bar. It wasn't a personal meeting, though; it was business. She hinted she would have liked it to be more personal but I told her I never wanted to get involved with her again.'

'I see.' Tia's heart skipped a beat as she looked into his eyes. It sounded as if he was telling the truth. Maybe there was a chance for her after all.

'**D**id you talk to him yet? About Juliet?' Saffy grabbed her and shouted into her ear as soon as they entered the dance floor on the upper level. The hypnotic thump of the techno-beat made it almost impossible to hear anything.

'He said he's not seeing her,' Tia yelled back, grateful that Josh was too far away from her to be able to hear her conversation.

Saffy looked bewildered. 'I meant have you asked about the share thingy? Is he going to defect to the dark side and let Rupert Finch make a hostile takeover?'

'No, I didn't know what to say.' She'd forgotten about Ravi and Saffy's suggestion that she try to persuade Josh not to sell his stake in Hellandback to Rupert or Juliet.

'You can tell me everything when we're back at yours later,' Saffy yelled, a meaningful look on her face as she danced past Tia, allowing Josh to move in closer. Tia doubted that Saffy would be sober enough at the end of the night for her to hold any kind of rational conversation with her. If she was, it would be a first, especially as she'd been drinking cherry bombs and sangria by the jugful.

Josh watched the array of expressions flit across Tia's face and wondered what was being said between her and Saffy. Ravi's phone call about Rupert Finch's share dealing had backed up what he'd unearthed already. Presumably, neither Rupert Finch nor any of Tia's friends knew that Juliet seemed to be playing a double game. Even though he had approached him anyway, Finch had known Josh would be reluctant to sell to him, perhaps he'd hoped that Juliet making the initial approach might soften him up.

Juliet, however, had suggested she buy the shares on her own account. Clearly she didn't trust Finch and planned to hold on to them to get what she wanted, or she intended to sell them on again to Finch. Unless, of course, she was buying them with Rupert Finch's money in the first place, which was another possibility. He hadn't told Finch about that at the meeting he'd had with him. He'd told him he would consider his offer, without any intention of selling to him at all.

The text message Juliet had sent Tia bore all the hallmarks of the Juliet of old. If she couldn't get what she wanted she would manipulate, cheat or lie to ensure no one else was happy either. Or until she had wheedled her way into obtaining whatever it was she was after in the first place. She'd even succeeded where he'd failed, it seemed, and managed to obtain Tia's closely guarded mobile number.

He watched Tia give herself up to the music, moving her slender frame in time to the beat. Looking at her now it seemed almost impossible that she had ever been Barbara. He caught her gaze for a split second as she looked up and her vulnerability showed in her eyes once more. Somehow he had to protect Tia from Juliet because one thing he did know for certain, Juliet was out to destroy Tia just as she'd destroyed Barbara all those years before.

Saffy had moved to dance nearer to Ravi and James so Josh moved into the space she'd vacated. When Ravi had called to discuss the shares and Juliet's connection, he'd been unable to resist suggesting that he invite himself along to the club. He'd guessed that Tia's hot date was really with her friends. She didn't seem the kind of girl who would two-time and after what they'd done together in her kitchen he was desperate to see her again.

He couldn't blame her for being wary. The messages on his phone and his reason for turning down her offer to spend the night must have seemed lame, especially as they'd spent the previous half-hour having the hottest sex he could ever recall.

The coloured spotlights from the sophisticated lighting system highlighted the faint dewy sheen of her skin as she moved to the rhythm. A deep-seated primal urge to grab her hand and pull her off the dance floor to some private place where they could be alone rose inside him.

Ravi cut in front of him, grabbing Tia by the waist and

twirling her around so that she laughed up at him. Josh was faintly surprised by the strength of the wave of jealousy that washed through him. He'd dated quite a few women since his schooldays but none of them had ever succeeded in getting under his skin quite the way Tia had. Kim would laugh her socks off if she knew, he thought ruefully. She had been hinting for weeks that Tia seemed as if she might be the girl for him.

Tia was glad of Josh's support in helping her get Saffy out of the car and into the house. Saffy wasn't completely smashed but she was definitely unsteady and the high heels of her shoes weren't exactly helping her balance.

As Josh deposited Saffy on to the couch in Ginny's front room she couldn't help wishing for a brief moment that her friend wasn't there. She banished the wish almost as quickly as it arose. There was not going to be a repeat of what had happened during Josh's last visit, however, much as her feelings had been building up inside her while they had been dancing.

There had been little opportunity to talk privately during the evening and she couldn't quite decide if she was glad about that or not.

'I'll have to go, the cab is waiting.' Josh made his way to the front door and stood with his hand on the latch.

'Thanks for seeing us home.' Tia had kicked off her shoes on entering the house and now wished that she'd kept them on for a little longer. Next to Josh she felt small.

'It was my pleasure. I'll talk to you soon.' He dipped his head and pressed his lips to hers, sending a dizzying thrill right down to her toes. Unable to resist, she wrapped her arms around him to hold him closer, deepening the kiss until the taxi driver sounded the horn of the cab to hurry them along.

'Night.' She closed the door behind him, her lips tingling from his touch.

Saffy staggered into the hallway to lean against the wall.

'Has Josh gone?' she asked, her voice sounding slightly hoarse and a little slurred.

'Yeah, the cab was waiting. Come on, I'll get us some coffee and some water.'

Saffy wobbled along the hall behind her, wincing when Tia turned on the bright kitchen lights. 'You really like him, don't you? And I still think he really likes you. I don't care what Ravi thinks he saw. You two have got chemistry.'

She struggled over the last word, bringing a smile to Tia's lips.

'Hmm, I don't know. Maybe physically,' she admitted.

'Oh yes.' Saffy grinned. 'I knew it. It's going to be good when the TV people are at the spa. They'll home in on you two, I bet. You could be the next Katie Price and Peter Andre – before the divorce and the bust-ups, I mean.'

Tia rolled her eyes and shook her head. 'You need coffee. Very strong coffee.'

*

Nevertheless, her friend's words lodged in her head and Tia couldn't help feeling a little bit sick when she arrived at the office on Monday morning. Ginny had arrived home from the hospital the day before, declaring herself fit, well and back to normal. Tia hadn't been quite as confident about her godmother's health so she intended calling her every few hours to make sure she was resting as per the doctor's instructions.

The TV crew were due to arrive at around ten to film general office scenes, the team editorial meeting and various pieces with staff in the different departments. The main focus, so Helen had said, would be on fashion, beauty and features as Ravi was due to interview the Flying Monkeys rock band for an entertainments piece that day too.

She'd taken extra care with her appearance, selecting a flattering new blue-grey sheath dress from her wardrobe and teaming it with the pale grey sandals which had set her back almost a month's salary earlier in the year. As always, her make-up had been applied with great care. The routine of applying creams and colours had proved soothing to her mounting nerves and the finished result helped her mask her feelings.

Juliet, unsurprisingly, was already in position, ordering Saffy around her department and terrifying Tia's intern. Tia slipped quietly into her cubicle clutching the large take-out stryrofoam cup of coffee she'd collected from the corner coffee bar on her way in. With luck she'd get a few minutes without interruption to get herself prepared.

As usual, her luck had gone missing.

'I thought I saw you come skulking in here.' Juliet appeared next to her desk.

She'd opted for her classic little black dress and Tia couldn't help smiling to herself when she realised Juliet was still wearing her sunglasses.

'I don't think I was skulking anywhere. I'm getting my projects in order before today's meeting,' Tia answered calmly and wished Juliet would clear off out of her office space.

'Did you have a good weekend?'

'Fabulous!' Tia couldn't resist exaggerating her reply to Juliet's brittle question, knowing that it would aggravate her to know her mean trick with the text hadn't worked.

'Oh don't give me that butter-wouldn't-melt-in-my-mouth business! Make the most of this week, because you may be looking elsewhere for employment by next weekend,' Juliet snapped.

'I think that would be up to Helen, don't you? And since I've never had any issues raised with me about my abilities to do my work, I don't think I'm going anywhere in a hurry.'

Juliet's lips thinned into a sketch of a smile. 'That's what you think.'

Tia shrugged. 'You might as well give it up, Juliet. I'm not about to let you push me around or bully me into quitting my job. You've done far too much of that kind of thing in the past.'

'We'll see. There's more going on higher up than you

would be aware of, so if I were you I'd do a search on situations vacant sooner rather than later.'

'Really? Well, maybe there is more going on than you know about.'

'I doubt it. Let's face it, I've got connections.'

'While I'm just a loser from Loserville. Give it a rest, Juliet, it's getting old already.' Tia couldn't resist throwing one of Juliet's favourite phrases of old, back at her.

Juliet looked at her strangely then turned abruptly on her Louboutin heels and marched out of the office.

Tia sighed and took a slurp of her coffee. It promised to be a very long day. She also had the horrible feeling that she'd said something she shouldn't have during her argument with Juliet. That was the trouble when you thought you'd said something smart – usually it came back round to bite you on the bum.

The TV crew consisted of a cameraman, a female producer and a sound girl. For only three people they created a surprising amount of disruption. Helen swept into her office shortly before the start of the meeting clad in an uncharacteristically bright green tailored suit and obviously fresh from the hairdresser's. The film crew did a short interview with her before settling in to tape the editorial meeting.

'Just pretend we're not here,' the producer instructed as Penny arrived in a wheelchair, her leg still heavily strapped, but clearly determined to be part of the programme.

'Like that's going to happen,' Saffy muttered as she took her seat next to Tia.

Everyone appeared to be on their best behaviour for at least the first fifteen minutes. There were many covert glances at the cameraman and polite interventions as they started going through the items on the agenda. Sales had produced very impressive bar charts to demonstrate their brilliance in what had to be a bid to plug their advertising skills. Ravi sported his best Armani suit and gold cufflinks while Gary from circulation had acquired a toupee.

The novelty of being filmed had worn off by the time the discussion reached the final items for inclusion in the anniversary edition and the normal sniping and inter-departmental bitching resumed. Tia outlined the plans for the photo shoot at the spa and dealt with Juliet's snide putdowns as patiently and politely as she could. Fortunately, Penny's presence meant Juliet's opportunities to take over the planning were limited to taking down instructions and seething quietly behind her sunglasses.

'Okay, thanks, everyone. That was great. We'll break for lunch and come around to film your individual pieces to camera this afternoon,' the producer announced after the meeting concluded.

The crew stayed behind to talk to Helen and Penny as Tia, Saffy and Ravi escaped and made a bolt for the stairs.

'Thank God that's over! Quick, get me out of here to grab a sandwich before Juliet realises I'm missing,' Saffy said, as they emerged breathlessly into the lobby of the building.

'Get me a prawn baguette, will you? I have to pop out

and see someone quickly before the Flying Monkeys get here for their interview.' Ravi thrust a five-pound note at Saffy and vanished through the revolving doors leading to the street.

'Now what's he up to? Honestly, this place gets madder by the minute. You know he's using Helen's office for the interview? Normally he'd go and see them at their hotel or at a radio station or something but oh no, because it's being filmed, we're being honoured with a visit. We'll probably come back to find fifty screaming teenagers camped in here if word gets out.' Saffy stuffed the note into her purse.

'Come on, I need some fresh air.' Tia slipped her arm through Saffy's and led her out into the sunshine.

'I didn't see her sneak past.' Saffy nodded her head towards the street corner where a familiar figure in a black dress was climbing into a cab. 'Now where do you suppose the evil one is going? Surely she isn't off to shag old Finchy today?'

'Probably off to get her broomstick serviced,' Tia quipped and made Saffy gurgle with glee.

26

By the time Tia had bought her sandwich, listened to Saffy's theories on where Juliet had gone and called home to make sure Ginny was okay, lunchtime was over. Ravi collected his baguette and hurried off to meet the Flying Monkeys, and waiting film crew, in Helen's office.

Tia contented herself with a quick peep as the band strolled through the department. She'd always quite liked Mikey, the drummer, and Ravi had promised he'd try to get her an autograph. Juliet hadn't yet returned from her mystery errand so Saffy had gone to make the most of her absence by trying to clear the mountain of work that had been deposited on her desk.

She gave the pile of freshly opened post on her own desk a cursory glance and sighed. She had to focus on her job. Everything would be better once this week was over. The photo shoot would be in the bag, the last of her articles finished and the anniversary edition put to bed. Then she would be able to switch her energy into dealing with Juliet. And this time she *would* deal with her. There would be no backing down or steering clear this time round.

On Saturday night, after Saffy had retired to the guest room, Tia had found herself lying on her own bed in the gloom, studying the hairline crack in the ceiling above the bed. Ever since Josh had discovered her past identity, Ginny's advice about telling Ravi and Saffy had been playing on her mind .

A few months ago she would never have contemplated the idea. If anyone had suggested it, she would have said she wasn't ready and gone into a complete panic. Much as she had when she realised that Josh knew. Since Juliet had returned and Tia had been forced to work alongside her, although she still disliked Juliet intensely, she realised she was no longer terrorised by her. It was as if being confronted by her demon had removed Juliet's power over her.

Once this week was over she would invite Saffy and Ravi out for a curry and tell them everything: who she really was, how she knew Juliet and Josh, everything. As for Josh, and where that relationship might go, who knew? Maybe she would have an answer to that by the time the filming was complete.

'How did it go? Did you meet the Flying Monkeys? Did the film people interview you?' Ginny levered herself up on the couch with her elbow, sending the pile of newspapers she had open on her lap on to the floor.

'It was okay. Yes, I was filmed, just a short statement to camera about my job role. Ravi got me the Flying Monkeys autographs, and as a bonus, I got a quick look when they left the offices. He's got me and Saf tickets to their concert at the O2 in a few weeks' time, too.' Tia perched on the end of the sofa as Ginny drew up her feet to accommodate her. 'More to the point, how do you feel now?'

'I keep telling you, I'm absolutely fine. I don't need all this cosseting.' 'She gave Tia's hand a reassuring pat. 'What's happening with Juliet?'

Ginny's brow furrowed in sympathy as Tia filled her in on the morning's confrontation. 'Honestly, she sounds as obnoxious now as she was back then. What that girl needs is a sharp smack on the back of her legs.'

Tia laughed. 'I think that might have worked when she was five, but it's a bit late now.'

'Well, it makes me cross. You've worked so hard to get to your position. There's no substance behind her threats, is there? You aren't really in danger of losing your job?' Ginny asked.

Guilt nibbled at Tia's conscience. She hadn't told Ginny the latest news from Ravi about his suspicions of a hostile takeover and Juliet's potential involvement. She'd been too concerned about her godmother's health to add any extra worry when she'd been in hospital.

'I don't think so. It's Helen who makes the decisions. Well, Helen and Sir Crispin. Probably Juliet's trying it on, trying to throw her weight around.'

Ginny's expression relaxed and she leaned back on her pile of cushions. 'That's good.'

Tia picked at the corner of a cushion, allowing the threads of the long, silky tassel to flow through her fingers. 'I've decided to tell Saffy and Ravi about changing my name and identity and everything.' She kept her gaze fixed on the threads as if removing the tangles was suddenly important.

'That's good. I think the time's right now, if you're sure that's what you want to do. When are you going to tell them?' Ginny's voice was warm and sympathetic although Tia could tell even without looking at her that her godmother was emotional.

'I thought it best to wait till this filming business is over.' She raised her gaze and, as she'd expected, Ginny's eyes were brimming with tears.

'I'm glad. They're good friends, of course they'll understand.' Ginny fumbled under her cushions for a tissue.

'I hope so.' Tia got to her feet ready to head to the kitchen to prepare supper.

Ginny blew her nose and sniffed. 'And Josh? What's happening there?'

'I don't know. I'll see him tomorrow at the spa during the shoot.' As usual Ginny had managed to place her finger firmly on the one thing that was still niggling her. Deciding to reveal her secret to Saffy and Ravi had taken a huge load off her shoulders but Tia still didn't know what to do or how she really felt about Josh.

She helped Ginny retrieve her newspapers and then made her way to the kitchen. She pulled ingredients from the fridge and began to prepare her evening meal on auto-pilot, her mind still busy wrestling with her feelings.

When she'd met him again for the first time she'd still

been harbouring schoolgirl fantasies about how he would somehow recognise her, sweep her off her feet and declare his true love for her. She smiled to herself as she switched on the hob and reached for a pan from the cupboard.

Then there had been the reality. He'd seemed to fall for her as Tia, and even when he'd learned about her past as Barbara, the fat, dorky girl from his schooldays, he still hadn't been put off. Her cheeks burned while she moved her ingredients from the kitchen table and she recalled what had taken place on that very spot. No, he definitely hadn't been put off.

She tipped a small amount of oil in the pan to heat and considered her thoughts. Was she still in the grip of her old infatuation where Josh was concerned?

She cracked some eggs into a bowl and added the seasoning.

The way he made her feel when he was near her, that hadn't changed. She still got tingles down her spine and flutters of excitement in her stomach. The sex had certainly been good. The sex had been better than good.

She reduced the heat under the pan as the oil began to smoke.

It was more than that. Underneath his hard business-man shell he was still the same boy who had cared enough about her feelings back at school to bike over to her house to check on her. The same man who hadn't betrayed her secret to Juliet and who had stopped to give her a lift in the thunderstorm. Which begged the question, did she trust him? Juliet was certainly trying her hardest to undermine that.

Tia picked up the whisk and began to beat the eggs, her pace picking up as she thought about Juliet. She dumped the contents of the bowl into the pan, jumping back as the hot oil fizzed and spat in protest. The edges of the omelette quickly turned pale golden brown and crispy as she moved the mixture around the pan.

Standing up to Juliet wouldn't be easy, but if Saffy and Ravi gave her their support, then she was sure she could do it. It was time to finally put the past completely away for ever. Although she did wonder, as she turned her supper out on to a plate, if perhaps, unlike her meal, it might be a case of out of the frying pan and into the fire.

Josh turned on his heel and surveyed the entrance to the spa. The builders had done it. All the work was completed. The glass walls were alive with coloured fish, swimming through their watery, aquatic world amidst mock-ruined Grecian temples and broken statuary. The floor gleamed with palest pink marble tiles, and a classically styled stone-effect desk decorated with carved Doric columns stood in place at the registration area.

Subdued ambient lighting gave the subtle effect of calmness and relaxation. The illusion would be shattered within the next half an hour when the models, film crew, magazine staff and sundry others arrived. For now, though, he was alone, the cleaners and the builders had gone; the reception staff and therapists were yet to arrive.

He strolled through to the changing rooms and checked that everything was ready for the shoot. The extra clothes rails were in place for the designer clothes which would be arriving shortly. Piles of clean white fluffy towels and robes stood on the sleek countertops. The mirrors gleamed unblemished silver under the bright lighting.

The treatment rooms shone pearlescent pink, the curved walls and ceiling giving the effect that he was standing on the inside of a delicate bubble. He wondered if Tia would like it when she arrived and saw the finished rooms. She'd really appeared to understand the whole concept of what he was trying to achieve when she'd looked around before. Somehow having her approval mattered to him almost more than the shoot proving a success.

'Here you are, darling. The man at reception said you were down here.'

Lost in his own thoughts, he'd failed to hear the click of Juliet's heels on the marble flooring. She lifted her sunglasses and rested them on top of her perfectly coiffed blonde head.

'Is everyone here already? I thought they weren't due for another thirty minutes.' He lifted his arm to check the time on his wristwatch.

'I'm a little early. I wanted to catch you alone, to see if you'd thought any further about my proposition?' She strolled the few short steps across the room to stand in front of him, the rich scent of her perfume heady in his nostrils.

'I already gave you my answer. Why are you doing this, Juliet? Just to be editor of some fashion magazine?'

She raised a shoulder in an off-hand shrug. 'I've got my reasons. It's a good offer – better than the market value, and' – she trailed her finger from where the edge of his shirt sleeve finished down his bare forearm – 'there could be fringe benefits.' Her lips curved suggestively.

He moved his arm away from her touch. 'I thought I'd been quite clear about where we stood on that front.'

Her full red lips curved into a pout. He recognised that trick of old, it was the expression she always used when she wanted to get her own way. 'We always had great chemistry together.'

'Had, Juliet, the word is *had*, back when we were sixteen. It was teenage sex, that's all. Times change. There is nothing between us now and never will be.' He kept his tone cool, hoping this time she would finally believe he wasn't interested.

'I suppose you have Tia, your new little playmate now.' Juliet's eyes narrowed and she pronounced Tia's name with a sneer.

'Leave Tia out of this.' Anger built within him when he thought of all the petty cruelties Juliet had inflicted on Tia.

'Oh, have I hit a nerve? I never thought you'd fall for a little mouse like her.'

'And I never thought you'd fall for a married man like Rupert Finch,' Josh countered and noted shock register on her normally blank face.

'Well, then, that's that, I suppose.' She took a step back, her shoulders rigid with anger.

In the distance he heard the murmur of voices and the sound of feet. 'I think our business is concluded. If you'll excuse me.' He walked past her towards the door.

'I hope you won't regret this.' Juliet's voice halted him in his tracks.

'Why would I have any regrets?'

She sauntered towards him, her sunglasses back in place shielding her eyes from his scrutiny. 'Things aren't always as straightforward as they appear.' The corners of her mouth curved upwards in a brittle smile. 'Let's hope you haven't been deceived.'

A noise from outside the room made him turn to see Tia and Saffy standing right behind him in the doorway.

'I'm sorry. Were we interrupting something?' Saffy asked, her gaze flicking between him and Juliet.

Tia stood at her side, loaded down with make-up cases and carriers full of props. Only the trace of heightened colour in her cheeks betrayed her confusion.

'Not at all. Juliet was on her way to meet you,' Josh said, and stepped aside to allow Juliet to sweep past.

27

There was a deathly hush as Juliet left the room.

'Brr, chilly in here, isn't it?' Saffy rubbed her bare arms, her eyes wide with mock innocence.

Josh's lips twitched in a fleeting smile. 'I'll see you later, I hope, Tia.'

He set off at a distance behind Juliet in the direction of the changing rooms.

'I think we interrupted something,' Saffy mused.

'Mmm, definitely. We'd better get this lot set up and go and see what's happening.' Tia dropped the bags and cases inside the door and wriggled her fingers to ease the stiffness. Saffy was right about the frosty atmosphere. When they'd inadvertently interrupted Juliet and Josh, he hadn't exactly hung around, either. Although he had said he'd see her later, something that gave her spirits an inexplicable little lift.

Tia led the way back to the main changing area where the scene was one of organised chaos. The photographer and his assistant were busy with metal boxes of photographic equipment and lights, the wardrobe assistant was hanging clothes on the rails while three tall, skinny models were studiously ignoring one another and texting on their mobiles. Josh and Juliet were both missing.

The make-up artist and her assistant staggered into the room carrying their kit followed by Tia's intern who promptly checked them off on her clipboard.

'Where's Juliet?' Saffy scooted over to help the wardrobe girl with the clothes.

Poppy shrugged. 'Maybe she went outside to meet the film crew.'

'She's supposed to be in here sorting this lot out, not poncing about in the lobby,' Saffy muttered.

Tia cast her eyes over the checklist and went to help the make-up artists get set up. She wondered where Josh had gone, if he was with Juliet. She had half hoped he might have been in the dressing area, waiting for her. Annoyed with the direction her thoughts were taking, she forced herself to concentrate on the job in hand.

'Watch where you're pushing me! I'm not a piece of luggage!' Penny rolled into the changing room, her wheelchair steered by a uniformed porter wearing a harassed expression.

Tia blew out a silent sigh of relief. The porter fled as Penny immediately took the clipboard from Poppy and started to issue a stream of instructions.

'Poppy, go and help with that screen, Tia, I want a display of the eyeshadow palettes, sort out the hot colours. Where're Saffy and Juliet?'

Caught up in a seemingly never-ending list of tasks, Tia missed Juliet's entrance into the room.

'Juliet, go and help Shane position that display of jewellery. I want that sequinned bag with the pearl necklaces and the jewelled hairclips. Put them in the shell room,' Penny dictated.

The mention of Juliet's name brought Tia's head up with a snap from where she had been engrossed in arranging eyeshadow palettes and make-up brushes into a decorative display next to a bronze sculpture.

Juliet caught her gaze and a satisfied smirk appeared on her freshly re-lipsticked lips. She picked up the items Penny had listed and, still smirking, left the room with the photographer's assistant to set up the props in the therapy suite, leaving Tia irritated and discomfited in her wake.

'Morning, everyone.' the producer said, as the film crew arrived into the now slightly overcrowded room. 'Just pretend we're not here.'

'Here we go again,' Saffy murmured, her arms full with sequinned designer dresses as she walked past.

Tia concentrated on her work, determined not to allow Juliet to rile her with her stupid mind games. All around her the hubbub of conversation, the sound of the hairdryer as the hairstylist worked, Penny's instructions, and Saffy humming tunelessly to some music playing in the background blended into an almost Zen-like, harmonious hum.

She straightened up and wriggled her shoulders to ease some of the tension from her neck. The photographer took some shots of the make-up displays they'd set up in front of the particularly nice statue of a

Greek god in the changing area while the models set off for the therapy suites in their first set of clothes. Penny commandeered Saffy to push her wheelchair after them accompanied by the film crew.

Her immediate tasks complete, Tia decided to take the opportunity to slip away for a coffee and a quick break before they all came back. She left the hair-stylist and the make-up artist happily chatting and set off through the spa reception area towards the hotel lobby. The spa looked amazing, every bit as good as Josh had described when they had taken their first tour and everything had been covered with construction dust.

Once she reached the lobby she fished out her phone to send Ginny a quick text. Her godmother had extracted a promise from her before she'd left that she would keep her updated on the shoot.

'Is everything okay down there?' Josh's question, spoken so close to her, made her jump. She'd been so deep in concentration, flicking her thumbs over the keypad, that she'd failed to notice his arrival.

'Um, everything's fine, I think.' She pressed send and dropped her phone back inside her bag.

'Good, I thought there must be a problem as you were out here.'

Tia shook her head. 'No, they've taken some of the cosmetics shots and now they're on fashion so I popped out for a break to get some coffee.' She noticed he'd changed his clothes. Before, he'd been dressed casually in jeans and a short-sleeved shirt; now he was clothed more formally in a smart lightweight grey suit, white shirt and blue silk tie.

'I thought you were deserting us.'

Tia blushed. 'No, just thirsty.'

'Didn't the girls on the spa reception tell you there's a drinks lounge down there?' He frowned.

'I didn't ask, I assumed that part of the complex wasn't ready yet.' Her face burned hotter under his amused smile.

'Kim's worked very hard to get things ready early so that it can be used. It's not open for guests yet as we're waiting on the wheatgrass people to sort out the health section, but we're all set up for tea, coffee and bottled drinks. I'll show you.' As they turned around to walk back to the spa entrance, he fell into step beside her, matching his long-legged stride to her shorter pace.

When they reached the spa reception area he took the corridor leading in the opposite direction to the therapy suites. This was a part of the complex she hadn't seen before.

'The restaurant, shops, gym and drinks area are along here with the lift to the water complex, sauna and salons. Of course the builders are still working down here to get this end finished,' Josh explained.

'Oh wow! This is amazing!' Tia paused in the entrance to the drinks bar.

The room reminded her of a film set. The floor was covered with a dark-blue marble tile and the bar itself looked like the prow of a sunken ship jutting up from below. The seats had been constructed to resemble giant shells. Classical-style statues stood next to tables which appeared to be made of huge boulders embedded with fossils of tiny sea creatures. It should have appeared tacky and artificial but instead it made her feel as if she had somehow been transported to Atlantis.

'You like it? You don't think it's too much?' Anxiety showed on Josh's face as he waited for her response.

Dumbfounded, she shook her head. 'It's amazing, absolutely amazing. Like Las Vegas or Disneyland but different, classier. I love it. Wait till Penny sees this.'

His face lit up at her comments and he seized her hands in his. 'I really wanted you to like it.'

Tia's pulse picked up speed as she looked into his eyes. 'Why? Was it important that I liked it?'

'I don't know why. It just was. I suppose when you first came here and looked around I felt as if you understood what I was trying to achieve.' He placed a gentle kiss on the tip of her nose and led her over to the bar where a pony-tailed waitress was busy polishing glasses and discreetly averting her eyes from their private moment.

'I'd better get you that drink.' His eyes crinkled at the corners when he smiled and she wished they were alone together.

'I'll have a coffee, but I need to get back before I'm missed.' Tia glanced at her watch. 'I only intended to step out for a few minutes.' She couldn't help feeling flattered that he'd wanted to know her opinion of the spa.

'It's okay, I have to get down there too. I'm supposed

to be doing an interview with the film crew. That's why I had to dash off and change earlier.' He accepted the drinks from the waitress and carried them over to one of the boulder tables. 'A few minutes' break and a shot of caffeine won't harm either of us.'

Tia sat on the edge of one of the conch shell-shaped benches and poked at the foamy froth on the top of her latte with the long-handled silver spoon. 'I never thanked you for not giving me away to Juliet. I've been thinking about things a lot over the last week or so. I've decided I'm going to tell Saffy and Ravi about being Barbara.'

'Are you sure?' His eyes were warm with concern, which lifted her spirits even higher.

'I wasn't ready before to tell anyone. Mentally ready, I mean.' She lifted the spoon carefully from her drink and allowed the drops clinging to the metal to fall back into the cup before she rested it on her saucer.

'And now you are?' he asked.

Tia nodded. She'd thought long and hard about her decision and her talk with Saffy about people who keep secrets had finally decided her. If Saffy and Ravi stood by her and accepted her, then she would confront Juliet too and finally lay that ghost to rest.

'That's good.' He took a sip from his cup.

Voices sounded in the corridor outside the room and Tia recognised Penny's strident tones.

'It sounds as if everyone is ready for a break.' Tia quickly drank some of her coffee and went to get up from her seat as Saffy wheeled Penny into the room. She knew the colour which had rushed into her face made her look guilty.

'I see some people have already decided to take their elevenses,' Penny observed, signalling to Saffy to steer her towards Josh and Tia.

'I'm afraid that was my fault. I wanted Tia to see the drinks lounge on the off-chance that you might want to use this area for the shoot too. Unfortunately, you were busy or naturally I would have come to you first.' Josh flashed Penny an apologetic smile.

Saffy made a grimace at Tia behind Penny's back, clearly not expecting Penny to fall for Josh's charm.

'Well, I suppose it would be quite good. Mmmm.' Penny manoeuvred her chair in a half-circle to take in more of the room, forcing Saffy to skip backwards or have her toes crushed.

'Let me get you a drink, Penny. What would you like?' Josh came to take Saffy's place behind Penny's wheelchair and steered her over to the bar.

'I wondered where you'd snuck off to.' Saffy sat next to Tia. 'Bloody Juliet keeps playing hooky too, and when she does come back she's on that iPhone and smirking away to herself like a cat that's got the flipping cream.'

'Just ignore her. Perhaps she's getting sexy pics from Rupert,' Tia suggested.

'You and Josh seem to be getting along fine too,' Saffy observed.

Tia glanced over to where Josh stood chatting with Penny. 'We were talking, that's all.'

'Talking, yeah right. I saw him kissing you on Saturday night in your hallway.'

Tia hoped Penny hadn't heard Saffy's comment.

'I left Juliet overseeing things. Tia, perhaps you could go and take over while she has her break. The next group of shots are in the reception area, think sequins and sparkle.' Penny trundled back to the table and fixed Tia with a steely glare. It appeared it would take more than a skinny latte and a Danish pastry to get back into Penny's good books.

'Of course.' Tia finished her drink.

Out of Penny's view, Josh gave Tia a wink as she left the others in the drinks lounge and went to take over from Juliet.

She knew there was something wrong the moment she re-entered the changing room. The hairstylist and the make-up girl fell silent and one of the models paused half in and half out of a vintage Yves St Laurent gown to openly stare at her. Tia turned and walked slowly from the room towards the therapy suite where the photographer and the film crew were working.

A sick feeling rose in the pit of her stomach as she took in the scene. The photographer and his assistant were still working but the film producer and cameraman were huddled around Juliet, looking at something on her phone. The photographer stopped shooting when he noticed her in the doorway and both of the models and his assistant turned to gape at her.

At the sudden silence, the film producer lifted her gaze. Her dark eyes bright with excitement.

'Tia, this is marvellous. Why didn't you tell us sooner? There really is no need to be so modest! Your transformation is fantastic. It'll be exactly the kind of human interest angle our viewers will adore. An expert who absolutely knows what she's talking about.'

Tia's ears buzzed and her stomach did a crazy somersault. For a split second she couldn't move as all the blood in her body headed towards her feet leaving her giddy and weak.

'I'm sorry?' She asked the question automatically although she already knew what must be on Juliet's phone.

'I told you: she is so modest about herself! But honestly, Tia, everyone is fascinated by how you managed to change from fat, frumpy Barbara into the woman you are today.' Juliet's words sounded sugar-sweet but Tia was in no doubt about the malice that lay beneath the surface.

As if sensing the drama of the situation the cameraman turned the camera away from Juliet's phone and on to Tia.

'You absolutely should tell everyone how you did it. I mean, that hair, all that weight, simply amazing!' Juliet added, her lips curving in a satisfied smirk.

Tia remained rooted to the spot feeling just as she had all those years before when she'd walked into Juliet's ambush in the caretaker's cupboard.

28

Juliet's face blurred until the only thing left in focus was the thin, spiteful red bow of her lipstick. The next thing Tia knew, she was running. She didn't know or care where, she had to get out. Far away from the avid faces of the film crew and Juliet's self-satisfied grin.

The whole of her body shook as she walked rapidly out through the lobby and into the warm sunshine of the car park. She made it around the corner out of sight of the front entrance and slumped against the brickwork, her breath coming in ragged gasps. The drink she'd so recently finished threatened to reappear and it was all she could do to keep from throwing up.

Her mind reeled. What should she do? She couldn't go back inside, not yet. God knows what they had made of her running out on them. They probably all thought she was completely crazy. Even worse, they had the whole thing on film. How had Juliet found out?

She had glimpsed the image on the phone just before everything went hazy and she'd bolted. It was a picture she'd never seen before. Obviously taken at school, presumably during sports day, it had shown Tia in her hateful school PE kit sitting on a grass bank drinking from a tin of pop.

A low groan of despair escaped her lips. She didn't think any pictures still existed of her days as Barbara, let alone any that showed the rippling rolls of fat round her belly and the ugly dimples on her thighs. The sun had been glinting off her glasses and her badly blonded perm while her double chin had been cruelly exposed, still visible even though she'd tilted her head to drink. The thought of anyone seeing that image made her feel sick.

She closed her eyes and sucked in a breath. The palms of her hands were damp with sweat and she wiped them against her hips as she tried to gather herself together. She focused on her breathing, allowing her racing heartbeat to steady and slow back into its normal rhythm.

Back in control once more, she exhaled slowly. This was not going to be like the last time. She wasn't a troubled teenager any more and she refused to allow Juliet to stomp all over her. She'd worked too hard building her new life and confidence to let Juliet win. That meant she had to go back inside and face everyone.

Her mobile vibrated inside her handbag and she guessed it had to be Saffy texting or calling her. She ignored it, instead pulling out her lip-gloss and opening up her small compact mirror. If she was going to go toe-to-toe with Juliet she intended to look her best. Relief flooded through her that, other than two high spots of colour on her cheekbones, outwardly at least she appeared to be her usual calm and competent self.

She stroked the tip of the gloss applicator carefully over her lips and checked her hair and make-up one more time. All the time her mind was busy planning what she intended to say when she got back inside. She spritzed herself lightly with perfume and squared her shoulders. Working in an industry where appearances were everything this had to be the best makeover of her life. This was it – show time – and she intended to take Juliet down.

She walked briskly back past the doorman and on through the lobby towards the entrance to the spa. Her heart began to thump faster, keeping time with the rapid tattoo of her heels on the marble flooring as she whisked past the spa receptionists and along to the therapy suites.

Her pace faltered a little as she drew nearer to the partly open door and caught the excited buzz of chatter inside the room.

'Of course, she always was a little unstable even when we were at school, poor thing. I mean, hiding her identity and changing her name, it's hardly normal behaviour, is it? Still, I suppose, looking the way she did, like a big barrage balloon—' Juliet snapped her lips shut when she saw Tia standing in the doorway.

The room fell silent and Tia was aware that the film crew had turned the camera to train it on her. It was as if time had been frozen and everyone in the room had entered some weird form of suspended animation. Penny was in her wheelchair holding Juliet's phone. Juliet stood next to the film producer. Whilst Saffy, next to Penny, stared at Tia, bug-eyed with astonishment.

Tia stiffened her spine. 'I apologise for running out on you all like that, but I'm sure you'll appreciate that having my deeply private affairs suddenly hurled into the public domain came as something of a shock.' She locked her gaze on Juliet.

'Oh, we wouldn't want to cause you any distress, it's just that when your colleague here brought your pictures to our attention, it seemed such an amazing transform-ation.' The producer was scarlet cheeked and gabbling.

Tia couldn't help felling a twinge of sympathy for the woman but she kept her tone firm. 'Then I'm sure you'll have no problems respecting my privacy. I'm quite happy to discuss this with you off camera and then perhaps we can come to some agreement about what's included in the final edit. And for now you can stop filming.' She tightened her grip on the shoulder strap of her bag to hide her trembling fingers as she spoke.

There was a moment of stunned silence. The cameraman looked at the producer. She gave him a sharp nod of her head and somewhat reluctantly he lowered the camera from his shoulder.

She started to apologise. 'Yes, of course, um, we'd be happy to—'

Tia cut her short as she returned her attention to Juliet. 'Perhaps my colleague would be good enough to explain where she obtained the photographs of me and why she felt she needed to share them with everyone without discussing it with me first?'

Juliet's mouth was slightly agape as if not quite believing that Tia had taken her on. Tia wished she could see Juliet's eyes behind her dark glasses. Her enemy's Botoxed frozen face revealed little of her inner thoughts.

'Darling, I couldn't help it. After my talk with Josh this morning when I realised who you were, I was so excited to find out it really was you. It seemed so incredible, I mean at school you were absolutely huge. I remembered Sasha, one of my friends, had some old pictures from sports day so I asked her if she'd still got them. I simply had to see with my own eyes.' Juliet held her hand out in a conciliatory gesture as if her actions were perfectly reasonable.

Tia caught her breath. Juliet surely couldn't be implying that Josh had betrayed her after all? The sensible part of her brain told her that it was merely the other woman being malicious once more but even so, she couldn't entirely eliminate the seed of doubt now it had been planted.

'I wouldn't have thought you would have been very excited to see me again. Let's face it, we weren't exactly close.' Tia ignored Juliet's outstretched hand. She was vaguely aware of the other occupants of the room looking on but her world had narrowed to the statuesque blonde standing in front of her.

'I remember, you did struggle a little at school, didn't you?' Juliet's tone managed to imply that Tia had been something of a dunce as well as a social misfit.

Tia forced herself to sound calm even though she itched to slap Juliet across the face. 'I won my place at

Longmorton on merit. I was a scholarship student, so I *earned* my place. I'm sure that was one of the factors you and your friends disliked about me.' She had the satisfaction of seeing a faint flush of colour appear in Juliet's cheeks and knew her comment had hit home. 'I think it's pretty clear to everyone why you've decided to indulge in a small piece of petty jealousy now. You resent my position at *Platinum*, and you hate Josh Banks being interested in me and not you.'

There was a collective intake of breath from the observers in the room as she spoke.

'You were strange back then, and you're even odder now. Odd and deluded!' The colour mounted higher on Juliet's cheeks. 'You think I'm somehow jealous of you because you've slept with Josh Banks! Let me remind you that I had a prestigious post in New York, I came back to *Platinum* as a personal favour to Sir Crispin and this is all the thanks I get.' She spat the words out.

Tia shook her head, doing her best to rise above the barb about her having slept with Josh. How could Juliet know that?

'I refuse to get drawn any further into this discussion. We're not at school any more, Juliet, and I will not allow you to try and bully me now like you did back then. I know *exactly* what you've been up to but, unlike you, I won't lower myself to your level and drag your tawdry secrets out in public.' She released her grip on her bag, adjusting it into a more relaxed position on her shoulder as if the last few minutes' confrontation with Juliet had meant nothing.

She smoothed her skirt and turned away from Juliet to face the film crew again. 'I think it's time we all got back to work. There's a lot to get through today.'

'Where do you think you're going? You don't imagine you can just carry on here as if nothing's happened.' Juliet stamped her foot in temper on the tile floor. Her heel made a metallic ringing noise that cut across the nervous hum of conversation which had broken out as soon as Tia had moved.

Tia didn't bother to look back; instead, she crossed the room towards the film producer ready to try and somehow salvage what she could of the documentary. Heaven only knew what the film crew must have made of all this. They were probably livid that they hadn't managed to capture it all on film.

Inside, her heart was still racing but she felt better for having finally confronted her demons. Elation rose up inside her like tiny bubbles inside a champagne bottle. She had done it, Juliet no longer had any kind of hold over her, real or imaginary.

'How dare you walk away from me! Get back here.' Juliet's voice went up a notch and Tia glanced over to see Juliet lunge forward, one hand rising as if to physically prevent her from walking away.

'Miss Gold! A word!' Penny rolled her wheelchair forward into Juliet's path, blocking her way. Her colour was as high as Juliet's and the steely glint in the fashion director's eyes betrayed her anger.

Juliet opened her mouth as if to protest but clamped it shut in deference to Penny's no-nonsense gaze.

Instead, she contented herself with hissing, 'This isn't finished' at Tia, before finally storming from the room with Penny hard on her heels.

A flood of conversation burst out as soon as Penny had rolled out of sight. Saffy hurried over to Tia.

'Oh my God! That was insane! Are you all right?' She pulled Tia into a fierce embrace. 'She's finally lost the plot completely! I thought for a minute then she was going to hit you.'

Tia fumbled in her bag for a tissue. 'I'm okay.' She wiped the corners of her eyes and blew her nose.

'You should have told me, about being Barbara,' Saffy said reproachfully. 'I'd have understood.'

Tia sniffed and blinked at the tears that threatened to pour down her face now the burst of adrenaline that had helped her through the last few minutes had finally evaporated.

'I know.' She hugged Saffy back. 'I was scared. It's a long story but honestly, I was about to tell you when all this was over. I'm sorry, forgive me?' Her voice wobbled as she asked the question.

'Daft cow! Of course I do, you're my best friend.'

The film producer emerged from her whispered conversation with her crew.

'We're so sorry about this, Tia. I do hope you'll talk to us and perhaps allow us to share some of your story with the viewers. It would be so inspirational to other people to show that you have real first-hand knowledge of all the tips and hints that you give people.' The woman smiled sympathetically.

Tia wondered if they would make an offer to Juliet too.

'She'd be delighted. I'm afraid Miss Gold, however, won't be continuing with the filming or the photo shoot.' Penny answered the question for her, rolling up to her side in her wheelchair.

Saffy poked Tia in the ribs indicating she should agree to the film crew's offer.

She was still struggling to grasp what Penny had said about Juliet. 'Of course. But maybe in a little while, when I've had a chance to sort some things out for the rest of the photo shoot.' Tia forced a weak smile.

'We'll all go and take a tea break and come back in a few minutes. Then maybe we could talk to you, Tia?' The producer smiled back at her and left with the rest of the film crew when she nodded her agreement.

Tia swallowed hard and braced herself ready to face whatever Penny had to say. She was sure it wouldn't be good, not after the scene that had just taken place.

'Miss Patterson, I believe you have work to be getting on with?' Penny arched her brow and looked meaningfully at her.

'Later,' Saffy whispered to Tia, and made herself scarce, taking everyone else with her.

At last, Tia and Penny were alone in the therapy suite.

'I'm sure you'll be relieved to know that I've asked Miss Gold to take some personal time away from work so she can reflect on her actions and decide if she wishes to continue working with *Platinum* magazine.'

Tia wished she could sit down. Her legs were shaking

once more as she waited for Penny to tell her she was suspended as well.

Penny's eyes narrowed and Tia prayed she wasn't about to be dismissed on the spot.

'I have never in all my years of working in this industry witnessed a scene quite like that one and, believe me, I've seen some things. I need to speak to Helen and Sir Crispin, obviously about what happened, but I think we can rescue this situation.'

Tia's heart leapt into her mouth. 'You mean you aren't sacking me?'

'I don't think either changing your name or losing weight is a disciplinary offence, do you? And it wasn't you that engineered that disgraceful scene which could have caused enormous damage to the reputation of the magazine. I actually think you handled it very well and with good grace, given the circumstances.' Penny reached out to pat her hand.

'I have no idea what Miss Gold thought she would achieve by showing those pictures and revealing your past to the world. Clearly she was motivated by some kind of petty jealousy involving your relationship with Josh Banks. However, if you are willing, then I think some good could come out of all of this.'

'Thank you, Penny.' Tia had always thought of the older woman as rather difficult and dry. She was touched to discover Penny was actually quite a kind person.

'Not at all. Now, shall we get a coffee before we try and get this shoot wrapped up?'

Tia nodded.

'Good, then you can push me back to the coffee lounge.' Penny settled back in her seat as Tia took hold of the wheelchair. It wasn't until they were almost back at the drinks lounge that Tia realised she hadn't noticed Josh while all of the action had been going on.

29

The film crew weren't in the coffee lounge when Tia and Penny arrived. Since Josh had said he'd come down to film his part of the documentary, she supposed it was possible that that was where they'd gone. At least he probably hadn't been present during the showdown with Juliet. If he had been, then it would have made a horrible situation even worse. Especially after Juliet had announced to the world that Tia had slept with him.

She collected a large cappuccino for Penny then left her colleague talking on her mobile with Helen while she fetched her own drink. Much as she would have liked to hear Penny's version of what had happened she didn't think her nerves could take much more stress. So, instead, she carried her cup of tea over to a different table, leaving Penny to talk privately. Wearily she settled back into the richly padded seat and closed her eyes.

It would be nice to think that Juliet wouldn't come back to work in the *Platinum* office, but somehow she doubted that things would be that simple. Sir Crispin would become involved as he regarded the magazine as his own personal flagship. Tia doubted that he would take the same understanding stance as Penny. Juliet appeared to be the golden child at the moment so it would take a lot to get him to send her back to New York or packing altogether.

Then there was the business with the shares and Juliet's involvement with Rupert Finch. What if somehow he or Juliet managed to get hold of enough shares to wrest control from Sir Crispin? Now, if Sir Crispin got wind of that, then he might well view Juliet's position at *Platinum* differently.

Even with her eyes closed she sensed Penny's gaze trained upon her. She opened her eyes and found she was correct. Tia longed to escape from under those watchful eyes so that she could go and talk to Saffy. Her friend was probably dying to get the low-down on her past life as Barbara and Tia longed to discuss her own fears about Juliet's next move.

She fished in her handbag for her phone to check her texts. As she'd thought, there were two from Saffy, and one from Ravi, presumably after Saffy had texted him to tell him what was going on. The messages had arrived while she'd been in the parking lot bracing herself for her confrontation with Juliet.

Quickly, she thumbed a reply back to Ravi, apologising for not telling him sooner about her connection with Josh and Juliet. She toyed with the idea of calling Ginny to let her know what had happened, but remembering her godmother's recent health scare she decided to wait until she got home. Perhaps she could deliver the news more gently that way.

She dropped her phone back in her bag and picked up her tea. Penny was still engrossed in her conversation with Helen. The elation she'd initially felt seeing Juliet leave had vanished, leaving her drained and emotionally unsteady. She tore open the sachet of sugar that had come with her tea and tipped it into the cup. Sugar was supposed to be good for shock, wasn't it? Maybe it would help her regain her sense of equilibrium, even if she didn't usually take the sweet stuff.

'Hi, Tia, may I join you?'

Tia looked up from stirring her drink to find Kim standing opposite her holding a cup.

'Of course.' Tia sat up a little straighter as Kim took a seat.

She liked Josh's straight-talking PA. She'd spoken with her many times in the last few weeks while they had been organising the photo shoot, and Tia thought she was direct and honest. She appreciated those qualities even more now, after dealing with Juliet's two-faced deceitfulness.

'I couldn't resist coming down here for my coffee break so I could see how things were going,' Kim confided, crossing her elegant legs.

It was obvious from the older woman's placid expression that news of the drama hadn't reached the penthouse office.

'It's going well. Thank you for all your hard work organising things at this end, we do appreciate it. This drinks lounge is amazing.' Tia waved her hand to indicate her surroundings, hoping to divert Kim from asking any awkward questions, such as where was Juliet.

'Thank you. I enjoyed it, and the spa is gorgeous, isn't it? Are the film crew around? I thought I might see them in here.'

Tia took a sip of her tea and shuddered at the taste of sugar. 'I think they must be off filming Josh. He was down here about an hour ago ready to film his piece.'

A tiny frown puckered Kim's forehead. 'No, I don't know if he's done that yet. I know he was all set to get the filming out of the way but then something happened and he had to dash off.'

'Oh.' Tia placed her cup down carefully on her saucer.

'Between you and me, I think it's something to do with that Juliet Gold.' Kim pulled a face, then looked around her. 'Oh, she's not here today, is she?'

'No, she's gone,' Tia reassured her. She pushed her cup away from her on the table, her drink barely touched. Even if she hadn't added the sugar, Kim's words had suddenly made the tea unpalatable.

'You look a little tired today, Tia. Organising this shoot has been such a lot of work, are you okay?' Kim peered at her, concern written across her warm expression.

'I am rather tired. Still, it'll soon be finished and we'll be out of your hair.' Tia forced herself to give the older woman a reassuring smile.

'Well, I hope I'll continue to see you around, even when this is all done and dusted.'

Tia knew this was a hint that she expected her to still see Josh after the shoot had ended and she wasn't certain how to respond. There were so many unanswered questions in her mind about how she felt about him. Out of the corner of her eye she observed Penny busy drinking her coffee, her phone call finished.

'I think Penny is nearly ready, so I have to get back to the shoot. Feel free to come and take a peep at what's going on. It was lovely to see you.' Tia stood, ready to go.

'It was good seeing you too. I expect I'll see you again soon.' Kim smiled confidently up at her as she took her leave.

'Are you, okay, sweetie?' Ginny asked, her voice warm with concern.

Tia nodded from where she sat slumped in the armchair wrapped in her favourite dressing gown. Saffy and Ravi had insisted on taking her out for a drink once the filming and photo shoot were done for the day.

One drink had turned into several and there had been much crying and laughing before they had finally poured her out of a cab outside her house. Now she was finally home and changed into her nightwear she could allow herself to relax. She had changed her mind and called Ginny from the bar early in the evening to give her the edited, softened version of the day's events.

Ginny listened to Tia's rather more detailed, rambling account with great patience. 'And you didn't see anything more of Josh?' she asked.

'No. I tried to find out if anyone knew where he might be, but I didn't want to be too obvious. Especially with them all thinking we were together, if you know what I mean.'

'It's rather odd that he went off like that, and that his secretary didn't know where he'd gone either,' Ginny mused.

'I know. I hope he didn't hear what happened and decide to go after Juliet.' Tia picked disconsolately at the hem of her dressing gown.

'It doesn't seem likely to me that he would. Not if what he's said to you is true about how he feels towards her. And you've no idea if Juliet will try to come back to work?'

Tia shook her head, the motion making her feel pleasantly woozy. 'No idea at all. Helen wants to see me in the morning and Penny has set up an interview with the film crew for next week to talk about my transformation.' She wiggled her fingers in the air as she said 'transformation'. It felt strange to think of herself as providing inspiration for other people.

'Hmm, I doubt if Juliet will reappear at *Platinum*. I expect she'll try Rupert Finch, if she's having a relationship with him, or she could go back to New York, I suppose,' Ginny said.

Tia bit back a yawn and raked her hands through her hair to try and rouse herself up a little. The champagne cocktails Ravi and Saffy had insisted on buying her were kicking in and making her sleepy.

'I dunno. She could go and see Sir Crispin; he always

seemed to think she was wonderful. It depends if he listens to her or to Helen and Penny.'

Ginny gave an unladylike snort. 'He's not stupid and he built that business up from nothing. I think he'll listen to Helen. He might have a weakness for a nice pair of legs but if word reaches him about Rupert Finch then she'll be toast. She's having an affair with his brother-in-law, for heaven's sake. Does she know that you know about that?'

'I'm not sure. I think she got the message that I knew when we were arguing. I don't know if Josh would have said anything to her.' She didn't want to consider what Josh might have said, or might *be* saying to Juliet. All day long, she'd tried not to think too hard about that.

Ginny looked at her. 'What exactly is going on now between you and Josh?'

'I don't know. I wish I did. He seems to really like me when we're together and he says he doesn't want anything to do with Juliet.' She fiddled with the Pandora bracelet encircling her wrist, straightening the charms as if she might find an answer in the sparkling glass beads.

'Do you believe him?' Ginny persisted.

'I've no reason not to believe him.'

'Then what's the problem?'

'It's just that Juliet has been doing her best to keep us apart and now today with him not being around when he was supposed to be, well . . . Plus there was Kim saying she thought the reason he'd disappeared was something to do with Juliet.' She trailed off, all her old doubts bubbling to the surface, making her feel wretched and miserable inside.

Ginny sighed. 'I always wondered with you and Josh, if it was simply the remnants of a teenage crush. First loves take a lot to shake off, sometimes.' She smiled at Tia. 'But, it's more than that, isn't it?'

'Yes.' Ginny was right, it was more than the remains of some adolescent fantasy. Much more.

'Do you love him?'

Ginny's gaze was fixed on her face and Tia longed to hide away from her scrutiny. The pleasant muzziness from the alcohol she'd imbibed was punctured by her godmother's rapier stare. A picture of Josh's face flashed into her mind, when he'd kissed her nose earlier that day before the confrontation. Pain knifed her between her ribs when she pictured him going after Juliet.

'Yes, I love him.' It was the first time she'd acknowledged the truth to herself, let alone anyone else, and the realisation stunned her. She loved the real Josh, the man she'd come to know over the last few weeks, not the boy from her teenage fantasies.

'Well, it seems to me that he feels the same way about you. He certainly had that moonstruck look about him when he was here the other night, although you haven't exactly made things easy for him.'

Tia blinked in surprise.

'He hasn't even got your mobile number,' Ginny reminded her.

Her godmother's words forced a wry smile from Tia. 'No, he hasn't.'

'Tia, if he's truly the man for you, then don't allow Juliet to come between you. I don't believe for one moment he's interested in her and, if you're honest with yourself, you don't believe he is either. I suspect he wanted to get to the bottom of this takeover business with Rupert Finch. You said that was more or less what he'd told you.'

'Yes, but . . .' Tia stared at her.

'Then what are you going to do about it?'

'Do?' Tia wondered how much alcohol had been in those cocktails.

'Yes, *do*,' her godmother emphasised.

'I'm not sure I'm with you.' Tia hoped Ginny wasn't suggesting what she thought she might be suggesting.

'Darling, I was in a similar position to you once. There was this man whom I really loved, but it was messy. He'd not long come out of a long relationship and I thought perhaps it was too soon and, well –' Ginny gazed misty-eyed into the empty fireplace – 'to cut a long story short, I didn't speak out when I should have done and he thought I didn't care. That I didn't trust him enough. By the time I'd plucked up enough courage to go and see him to tell him how I felt, it was too late. His mother told me he'd gone. He emigrated to New Zealand and I never saw him again.'

Tia slipped from her seat to cross to Ginny's side and hugged her. 'Is that why you've never married? Mum always said you'd had someone special but something went wrong.' She remembered when she'd been a little girl asking her mother one day why Ginny wasn't married. It had baffled her at the time why her pretty, clever godmother was always on her own.

'Then don't make my mistake. I left it too late to tell the man I loved how I felt. You need to be honest with Josh and talk to him,' Ginny urged.

'But what if he doesn't feel the same way? What if I've made a horrible mistake?' Tia wished it was that simple.

Ginny smoothed the tangles in Tia's hair with a loving hand. 'At least you'll know.'

Alone in her room later that evening Tia thought about what Ginny had said. What other choice did she have? She supposed she could wait around for Josh to contact her through her email or by turning up at her office, speculating and worrying all the while that he was with Juliet. Or, she could take control, call him and see if he wanted to meet her.

She carefully cleaned off her make-up in front of her dressing-table mirror. There was tomorrow to get through, first. Helen hadn't given her any kind of clue of what was likely to happen when she'd called and ordered her into a meeting. She tossed the soiled cotton wool ball into the wastepaper basket and prepared to apply her toner.

From what Penny had said she didn't think Helen was about to sack her. Unless . . . she paused in her application of the cool lime-and-rose-petal tonic. No, Sir Crispin wouldn't – well, not until she'd recorded the interview with the documentary team and rescued his beloved *Platinum*'s image.

She finished with her toner and unscrewed the stopper on the sample of expensive moisturiser she was testing for a column. There was no point speculating and stressing. Tomorrow she would see Helen and find out her fate and then she'd think very carefully about what she planned to do about Josh.

By the time she arrived at the *Platinum* offices the following morning, Tia's nerves were in overdrive. She hadn't even been able to face her usual coffee on the way in. Her head still ached from the cocktails she'd drunk the previous night and the painkillers she'd choked down hadn't yet kicked in.

Ravi and Saffy were huddled together around the watercooler waiting for her in a show of support.

'Stop looking so nervous! You haven't done anything wrong,' Saffy admonished her.

'Yes, look on the bright side, the witch queen is gone and Saffy might finally get that promotion to senior fashion editor. That's assuming Helen gets desperate.' Ravi winked at them as Saffy promptly poked him hard in his ribs.

'Thanks, guys.' Tia managed a small smile. 'I can't tell you what it means having you to support me.'

'Three musketeers, all for one and one for all and all that crap,' Ravi said.

'Yeah, what he said,' Saffy added. 'You'll be fine, honest.'

Tia hoped they were right. She helped herself to a beaker of water and headed for her cubicle. Looking around at the piles of make-up samples, publicity leaflets and promotional packs, she wondered how many cardboard boxes she would need to hold her belongings if Helen decided to fire her.

'Tia, I've got the post here.' Her intern entered the office laden down with letters.

'Thanks, Poppy.' Tia turned to take the mail from her.

'I thought you were very brave yesterday, and wow, I saw the picture on Juliet's phone. I wouldn't have known that was you. Honestly, you look so amazing now. You're my hero.' The intern blushed.

Tia gave a small shrug, embarrassed by the open admiration in her assistant's eyes. 'It was a long time ago. I suppose it proves that some of the stuff we write about really does work.' She smiled at the girl and was relieved to see her smile back.

'Yes, I suppose it does, doesn't it?' Still blushing, Poppy headed back to the copier to finish the rest of her tasks.

Tia glanced over at Helen's office. There were no signs of life. She decided that must be a good sign if Helen hadn't strayed out of her usual routine to come in early to see her. She pulled the pile of post towards her and tried to concentrate on her work, waiting all the time for her phone to ring with Helen's summons.

Finally, she saw Helen enter her office. Unable to focus any longer, Tia put down her pen and decided to nip to the ladies' before she was called in to face the music. Her nerves must be irritating her bladder. This was the third time she'd needed to pee in less than an hour and she'd only managed a few sips of the water she'd placed on her desk.

She smoothed her hair in front of the mirror in the toilets. At least outwardly she looked okay. She'd toned down the make-up she usually wore. It was funny, perhaps she didn't feel the need to hide behind her cosmetics any more. Inside, though, she was still a quaking mass of nerves, wondering what Helen would say about the whole embarrassing debacle yesterday.

She'd no sooner taken her seat back at her desk when Helen rang.

'We're to go to the Broadoak Imperial hotel; Sir Crispin will meet us there. Be downstairs in five minutes.'

Tia replaced the receiver with a shaking hand. She shouldn't have been so blasé about Helen coming in at her usual time. If Sir Crispin was involved and they were to go to Josh's hotel, then it had to be very bad. Five minutes didn't even give her time to go to the loo again.

She gave her intern instructions for the morning and descended to the lobby as quickly as she could. Helen was already waiting for her, and Tia followed her into the back of a black cab. Deep in conversation on her mobile, Helen said nothing other than a brisk 'good morning' to her for the whole of the journey. Consequently, by the time the taxi pulled up outside the hotel entrance, Tia's imagination had conjured up sixty different scenarios for the meeting that lay ahead, and none of them were good.

Within minutes of their arrival at the hotel, Kim appeared in the lobby to take them up to Josh's office. Tia's stomach turned somersaults as the elevator travelled swiftly upwards and only Kim's friendly smile stopped her from being physically sick. Somehow she managed to exchange pleasantries with the PA although Helen remained silent.

Tia's heart sank and her pulse hammered in her ears when she saw Sir Crispin seated at the large glossy table in Josh's office with Josh alongside him. Sir Crispin's expression revealed nothing, although he fixed Tia with a hard stare as she entered the room. Both men stood to greet them before resuming their seats, only to stand again a moment later as Juliet made her entrance.

Juliet had foregone her trademark black fitted dress and severe chignon in favour of a short, white prom-style dress showing off her long tanned legs. Her shiny blond hair was loose around her shoulders, held back with a white Alice band. She walked into the room with the air of a film star honouring them with her appearance, and, ignoring Tia completely, she took her seat at the table.

Josh's face was sombre and he avoided Tia's eyes as he took his seat. By now Tia's legs were shaking so much she had to press her feet hard against the floor to stop the noise of her heels from sounding out loud in the room. She folded her hands in her lap and kept her gaze fixed on the tabletop while she tried to control her breathing.

'Miss Gold, Miss Carpenter, thank you for joining us.'

Tia lifted her head as Sir Crispin spoke.

He leaned back in his seat, his eyes narrowing as he surveyed them all. 'I must admit, I was perturbed yesterday when Miss Gold first contacted me and I learned that my fashion editor had been suspended.' He turned his gaze on Helen.

She flushed under his scrutiny while Juliet looked smug.

'Then I had a telephone call from Mr Banks, here.' Sir Crispin gestured towards Josh who continued to look grave. Tia swallowed and wondered what Josh could have said to Sir Crispin. Had he pleaded Juliet's cause for her?

Juliet was positively smirking now and Helen shuffled on her seat as if wishing to speak but Sir Crispin continued without allowing her to do so.

'Miss Carpenter, I was astonished to learn that you, of all people, had apparently been the catalyst for this astonishing behaviour.' Colour bloomed in Tia's cheeks as Sir Crispin turned his formidable gaze in her direction. Indignation rose inside her. According to whom? She hadn't been the person who had disrupted the photo shoot or the one levelling accusations about the past.

'Most extraordinary. Thankfully, I'm given to understand by your seniors that any potential damage to *Platinum* from this episode may be contained and even possibly turned in our favour.'

Juliet's expression hardened and Tia guessed this last piece of information hadn't pleased her.

'Is there anything you wish to say on the matter?' Sir Crispin asked.

Tia cleared her throat and prayed her voice wouldn't sound wobbly. 'Not really, sir. I was put in a very difficult position and I handled it the best way I could at the time, given the circumstances.'

There were a lot of things she could have said but they were either embarrassing or would make her sound petty and spiteful. She had to trust that Helen and Penny had given Sir Crispin a far more balanced account of events than the one he would no doubt have received from Juliet. What she didn't know was what Josh had said. Had he told Sir Crispin about Juliet's liaisons with Rupert Finch? Possibly not, from the way she was acting.

'Miss Gold, is there anything you wish to add?' He turned his head towards Juliet.

'I believe I gave you an accurate account of Tia's deplorable behaviour yesterday.' She widened her eyes as she replied, looking the picture of innocence and maligned virtue.

'Very well.' Sir Crispin nodded and Juliet settled back in her seat looking satisfied with his response.

Tia wondered if it were possible to pass out if you were seated.

'I must say, I was most shocked by the whole incident and Miss Gold's account of what had occurred sounded very alarming, with both Miss Tia Carpenter, who has been in my employ for quite some time, and Miss Penny Taylor, my fashion director, both appearing to behave in a manner most unlike themselves.' His craggy features creased into a frown and Tia wished he would just cut to the chase. If he intended to dismiss her he could get on with it and not spin this hideous torture out for much longer.

'However, acting on further information I received yesterday, I have since conducted some investigations of my own, with the aid of Mr Banks and some other interested parties.' He paused and Tia noticed Juliet's expression change. Something akin to panic flickered across the smooth skin of her face as she watched Sir Crispin.

'I had hoped to persuade my esteemed brother-in-law, Mr Rupert Finch, to join us here this morning; however, I believe he had pressing business elsewhere. A *family* matter, I think.' He paused and looked hard at Juliet.

'There is also, so Helen tells me, the small matter of some missing confidential files which had been removed from a locked cabinet in her office. I understand they have now been recovered from your desk, Miss Gold.'

The colour drained from Juliet's face, leaving her complexion as white as her dress. Tia guessed she finally had the answer to what Juliet had been carrying in the large brown envelope when she'd caught her leaving Helen's office shortly after Juliet had started at the magazine.

'Miss Gold, I'll ask you once again, is there something you wish to say at this point?' Sir Crispin fixed his steely glare directly at Juliet and Tia's spirits began to rise. There was no mistaking the subtext of Sir Crispin's words. He knew about Juliet's affair with Rupert Finch. and, from the sound of things, so did Rupert's wife. He also knew Juliet had been rifling through confidential papers from Helen's office, presumably so she could pass information to her lover.

Juliet shook her head, her eyes still fixed on Sir Crispin as if not quite believing she had been caught out.

'I see. Then you should know that I shared my information with Helen this morning and we are both of the opinion that it would not be in the interest of *Platinum* magazine for you to continue working for us. You are, of course, at liberty to contest this decision, but I would venture to suggest that an employment tribunal might reveal all manner of things which might not be pleasant for you to have made public.'

Where before Juliet's face had been white, her complexion had now changed to crimson and she rose quickly from her seat, snatching up her bag.

'So that's the way it goes, is it?' She turned on Josh, 'You did this, didn't you? She's got you right where she wants you. Sitting there like a pathetic little mouse. I can't believe you've chosen that loser, that ex-blimp, over me.' She thumped her handbag down on the table, her knuckles white with rage.

Josh's jaw was set. 'I think you've said quite enough, Juliet.'

'Then I'm off!' She glared at Sir Crispin before turning her attention to Tia. She pushed her face closer to Tia's, and Josh rose slightly from his seat as if poised to step in.

'Well, I hope you're happy now! You finally got your revenge! I'm glad I read those files and exposed you for the loser you really are. I've known for a couple of weeks that you were Barbara Baker. It was easy to find out once I started digging through your records and found the photocopies of your old exam results. Don't think this is the last you'll hear of me. I've got friends in high places, I can make sure that you'll be finished in this industry inside of twelve months.' She stormed off towards the door where Kim was already waiting to see her out.

There was a moment of stillness in the room after Juliet's departure. Tia released the breath she had subconsciously been holding during the last part of Juliet's speech.

'Awful, ghastly woman. Please take no notice of her empty threats. I can't believe she stole confidential employee records from my office. I always keep them under lock and key, only HR have a duplicate set.' Helen shook her head as if unable to believe the scene she'd just witnessed.

'Miss Carpenter, please accept my apologies for putting you through this meeting. Sadly, Miss Gold is the type of person who is apt to manipulate situations to suit her own purposes. I had to ensure that her dismissal would be seen to be fair and equitable and that she'd been given the opportunity to defend her actions. Not that I consider them in any way defensible.' Sir Crispin smiled gently at her from across the table before continuing.

'I also want to thank you for agreeing to allow your

personal affairs to be used by the documentary makers. I sincerely regret that this was forced upon you by Miss Gold's thoughtless actions. I'm sure, however, that the programme can only reflect well on *Platinum* magazine and on you personally. Obviously, Helen will issue an official statement regarding Miss Gold's departure and I know that you will keep the information from this meeting confidential. Along with the other matters which were only alluded to here but of which I believe you to be fully cognisant.' He raised one bushy eyebrow and Tia guessed he was referring to Juliet's role in the hostile takeover attempt as well as the affair with Rupert Finch.

Somehow she managed to find her voice to respond. 'Of course, you can count on my discretion.'

'Thank you, my dear. Now, if you'll excuse me, I have some matters I need to discuss with Helen.' Sir Crispin stood and shook Josh's hand. 'My thanks for your help in resolving this matter.'

He turned and nodded at Tia. 'Miss Carpenter. Helen, my dear, accompany me downstairs.'

Helen rose and followed Sir Crispin to the door, leaving Josh to retake his seat at the head of the table. Tia wiped the palms of her hands on the soft pale-blue cotton of her dress and waited for him to speak. She still felt shaky from Juliet's verbal vitriol.

'I'm sorry you had to sit through that,' Josh said, his expression unreadable. 'Sir Crispin does like his melodrama.'

'Hey, I'm still employed.' Tia made a feeble joke. She

couldn't help feeling nervous about what Josh might have to say to her now the others had gone. She nibbled on her lower lip trying to find the right words to steer the conversation around to the two of them.

'There was never any doubt that you wouldn't be. Sir Crispin is pretty astute. He knows who pulls their weight.'

Her heartbeat kicked up a notch as she looked into his eyes. 'He said you called him yesterday. Is that where you went?' She needed to know exactly what he'd said to Sir Crispin. It would tell her everything about how he truly saw her; if he could love her past as Barbara, as well as her present as Tia.

Josh stood and strolled over to the window next to her, his hands in his pockets.

'The spa receptionists told me there was some kind of drama happening in the therapy rooms. I caught the tail end of Juliet's performance. Then, after Penny had sent her away, Juliet came after me. After outing you as Barbara had backfired on her so spectacularly she tried to convince me to back her instead of you. I think it was a kind of last throw of the dice.'

'Oh.' Tia watched him and waited for him to continue.

He turned to face her. 'I managed to piece together the story and I found out she planned to go straight to Sir Crispin. She was confident that he'd see her side of things and sack you. What she didn't know was that your friend Ravi and I had already given Sir Crispin some proof of her double-dealing over Rupert's planned takeover of Hellandback. You have good friends, Tia.'

'Sir Crispin believed you?'

Josh smiled. 'Oh yes, and so did Celestine, his sister. She and Rupert are now in the Caribbean where I believe Rupert is having to do some pretty heavy-duty grovelling in order to keep his marriage on track.'

'Then I suppose I should be thanking you and Ravi for helping to save my job.' Her voice sounded husky.

Josh came towards her, his deep-blue eyes fixed on her face. 'You don't need to thank me. I think Sir Crispin had probably figured out what Juliet was really like all by himself.'

He traced a finger lightly down the side of her face and somehow she was on her feet and in his arms. His mouth closed on hers and she wrapped her arms around him, savouring the hard, muscular feel of his body against hers. Desire coiled low in her belly as she revelled in the taste of him.

She was dimly aware of the office door clicking open and then closing again as he lifted his head to smile at her. 'I think that was Kim making a tactical retreat.' He drew his finger along the curve of her cheek once more, his action sending a delicious shiver of want through her body.

'That's embarrassing.' Tia smiled back at him, glad he was still holding her close.

'You don't want to be seen with me?' he teased.

Tia answered him with a very satisfactory kiss on his lips. 'You're happy to be seen with me? Especially when the documentary goes out and the whole world knows I used to be "Big Barb, tub of lard"?' she asked, although deep in her soul she knew his answer already.

His gaze locked with hers. 'I'll always be proud to be seen with you. Beauty is what's on the inside, Tia, not the outside. You should know that, Ms Beauty Editor.' He stroked a finger along her cleavage making her knees feel weak. 'Although your outside is incredibly gorgeous too.'

'Ginny told me to tell you how I feel about you. That we should talk more.' She ran the flat of her hand across his shoulder blade.

'Oh, and how do you feel about me?' His tone was light but his eyes were dark and serious as he waited for her to reply.

'I think I should let you have my mobile number so you can call me.' She pressed another kiss on the corner of his mouth, revelling in the faint masculine roughness of his chin against her lips.

His mouth closed on hers once more and she gave herself up to his kiss.

'I'm not sure I'm keen on talking, there are a lot more fun things I'd rather do with you,' he murmured.

'Kim might come back.'

'She won't disturb us; she told me to make sure I didn't let you go.' He finally allowed her to catch her breath.

'Oh?' Tia trailed her fingers through the short dark curls at the nape of his neck, revelling in the silky texture of his hair. 'I like your PA.' Joy bubbled up inside her, a giddy happiness erupting in her chest.

'Yeah, she seems to think that you're the one.'

Tia's fingers stilled and she felt as if she could hardly breathe. 'Oh?'

Josh smiled down at her. 'Don't tell her I said this, but my PA is very rarely wrong.'

Tia smiled back and moved her hand to slacken the knot on his tie, anxious to touch and taste more of his skin.

'Really.' She couldn't remember when she'd ever been this happy.

'Really.' He nibbled on her earlobe, making heat build in her stomach. 'I suppose if we have to thank anyone, it's Juliet; without her helping hand you and I might not have found each other again.'

'I suppose not,' Tia agreed.

'Yeah, and just look at us now.' He silenced anything else she might have been intending to say by capturing her lips with his once more.

Pick up a *little black dress* – it's a girl thing.

978 0 7553 3513 8

THE KEPT WOMAN
Susan Donovan
PB £4.99

It's purely business – all Samantha has to do to achieve a better life for her kids is play happy families with womanising Jack Tolliver when he's running for the senate. But then they share a knee-trembling, electric kiss . . .

MEMOIRS ARE MADE OF THIS
Swan Adamson
PB £4.99

978 0 7553 3366 0

Venus Gilroy is determined to get ahead in her job as PA to glamorous journalist Susanna Hyde. But is Venus proving rather too good at covering Susanna's column and hitting it off with her ex-toy-boy, Josh O'Connell?

In the bestselling tradition of *The Devil Wears Prada*

Pick up a *little black dress* – it's a girl thing.

978 0 7553 3459 9

SEX, LIES AND ONLINE DATING
Rachel Gibson
PB £4.99

When undercover cop Quinn McIntyre poses as an internet dater, the last thing in his mind is falling for the chief suspect in his hunt for a female serial killer. Lucy Rothschild just doesn't seem like the killing kind ... does she?

BLUE CHRISTMAS
Mary Kay Andrews
PB £4.99

Eloise Foley is looking forward to a magical Christmas filled with friends, family and festive fun, but it doesn't seem as if everyone around her is feeling the same seasonal goodwill.

Will Eloise get the fairy-tale celebration she desires or is she heading for a blue Christmas?

978 0 7553 3280 9

Pick up a *little black dress* – it's a girl thing.

THE BALANCE THING
Margaret Dumas
PB £4.99

Becks Mansfield has never put much effort into her relationships with men, but now she's lost her hot-shot job as well. Surely it's more important to sort out her career than her love life? Or is life trying to tell her she needs a little more of *The Balance Thing*?

978 0 7553 3731 6

SIMPLY IRRESISTIBLE
Rachel Gibson
PB £4.99

Georganne Howard knows she's irresistible, but when she's rescued by John Kowalsky he proves impervious to her charms and packs her off after one night.

Ten years later, she's back and this time Georganne is playing hard to get. She's also hiding a very big secret . . .

978 0 7553 3742 2

You can buy any of these other
Little Black Dress titles from your
bookshop or *direct from the publisher*.

FREE P&P AND UK DELIVERY
(Overseas and Ireland £3.50 per book)

TO ORDER SIMPLY CALL THIS NUMBER

01235 400 414

or visit our website: <u>www.headline.co.uk</u>

Prices and availability subject to change without notice.